FEARLESS HEARTS

Taleah was certain that nothing physical would happen between them, but she didn't think of it as the worst thing that could occur. In fact, making love to Lorenz would fill her up in every way. It would definitely rid her of all her pent-up frustration. "It's not going to happen," she whispered. "It can't happen. Go to sleep and stop the agony of thinking of the ecstasy."

Taleah quickly closed her eyes when she heard the bathroom door open. She listened intently for the sounds of his every movement. Would he just go to bed if he thought she was asleep? Maybe he'd turn on the television. The hotel did have cable. Her heart nearly stopped when she felt his weight on her bed. He was seated on the side of her mattress. What was he about to do? Taleah fought hard to remain calm, but her heart was already thumping erratically.

Lorenz leaned over and kissed her forehead. "I guess you just couldn't hang on. Sleep tight, precious angel." He then kissed each of her eyelids as he smoothed back her silky hair.

Taleah dared to breathe after he'd moved away from her bed. After a couple of minutes had passed, she turned her back and faced the wall. As she thought about his gentleness, tears slipped from her eyes. Taleah knew without a shadow of a doubt that she loved him, loved him like crazy.

BOOK YOUR PLACE ON OUR WEBSITE AND MAKE THE ARABESQUE ROMANCE CONNECTION!

We've created a customized website just for our very special Arabesque readers, where you can get the inside scoop on everything that's going on with Arabesque romance novels.

When you come online, you'll have the exciting opportunity to:

- View covers of upcoming books

- Learn about our future publishing schedule (listed by publication month and author)

- Find out when your favorite authors will be visiting a city near you

- Search for and order backlist books

- Check out author bios and background information

- Send e-mail to your favorite authors

- Join us in weekly chats with authors, readers and other guests

- Get writing guidelines

- AND MUCH MORE!

Visit our website at
http://www.arabesquebooks.com

Linda Hudson-Smith

FEARLESS
HEARTS

BET Publications, LLC
http://www.bet.com
http://www.arabesquebooks.com

ARABESQUE BOOKS are published by

BET Publications, LLC
c/o BET BOOKS
One BET Plaza
1900 W Place NE
Washington, DC 20018-1211

All Kensington Titles, Imprints, and Distributed Lines are available at special quantity discounts for bulk purchases for sales promotions, premiums, fund-raising, and educational or institutional use. Special book excerpts or customized printings can also be created to fit specific needs. For details, write or phone the office of the Kensington special sales manager: Kensington Publishing Corp., 850 Third Avenue, New York, NY 10022, attn: Special Sales Department, Phone: 1-800-221-2647.

First Printing: June 2004
10 9 8 7 6 5 4 3 2 1

Printed in the United States of America

This novel is dedicated to the loving memeory of
T.W. Miller
Sunrise: December 13, 1917
Sunset: July 2, 1990

And to my very special Texas connections:

Your love, friendship, and loyalty defy description.

Brenda Bailey, Drusilla Smith, Sherra Miller, Charlie Brown,
Linda Robinson, Clay Robinson, Mattie Meeks, Robert
Meeks, Frank Walker, Dr. Phyllis Tyler, Tannie McGregor,
and Sylethia Jones.

One

Taleah Taylor set her tennis racket down on the light ash hardwood coffee table in order to answer the telephone. Her golden brown eyes glistened with satisfaction as she looked around her recently cleaned apartment. Taleah resided in an upscale neighborhood, inside a beautifully furnished two-bedroom apartment located in the Fox Hills section of Los Angeles, only two short blocks from her parents' lovely home. The color scheme of her modern-deco furnishings and accents was done in various shades of cream and soft antique greens. Sparkling ceramic tile and hardwood floors were laid throughout the spacious living quarters.

Upon hearing her mother Allison Taylor's sweet voice on the line, Taleah smiled brightly. "Hey, Mom. I was just leaving to come up there. Is everything okay?"

"Things are fine. Your daddy is patiently waiting for you to get here so he can drive you to your tennis lesson."

Taleah smiled at the mention of her dad. She was Jack Taylor's little girl, and she was proud of it, never made any excuses for it. In fact, all three of Jack's daughters, Lynette, Marsha, and Taleah, were Daddy's girls. Taleah was the youngest of the Taylor daughters and two sons, Joshua and Jared. Jared and Taleah weren't twins, but the two siblings were as close as any two siblings could ever be. Jared was two years older than the baby sister he adored.

Although Taleah was twenty-seven years old, she'd never gotten her driver's license. She'd failed at the driving test the first time out. A short time later, after suffering a broken pelvis as a passenger in a co-worker's car, which was involved in a terrible accident, Taleah had tossed out any desire to ever drive an automobile. Her life could've been lost that fateful day had she been encumbered in a seat belt. Getting around Los Angeles on the city buses was just fine and dandy with Taleah when her father was unavailable.

As an administrative assistant to several dentists in a private dental practice, she lived only a few blocks from her job, which allowed her to walk the short distance whenever she chose to. The great L.A. weather made it possible quite often.

"I was almost out the door, Mom. Tell Daddy I'm on my way."

"I will, Taleah, but that's not why I called. Do you have any plans for the weekend?"

"Yeah, I do. I'm going camping tomorrow with several of my friends. But why do you ask? Do you need me to do something for you?"

"Your brother-in-law just called. As you know, Mark's TDY at March Air Reserve Base in Moreno Valley, and he wants you to meet one of the guys who is also there TDY. His name is Lorenz Hampton. Mark already knows this guy, but he didn't say how long or from where. Mark was thrilled to run into him this way. He's bringing Lorenz down this evening. They plan to stay over until Sunday. Think you could change your plans?"

Taleah laughed with undisguised sarcasm, pushing her sable-brown bangs back from her pretty face. "I can't believe Mark Jefferson's playing matchmaker again. The last blind date he chose for me turned out to be married. Why does everyone keep trying to hook me up? I'm not looking for anyone to hook up with. I'm not interested in meeting *Mr. Right* and surely not another *Mr. Wrong*. I like things just the way they are, Mom. A few casual dates a month works fine for me. Don't want to be committed to anyone. Besides, I never want to even think of getting married or engaged again. One failed personal relationship is enough to last me a lifetime. It didn't even last a measly year and it's already been over with us for nearly four."

"Taleah, who said anything about marriage? Your engagement to Bradley Fields was just a youthful indiscretion at twenty-three years of age. We all know that you two never should've gotten yourselves into that serious of a situation. Mark only wants you to meet one of his new friends, not set up housekeeping with him. Anyway, Mark is bringing his friend down this evening. Lynette came all the way out here from Maryland to stay with us while Mark's here, so you might want to at least consider your sister's feelings in your decision. It may not be fun for her to have an extra man around with no one to entertain him but her husband."

Taleah groaned loudly. "Okay, go ahead and put Taleah Denise Taylor on a guilt trip. I'm sure she won't mind!" Taleah laughed softly. "See you in a few minutes, Mom. I promise to think about what you said on my short walk to your house. We both already know that this is a no-win situation for me. If I agree to this madness, Mark's gonna owe me big time."

Allison laughed heartily, even though she felt sorry for Taleah. It seemed that everyone but Taleah was looking for the right man for her youngest child. Taleah had been so young when she'd gotten hurt so horribly bad. That she still hadn't completely recovered from her pain was a major concern for her family and friends.

Four years had come and gone since Taleah had broken off her engagement, after learning that her fiancé had another woman on the side.

"Thanks for at least thinking about it, Taleah. Don't see meeting this guy as any more than it really is. Don't set yourself up for failure. According to Mark, he's stationed in Japan."

Taleah blew out a gust of breath. "Japan! Thanks for that bit of good news. Things are starting to look up, since it looks like I won't have to worry about him after this weekend. That is, if I should decide to cancel my camping plans with my friends. Bye for now, Mom."

"Bye, Taleah. Love you, honey."

"Love you, too, Mom."

Taleah immediately grabbed up her tennis racket and purse and started for the front door. Before leaving, she quickly turned back around and ran into her bedroom, where'd she'd left the backpack that held her clean change of clothes. Taleah always showered at the park after her tennis lesson was over. She also looked forward to seeing her instructor every Friday afternoon.

If he wasn't engaged to Marvella Ganion, a sexy beauty queen, Taleah thought Jonathan Moreland might just be able to change her mind about men. Tall, dark, muscular, and extremely handsome, Jonathan, a professional tennis player, was what most women would consider the total package. His personality was champagne-bubbly and his wit was crisply refreshing. Jonathan was also a very sensitive and caring man. Although Taleah wasn't anything akin to a man-hater, she was still very cautious around, and somewhat distrustful of, the opposite sex.

Taleah Taylor had the tendency to guard her heart as if it were Fort Knox.

Taleah hit a tennis ball wide, sending it scurrying across the court. Feeling horrible about how badly she'd hit the fuzzy yellow ball, Taleah watched as Jonathan chased it down, wondering if she'd ever master this game. She'd been taking lessons for more than a year now. Maybe she should just give it up. Since surrendering to defeat was not in her makeup, it was easier for her to decide to keep plodding away at it.

Jonathan came up and stood behind Taleah. Standing close enough to her to make her feel slightly uncomfortable about his gorgeous body leaning into hers, he guided her elbow and arm through the motions of a perfect stroke. "Your elbow and arm have to flow as one, Taleah. You have to stop bending your elbow."

Jonathan then demonstrated for Taleah how her elbow and arm should be level with her chest before swinging them out in a single fluid movement. He then reminded Taleah of how she should keep her feet firmly planted.

Taleah laughed heartily when a group of women stopped to boldly check out the tennis pro from head to toe. The catcalling and whistling began only seconds later. Jonathan was often embarrassed by the special attention he received from the ladies jogging or walking through the park. It was when they stopped and stared right at him that made him the most uncomfortable.

Jonathan's discomfort over the probing eyes caused him to make a bad serve. "Sorry about that, Taleah. Flirtatious females sure know how to make a guy feel nervous."

"You shouldn't be so darn fine, Jonathan Moreland," Taleah teased.

"Fine and taken. These modern-day women seem to have no shame in their game. They sure know how to stare a brother down."

"Oh, please, as if you guys don't do the very same thing. At least they weren't all up in your face asking for the digits before they even asked your name."

Jonathan chuckled. "Good point. Now you need to score some points on this court."

Taleah smiled with the brightness of an angel's halo. Though it was difficult, she managed to stifle the giggles bubbling inside her. "Hey, Lorenz Hampton, nice to meet you."

"Same here, Taleah."

Taleah Taylor, Lorenz mused. *Nice name.* Mark hadn't told him that his sister-in-law was such a bombshell, a pretty hot one, too, from what he could see. Lorenz couldn't believe how easily Taleah's outrageously sexy one-piece black bathing suit had turned him on. The swimwear wasn't too revealing, but she was tantalizing enough in it to make a man's mind wander all over the place. Even her voice was the bomb, sweet, soft, and lusty.

This wasn't the first time Lorenz had ever been introduced to a woman wearing a bathing suit, but none had ever turned him on in such a way as this.

Taleah had been outdoors lazing by the complex's pool when they'd first arrived; much sooner than she'd expected them to. Soft and pretty, this woman was built like a compact brick house.

Taleah couldn't tear her golden brown gaze away from the gorgeous face of Lorenz Hampton, a member of the United States Air Force. Six one, at least, she guessed at his height, marveling at his beautiful night-black eyes. His copper-brown complexion looked silky smooth and was clean-shaven. She even imagined her fingers slow-dancing over his baby-soft skin.

His muscular athletic build nearly had Taleah drooling. She couldn't see his abs beneath the white polo shirt he wore, but she was willing to bet that a quarter could be bounced off what she envisioned as rippling muscles. Everything else on his anatomy was also packed tightly. The brother had a body on him that defied description. She loved his broad chest, tapered waist, and the long, muscular legs. The casual shorts he wore revealed powerful-looking lower extremities.

Lorenz simply had the statuesque physique of an athletic phenomenon.

Taleah's glistening eyes then took in Lorenz's dark brown hair, silky with waves. His hair was cut short and neatly trimmed. Within military regulations, she guessed, aware that her military brothers-in-law also had to wear their hair a certain length.

Taleah knew very little about military life despite the fact that she had two sisters with military spouses. Both Mark and Miles were in the air force. Mark and Lynette were stationed at Boling AFB, Maryland. Miles and Marsha were assigned to Andrews AFB, Maryland. The two bases were in close proximity to each other, which afforded the two sisters constant contact.

Jack Taylor had also served in the military, the United States Army, but had retired three years after Taleah was born. Taleah only knew that which she'd heard about her dad's military career through his animated stories of peace and war. Although she had visited her sisters at their base homes, Taleah knew next to nothing about the kind of lives her older sisters really led.

Taleah felt completely hypnotized by Lorenz's beautiful dark eyes. It was as if she'd fallen under a magical spell of some sort. Tearing her eyes away from him still seemed impossible, glad that he was seated next to her at the kitchen table—and not on the sofa clear across the room. He was close enough for her to smell the enticingly scented cologne he wore.

Maybe he's the one! Taleah immediately scolded herself, shaking her head from side to side. What was she thinking? The one for what?

Because Taleah thought he was a young, raw recruit, she had to laugh inwardly. Lorenz didn't look a day over twenty or so. She couldn't imagine him teaching her a thing. But she couldn't stop herself from thinking about what delicious things she might be able to teach him. She silently scolded herself on that thought, too. She had gotten way out of line in her thinking.

Lorenz figured himself to be a head taller than Taleah, which should put her at five one. He loved the petite packaging; sure she packed quite a wallop in spite of her size. Her shoulder-length sable-brown hair looked like spun silk, as he imagined his fingers running all through it. The diamond-studded sparkle in her golden brown eyes mesmerized him. This fabulous-looking girl was Lorenz's dream come true. Taleah had instantly awakened his spirit. As if he had no control over them whatsoever, his night-black eyes locked onto her full, luscious mouth.

Taleah blushed, pointing at her bathing suit. "Sorry about my attire. I took to the pool because I wasn't expecting you guys until much later. I was only floating on my inflated pool lounger. If you'll excuse me a moment, I'll go into the other room and slip on a cover-up."

Don't want your eyes to fall any farther out of your head, Lorenz Hampton!

Taleah chuckled as she left the room, still thinking that *Mr. Right* had possibly landed, yet relieved that *Sir Fineness* would be landing back in Japan in less than four weeks. Despite her desire not to get bogged down with any romantic entanglements, Taleah couldn't help singing out loud, "What a man, what a man, what a beautiful man!"

The Kentucky Fried Chicken had been freshly cooked to order while the foursome had waited to take delivery, chatting away freely as they'd done so. A quick stop at the convenience store to pick up sodas and chips had been the only other delay in getting back to the apartment.

While setting out the china plates on the dining room table in her apartment, Taleah felt bad for having asked everyone to pitch in on the purchase of the KFC meal. But she was so short on funds. Besides, all the others had good-paying jobs. Why should she have to feed grown folks on her limited budget? Lorenz was actually Mark's guest, not hers. Mark had invited everyone to her place, not the other way around. Lynette was staying with their parents.

Taleah knew if she'd had the money she wouldn't have minded paying for everyone. Although she held down two jobs, she was still strapped for cash. Taleah had only taken on the second job to pay off all her credit cards. Using the ever-handy plastic had nearly driven her into bankruptcy court. It wouldn't be long before she was debt-free, one of her most important goals.

Once everyone started talking about going out to party, the low funds caused Taleah to think about the cost of the evening's activities. She didn't even have enough for the ten-dollar cover charge that most clubs charged, though she could borrow it from her parents if she had to.

Realizing she had to find out a thing or two about the group's expectations for their brief stay-over, Taleah briefly fixed her eyes on Lorenz. She then captured Lynette and Mark in her inquisitive gaze. "Tonight, guys, what do you have in mind for fun?"

Seated on the same body-contour chair with her tall, good-looking husband of eight years, Lynette smiled at her baby sister. Anyone could tell at a glance that the two women were somehow closely related. Lynette, five years older than her younger sibling, had a more sophisticated, polished look than Taleah. All three sisters shared the same eye and hair coloring, inherited from their mother. Lynette and Marsha were both several inches taller than Taleah.

"I thought we'd go out to a club," Mark responded, before Lynette had a chance to. "Have a good one in mind, Taleah?"

"Several good ones come to mind. I'm sure I'll have one picked out well before the time we leave. A Walk on the Wild Side up in Hollywood is pretty much the liveliest club around. But it's always packed tight every single night. Not much room to breathe in there, let alone move around." Taleah was definitely not a lover of huge crowds and crammed spaces.

Taleah turned her eyes on Lorenz. "Since we're all talking about going out tonight, I'd like to know if you're my date, or are you just out to catch?"

Lynette and Mark cracked up. Mark realized he'd forgotten to warn Lorenz about his sister-in-law's sharp wit and her knack for making colorful and right-out-of-the-blue comments.

Lorenz's surprised expression made it clear to everyone that he'd been totally caught off guard by Taleah's pointed question. However, it didn't take him long to recover. The dangerously sexy smile Lorenz tossed her way nearly brought Taleah to her knees. He had the most gorgeous white teeth she'd ever seen—and she worked in the field of dentistry.

It was Taleah who was now in need of some serious recovery time.

Lorenz's night-black eyes darkened even more as they made direct contact with Taleah's. His mesmerizing eyes appeared to hold the secret tale of a deep, dark mystery; a story that Taleah was extremely eager to probe into and eventually unfold, slowly.

Lorenz stroked his chin, looking thoughtful. "It was my understanding that Mark had already set you and me up for the entire weekend. Are you okay with his plan? It works for me."

Taleah blushed like crazy. "A-okay!"

Taleah wasn't a big fan of clubs and hot nightspots, but tonight felt different. She didn't feel like she was on the prowl. She actually had a date with a handsome, charismatic gentleman. Taleah hated waiting for guys to ask her to dance, but she wouldn't think of taking the initiative in that area. She'd even dance with people whom she'd never think of stepping outside the club with, if she wanted to dance. Hurting the feelings of others wasn't something she indulged in, nor would she enjoy it. She'd had her feelings hurt enough to know exactly how it felt. Horrible.

Dressed in a moderately conservative, curve-hugging navy blue pantsuit and white low-cut shell, Taleah smiled brightly at Lorenz, wondering what in the world he was thinking. He was a hard read for her even though his eyes had barely strayed from her since they'd first met. If nothing else happened between them, their eyes had already made a serious love connection.

Taleah loved the brown leisure suit Lorenz wore. It looked good on his tall, lean frame. Muscles bulged beneath his beige silk T-shirt and his pants fit him in all the right places.

After finally managing to drag her starstruck gaze from Lorenz, Taleah looked all around the popular club Shades of Color. Taleah never knew the story behind the club's name, nor had she ever bothered to inquire of it. Since it was a multiracial venue, she thought the name might refer to the host of ethnic groups that patronized the place.

Lorenz moved his head forward until his mouth rested close to his date's ear. "Would you like to dance, Taleah?"

Taleah shook her head in the negative. "I'd like to wait until there are others out on the floor. I'm not comfortable being out there alone."

Chuckling softly, Lorenz raised an eyebrow. "Alone? Am I suddenly invisible?"

Taleah laughed heartily. "I'm sorry for that. You are definitely a visible presence." *A physically stimu-*

lating presence at that. "But do you mind if we wait a bit longer?"

Lorenz shrugged. "No problem. I'm all for whatever pleases you, Taleah."

"Thanks, Lorenz."

In just a matter of minutes the dance floor had quickly filled to near capacity. Taleah had no more excuses. Not that she needed one. If she wasn't interested in dancing at any given time, she believed that it was in everyone's best interest for her to be open and honest about it.

Deciding that she should go ahead and make the next move, since Lorenz had already asked her to dance, Taleah looked him right in the eye and nodded toward the dancing arena. Taleah had somehow gotten the feeling that he might not ask a second time. That had prompted her into wasting no more time in revisiting his request.

Lorenz smiled as he got up from his seat. He then reached for Taleah's hand. She felt the sparks of heat pass right through her at the same moment she nestled her hand into his warm grasp. The short distance to the dance floor had her feeling as if she floated on cloud nine.

A few minutes into the music Taleah saw that Lorenz was rather behind on the latest dance steps. His funky moves had come and gone more than a year ago. Perhaps his part of the world wasn't up on the newest dance crazes. Despite it all, he was an incredibly smooth dancer.

Japan *was* thousands and thousands of miles away from the part of the world she loved so much, sunny southern California. Taleah had no desire to live anywhere else on the planet.

The idea of her visiting Japan was a fleeting one. Taleah recalled with fondness her vow to one day visit Tokyo, Japan, after her geography teacher had shown her eighth-grade class numerous film slides from her summer vacation visit to the colorful and intriguing country. That had been a very long time ago, but the sharp images were still crystal clear in Taleah's mind.

The music eventually turned slow, which brought out even more dancers onto the floor. Taleah went straight into Lorenz's arms, as if she'd always belonged there. Without the least bit of reluctance on her part, Taleah's head quickly found its way to Lorenz's broad chest. Each step brought them closer and closer, holding each other tighter and tighter, until there was nothing between them. Taleah's body tingled with joy at the close physical connection it had made with Lorenz's. His embrace was warm, fostering in Taleah a sense of security and sweet peace.

Taleah was surprised when Lynette and Mark announced to her and Lorenz their intent to visit the club's restaurant for a bite of dessert. Since they hadn't offered for the other couple to tag along, Taleah realized she was going to be alone with Lorenz for the first time. She couldn't help wondering if her family had set her up. But they probably needed some time alone, since Lynette and Mark were away from each other during the entire week, she concluded. Spending time alone with Lorenz both frightened and thrilled Taleah, all at the same time.

The couple managed to converse over the loud music, but it was only possible by keeping their heads closely together. The climate between them seemed rather intimate in Taleah's opinion. She was really shocked to learn that the man who looked like a raw recruit was actually thirty-one years old, four years her senior. He looked so much like a young

kid to her. He was also a veteran with thirteen years
of active duty time under his belt. Maybe he could
teach her a thing or two, after all. She certainly
had a few captivating ideas in mind for a first lesson.

As if Taleah hadn't already been shocked senseless, his marital status—he was married!—had her
shaking all over. She felt like screaming at the top
of her lungs. Why did these sorts of things always
happen to her? If it wasn't for bad luck, Taleah felt
that she wouldn't have any luck at all. Not wanting
to hear any more details about his personal life,
Taleah quickly excused herself, leaving Lorenz in
pretty much the same state of mind she was in.
Confused and stunned.

Taleah's legs couldn't carry her fast enough to
the club's restaurant. Mark was going to hear from
her in no uncertain terms. How was it that her
brother-in-law kept hooking her up with married
men? Granted, he didn't know the last guy was
married, but Taleah thought he would've made sure
this time around. Taleah felt like crying. The possibility of a *Mr. Right* was just another *Mr. Wrong.*
Taleah hated any sort of confrontation, but Mark
had to be confronted.

Taleah dropped down in the chair at the table
where her family was seated. Without any warning
to Mark, she reached over with one hand and
grabbed his shirt by both ends of the collar. "What
have I ever done to you to make you have such a
low opinion of me?" Taleah's ability to reason no
longer existed. All the volatile thoughts that had
run through her head on the short trek to the restaurant had caused her anger to rapidly build out of
control.

Mark gently removed Taleah's hand from his
collar, since he was nearly choking from the tight

hold she had on it. He gulped hard. "Calm down, Taleah. What's this all about?"

Taleah glared fiercely at Mark. "Your friend out there in the club. He's married! Mark, why do you keep doing this to me? I don't understand it. I'd never date a married man."

Lynette looked on in utter amazement, eager to hear what her husband had to say for himself. Neither could she believe that Mark would allow this to happen twice to her sister.

Mark shook his head. "Lorenz is separated, Taleah. His divorce is nearly final. He hasn't lived with his wife in four years, but he only filed the paperwork less than a year ago. I'd never do that to you on purpose. I asked Lorenz his marital status before I ever thought of introducing you to him. He's a great guy, Taleah. I already know that much."

"How could you possibly know how great he is or isn't? You haven't known him much longer than I have, Mark. I just don't believe any of this is happening."

"I beg to differ, Taleah. Lorenz and I were at Buckley Academy together for two years. We weren't best of friends, but he was one of the most respected guys on the Dallas campus."

"So you do know him. Big deal! What does that have to do with his marital status?"

"Come on, Taleah, you're being unreasonable," Lynnette charged. "If I thought Mark was lying to you about Lorenz, I'd be all over him myself. Little sister, this is just a blind date. You'll probably never see Lorenz after this weekend. Why are you so worked up?"

Because I'm falling for him like a ton of bricks! That's why I'm in such a tizzy. Taleah would never admit to her family how very taken she was with Lorenz Hampton. It just seemed way too soon for that. She had already gotten caught up in one whirlwind relationship; one was enough. Still, there were just so many things about Lorenz that intrigued her. He was also a gentleman and he'd shown her nothing but the utmost respect.

Taleah really didn't know how she felt about Lorenz being nearly divorced. That was the same as being almost married. No matter how you looked at it, he still wasn't free. But why should that matter? she wondered. The guy was only visiting her for the weekend and he also lived on the other side of the world, she reminded herself. This was a no-brainer.

Taleah got up from the chair, smiling weakly. "Guys, I'm going to go back to Lorenz and try to explain why I ran out on him the way I did. I owe him a sincere apology."

"No, I'm the one who owes an apology, Taleah."

Taleah turned around at the sound of Lorenz's deep voice. She looked stunned to see him standing there. She had to wonder about how much of the conversation he might've overheard.

Lorenz pointed at an empty table at the very back of the restaurant. "Why don't we sit over there? I see that I need to clear up a few things for you. I'd like to do it over something to eat and drink. Okay?"

"Fine with me, Lorenz." She turned to Lynnette and Mark. "See you guys later."

Taleah's heart skipped several beats at the sad expression on Lorenz's face. She had probably hurt his feelings by the way she'd jetted out of the club. This was one person she didn't think she could stand to hurt in any way. He seemed so sensitive. She didn't know why, but she felt that someone had possibly hurt Lorenz as bad as she herself had been hurt. On the other hand, had he been trying to play himself off as a single man, when he wasn't, Lorenz would've gotten more than just his feelings hurt. Taleah hated to be lied to by anyone.

Immediately after the waitress took the food and drink orders Lorenz apologized to Taleah for how he'd carelessly mentioned his marriage. He then began to tell her more and more details about his personal life. He had started out with where he'd been in his life and the direction it was now headed in. Just as Mark had told Taleah, Lorenz reiterated for her that he and his wife had been separated for four years.

Taleah sensed Lorenz's reluctance to get too deeply into the reasons for the marital problems. However, he did mention that the separation hadn't been his desire. He also stated that his wife had never really been able to adjust to military life, which made it extremely hard for her to support him in his chosen career field.

Although the couple hadn't had children together, Lorenz had been a stepfather to his wife Loretta's son, Amir. From the things Lorenz said to her about his stepson it was apparent to Taleah that Lorenz terribly missed the company of the little guy.

Amir had been only two when they were married and the separation had come before his fourth birthday. Amir's natural father had always paid child support for his son. On top of the money Lorenz sent for the running of the stateside household his estranged wife presided over, he had also set up a college fund for Amir, which had occurred long before the separation.

Lorenz spoke highly of how the military accepted stepchildren, providing them with the same wonderful benefits offered to natural children of service members. He thought it was an exceptional practice for the U.S. Government to have implemented. Because he and Loretta hadn't been married long enough for her to keep her military benefits, Amir would lose his also once the divorce was final. Had Amir been Lorenz's natural son his coverage would've remained in force. Children of military parents didn't receive military ID cards until they reached the age of ten. Amir hadn't yet reached the age for the issuance of such an identification card.

Although it had not been her intent, Taleah soon found herself baring her very soul to Lorenz. Soul-stirring words poured from her mouth, yet she kept her emotions under control. He was easy to talk to and she could see that she held his undivided attention. Taleah had no problem sharing the details of her broken engagement without placing blame on Bradley. She couldn't hold anyone responsible but herself for her problems with her ex-fiancé.

Taleah then told Lorenz private things that she hadn't ever shared with anyone, not even with any of her siblings or her three very best friends, Drusilla Smith, Sherra Miller, and Brenda Bailey. The more she got off her chest, the more relieved she felt. No one could ever have made her believe that she'd discuss so many intimate details of her life with a perfect stranger.

It suddenly dawned on Taleah that she didn't even think of Lorenz as a stranger. Nothing about him seemed strange to her. Taleah had made some sort of miraculous connection with Lorenz. It seemed as if she'd known him all her life, as if he were a dear, old friend.

Could Lorenz Hampton be her soul mate?

Lorenz leaned over and gently brushed his knuckles over her cheek. "It sounds like we're in the same sinking boat. Maybe we can throw each other a life raft. You think?"

Taleah smiled softly. "I'll make sure to keep one inflated, just in case you need rescuing."

He grinned. "I need to be rescued right now, Taleah. I just don't know from what or perhaps from whom. If you got that life raft handy, maybe you can help me figure it all out."

Taleah returned his gesture of comfort by kissing the back of his hand. "At your service!"

While Lynette and Mark danced the night away, Taleah and Lorenz had the desire to just spend the rest of the evening getting further acquainted. It seemed that they had so much to talk about and appeared to have so much in common.

His air force career field impressed her. She'd never met a real live meteorologist before now. All she ever knew about it were the weathermen on television. When she mentioned her limited knowledge about his field, he was quick to let her know that all the TV weathermen weren't really meteorologists. The majority of them were communications specialists.

Taleah thought that he had to be awfully intelligent to be in that line of work. Although he'd eventually received his degree in meteorology, compliments of Uncle Sam, Lorenz told her that he had opted to stay in the air force as a noncommissioned officer. She later learned that he loved to play softball and basketball. After boasting in a nonegotistical way about how good he was at his favorite pastime passions, Lorenz informed Taleah that he played each game with organized sports teams on Yokota Air Base, his assigned duty station in Japan. He was also a cross-country runner and a jogger, pretty much an all-around athlete.

Taleah clearly saw the evidence of such written

all over Lorenz's fine-tuned, sculpted body. The brother was one big hunk of milk chocolate delight. She couldn't wait to find out what delicious flavor existed in his soft center. A sudden image of her biting into a chocolate-covered cherry caused her to involuntarily lick her lips.

Taleah laughed like crazy as she talked about how horrible she was at playing tennis, the sport she loved and had wanted to learn to play for as long as she could remember. Taleah enthused about how she could be found in front of the television set every time the Williams sisters took center court. She thought the two women were in a class all by themselves.

Embarrassment struck Taleah hard as she told Lorenz how she often kept her pro instructor running all over the place after her wildly driven tennis balls. Taleah had a nonexistent backhand and her forehand was just as lousy. Despite all her errors and mishaps she was determined to stick with it. Taleah never quit at something once she started it.

The sleeping arrangements had become a little problematic for Taleah when Lynette and Mark suddenly made their announcement to spend the night at her place rather than going back to the elder Taylors' home. The lateness of the hour was cited for the change in plans—they didn't want to wake anyone up.

Taleah only had two bedrooms, one of which served as an office/exercise room. She felt obligated to give her bedroom up to Lynette and Mark, as if there were any other way to solve the issue. She certainly wasn't going to offer to sleep in her bedroom with Lorenz. After mulling the delicate situation over a bit longer, Taleah decided that she and Lorenz would have to deal with the sofa and love seat. It was the only workable solution, unless he liked sleeping on the floor.

With Lorenz as a guest in her house, and her being the shorter of the two, Taleah knew she'd have to be the one to brave the smaller couch. Just thinking about being so cramped up in such a small space caused her to wince in agony. Not much sleep would occur for her tonight, Taleah mused. She hated to have to forgo her delicious dreams, especially tonight. She had planned to dream about the gorgeous man who'd already begun to break down the protective barricades surrounding her precious heart.

Taleah announced the sleeping arrangements as she gathered enough linen to make up the two sofas. She kept extra pillows on hand just for unexpected situations like this one. It really surprised her when Lorenz jumped right in and helped her prepare the sofas for sleeping on.

"Lorenz, do you want to hit the shower first? Or would you rather wait and shower in the morning?" Taleah asked, thanking God that she had two bathrooms.

He laughed. "After all that dancing we did, I'm sure I'm pretty ripe about now. Thanks for the offer. I can use the same towel and washcloth you gave me earlier. I hung it back up just for that purpose."

"That's great. I'm going to fix myself a cup of tea. Would you like some? Or do you prefer coffee?" Taleah drank a cup of soothing, relaxing blend of Lavender Warm Spirit tea every night before going to bed.

"The tea sounds nice if it's herbal, Taleah. I don't drink anything with caffeine in it."

Taleah smiled at him. "It's herbal. I'll have it ready by the time you're all through." Taleah's nightly ritual of falling asleep to soft music suddenly came to her mind. "One more thing. I normally sleep with one of the digital cable music stations on. Will that bother you?"

Lorenz had to laugh. "I don't think so. I'm also a disc jockey, Taleah. Music is in my blood." Before she could comment, Lorenz had already started for the guest bathroom.

Smiling broadly, Taleah raised an eyebrow. "A DJ, too."

His personal resume got more and more interesting by the moment. "I wonder what type of music he likes to rock his woman's world to." Taleah patted her cheeks in a gesture of scolding herself. "Bad girl, bad girl, you'd better behave yourself. You are so out of line. It's definitely not going to be that kind of party up in here tonight. Save it all for your dreams."

Taleah chuckled inwardly at her own silliness.

TWO

Taleah felt alert and chipper despite the fact she and Lorenz had sat up talking and listening to music for several more hours after they'd both taken showers. Their unusual soulful connection still blew her away. However, she wasn't too happy with Lorenz taking the initiative to clean up her kitchen without asking if she minded. She had awakened to find him standing at the sink washing the dishes left from the previous evening's meal. For whatever reason, him taking care of her household chores didn't set too well with her. It seemed somewhat intrusive.

Although Taleah had rinsed the dinnerware off with hot water right after dinner, she had left it all in the sink instead of stacking it in the dishwasher. Lorenz was washing the dishes by hand. Because she didn't know how to address the situation in an appropriate manner, she decided to let it go. Her consideration hinged on the fact that he'd only be there for the weekend.

Since everyone was invited up to the Taylor house

for breakfast, Taleah said her cheerful good mornings to Lorenz and then greeted and hugged her family members, who were also up and dressed. She then rushed off to shower and get herself prepared for the day.

Taleah had noticed that Lorenz had already attired himself in navy shorts and a short-sleeve, open-collar shirt. She thought he looked pretty cool and relaxed. She hoped he'd fared better on the couch than she had cramped up on the love seat. He had offered her the full-size sofa, but she'd insisted on him sleeping there. Lorenz had even told her he had no problem sleeping on the floor, one of his favorite places to stretch out. He'd also mentioned that he sought out the hardness of the floor during the rare times he experienced back pain or muscle spasms.

The atmosphere in Taleah's spacious bedroom was like a fresh breath of spring. The room was showered in pastels, a lovely complement to the antique-white furnishings and white plantation shutters. The magnificent patchwork quilt draped over her queen-size bed was handmade. Her gentle-colored sleeping quarters were quite serene yet softly animated.

Taleah's mind stayed steadfastly on Lorenz as she showered. She thought that he was a really great guy, from what little time she'd spent in his company, but she knew how these things worked. Life was a bed of roses for most new couples. That is, until the dagger-sharp thorns started to pop out everywhere. Everyone and everything was always great in the beginning.

"The beginning of what?" Taleah asked herself.

"There is no beginning here; nothing but an inevitable ending to what has so far been a great weekend."

That bit of relative information was something she'd better get used to. How many times did she need to remind herself that Lorenz Hampton lived on the other side of the world? *Until it finally sinks in,* she mused, feeling sorry that no chance whatsoever existed for any sort of serious relationship to develop between them. Her already fragile heart couldn't even stand the thought of a long-distance relationship, let alone getting involved in one.

If she couldn't trust someone living in the same city with her, how could trust ever build between two people living on separate continents? It was impossible.

"Pen pals," she practically sang out. "We can at least be pen pals. That is, if he wants to correspond with me half as much I'd like for it to happen."

The thought of them writing letters to each other from across the miles on an occasional basis suddenly lifted Taleah's flagging spirits. The thought of never seeing or hearing from Lorenz again had saddened her. As much as she hated to admit it, she was going to miss him when the weekend was over. Would Lorenz miss her, too? She couldn't help wondering.

With her mind now locked in on the day's activities, Taleah generously lathered Avon's Soft & Sensual Skin So Soft lotion all over her evenly tanned body. She then put on fresh underwear and pulled on a pair of cute white zippered-front shorts. A few seconds later she pulled down a bright orange tank-style T-shirt over her head and slipped her feet into white sandals.

Taleah loved bright colors, especially in the spring and summer. Spring had just recently come into bloom, so she had several months ahead of her to wear the bold hues. Their brightness definitely enhanced the seasonal tan she worked so hard to maintain during the spring and summer months. She didn't concern herself with tanning in the fall and winter seasons.

After thoroughly brushing out her long hair and then leaving it to hang loose about her shoulders, Taleah put on a colorless lip gloss and brushed onto her cheeks a slight amount of blush. A light pulse-point spraying of Casual, one of her favorite perfumes, had Taleah ready to meet both the joys and the challenges of the promising day that lay ahead.

Satisfied with her springlike appearance, and in eager anticipation of joining her overnight guests, Taleah grabbed her colorful beach-style bag and left her bedroom. Though she felt like whistling a happy tune, she refrained. God forbid that anyone should find out that her brief but exhilarating encounters with Lorenz had already stopped her heart from singing nothing but the blues. How long the sweet new love tunes in her heart would last was anyone's guess.

As soon as Taleah reached the living room, Mark got to his feet. "It's about time, Miss Taleah. Why does it always take you women forever?"

Taleah cast Mark a bold look of defiance. "Don't start with me! Women can't help it if you men have very little to take care of. Our hair alone takes us a lot of time. So get over it."

"If it's that much of a problem, cut if all off," Mark shot back in a teasing manner.

"Oh, I know you didn't go there. You'd have a fit if Lynette even got her hair so much as trimmed.

I'm not your wife, so you have no say in what I do or don't do with my locks. If I were married to you, you still wouldn't have any say. So there." Taleah stuck her tongue out at Mark.

As an only child, Lorenz enjoyed the spirited exchange. It was nice for him to see that Taleah could hold her end up on the battlefield, although nothing more than a friendly war had just been waged. In Lorenz's opinion, Taleah was the victor. Mark had challenged the wrong opponent. It seemed to him as if Taleah and Mark had thoroughly enjoyed their huffy exchange.

Laughing, Lynette got to her feet. "You two need to give it a rest. Let's get to Mom and Dad's so we can do this breakfast thing. Mark and I haven't showered, since we didn't bring a clean change of clothes, so that's the first thing on our agenda when we get there. Let's move it."

Taleah and Lorenz headed for the door. Once everyone was outside, Taleah secured the locks before getting into Mark's late-model Infiniti. She would've preferred to walk, but she was included in what one might call a foursome. Always considerate of others, Taleah thought she should go along with whatever the program, especially in this instance.

It was such a beautiful day, Taleah mused. The sun was out and the skies were clear and blue. The cool breeze blowing made the weather conditions perfect for a leisure stroll. Perhaps Lorenz would like to walk, too, she mused. "Hey, guys, I'm going to walk up to the house. Lorenz, I'd love for you to join me if you don't mind. It's not that far. Just a couple of blocks."

Lorenz nodded. "I know. We stopped by your parents' home to pick up Lynnette before we came to your place. I'd love to walk with you. It'll be a real treat with the cool breeze."

Taleah smacked her forehead with the palm of her hand. "That's right, you guys did stop by there. I wasn't thinking. That's not so unusual for me. Lately I've been a little ditzy."

Lorenz laughed inwardly at the comically perplexed expression on Taleah's face.

Taleah and Lorenz waved to Lynette and Mark as they pulled off in the car. The couple then started out for the short walking distance to the Taylors' home.

Lorenz wanted to hold Taleah's hand, but he wasn't sure how she'd react. Nothing more intimate than a kiss on the cheek had occurred between them. But he really didn't expect anything more than what had already happened. A passionate kiss or two would be nice. But Taleah still had a broken heart. Though he no longer carried the torch that once burned so hot for his wife, his heart had probably been in worse shape than Taleah's a few years back.

Taleah pointed to an apartment building across the street from hers. "Two of my best friends live there, Drusilla and Sherra. My other best girlfriend lives in the same building as I do. Brenda was out last night on a date, or she would've already come down to check out my blind date. We all talked this morning. We're all up in each other's business. One of us is no worse than the other. We always have to know what's going on in each others' lives."

Lorenz cracked up. "No secrets, huh?"

"Well, I know I have a few secrets. I'm sure they do, too. I guess some things are sacred. I told you a few secrets last night, some that I've never told anyone."

He eyed her curiously. "Really! I'm glad you trusted me that much. What were some of the secrets you told me?" Lorenz wasn't even sure Taleah liked him, let alone trusted in him.

Taleah laughed. "I'm not sure if I'd call it trust, since I haven't known you long enough for us to have built that kind of rapport. As for the secrets, they don't bear repeating. However, I was sure I'd never hear them again, especially from anyone I knew."

"Why's that, Taleah?"

" 'Cause you're going back to Japan. And I don't know anyone in that part of the world."

Lorenz chuckled. "You got a point there. But I know Mark. That doesn't concern you."

"Not a bit. Besides, you don't know what was a secret and what wasn't."

Lorenz shrugged. "But I could tell him everything."

Taleah stopped dead in her tracks and turned to face Lorenz. "You wouldn't do that, now, would you? I didn't sense that you were that kind of person. That's why it was so easy for me to open up to you like I did. Did I make a mistake in judgment?"

His desire to bring the vulnerable-looking Taleah into his embrace burned white hot. Instead, he stroked her cheek with his forefinger. "Trust is a very fragile thing, no matter how long you've known someone. Your secrets are safe with me. I'd never utter a word you've said to me to anyone. Feel better now?"

Taleah smiled gently. Fighting back a surge of emotions, she resumed walking. "Much better. But I already knew you wouldn't give me up. Don't ask me how I knew. I just did."

The expression in his eyes had softened at her last statement. Her comment seemed to suggest that she had somehow tapped into who he was as a person, that she already knew him despite the fact they'd only met yesterday. He had felt a powerful connection to her from the very beginning. There was a strong spiritual force at work here. The odd mixture of feelings he had been experiencing was totally unexplainable.

Could his connection with Taleah be a spiritual awakening or perhaps a miracle?

Taleah was intriguing, also very confusing. Her coolness was somewhat of an enigma for him. Although he felt her presence, she sometimes seemed detached, as if she were somewhere else. Taleah had gone into quite a bit of depth regarding her broken engagement. That she'd taken it extremely hard had come through to him with crystal clarity. He couldn't help wondering if she had built an impenetrable prison wall around her heart. Considering what she'd already been through, it was no wonder.

Although Taleah was friendly enough he didn't get the impression that she had any real interest in him on a romantic level. Although they'd spent an incredibly wonderful evening together, he didn't see much hope for anything beyond the weekend. Since he was going to be in the state for another few weeks, he'd really like to see her again. The weekends were the only free time he had. It would really be nice if Taleah wanted the same thing. Fat chance, he mused.

"I understand you're going to be here for about three more weeks. Think you'll come down to L.A. with Mark again?"

Lorenz's heart nearly stopped. How could she have known what he was thinking? Was she a psychic or what? This constant weird stirring within his heart was starting to make him crazy. Taleah was getting inside more than just his head. "I guess I'd have to be invited before I could make that determination. Mark may not want to bring me again since his wife is here. They may want to get away for a weekend and be alone, since they're apart during the week."

Taleah's heart raced like the wind inside her chest. "What if I invited you back, Lorenz? Would you accept?" In anticipation of his response, she sucked in a deep breath and held it.

He looked at her in stunned disbelief. "Are you actually extending an invite? Or was that just a hypothetical?"

Taleah released her breath. "It's definitely an invitation. I'd love to see you again."

Taleah didn't know where the sudden boldness had come from, but she hoped she wouldn't regret it showing up. It was really too late to worry about it now. She had laid her cards out on the table. It was now Lorenz's turn to show his hand. Taleah hadn't given any thought to the possibility that he might turn down her invitation.

If that were to happen, Taleah would be mortified. For whatever reason, she felt confident that it wouldn't occur. She believed Lorenz would only turn her down if it weren't possible for him to accept. She didn't think he was in any way an insensitive man.

Then it occurred to Taleah that Lorenz could be deeply involved with another woman. That hadn't been discussed. As good looking as he was, she'd find it hard to believe that he was completely unattached. He *was* in the midst of a divorce, though. Still, he hadn't lived with his wife in a very long time. If he did have someone special in his life, not only did he think of going on a blind date, he'd accepted Mark's offer to meet and go out with his sister-in law. Even so, Lorenz wasn't guilty of betrayal. Everything to do with them had been totally innocent.

Intriguing thoughts, Taleah concluded, wishing she'd found out if he had a girlfriend in Japan before extending the invitation. If he did accept, she vowed to find out.

Lorenz once again fought the temptation to take her hand. "I'd love to see you again, too. But we still have to consider Mark since it's his car that brought me here. He may not want me to tag along next time." Was her invitation to him a dream come true or what?

Taleah grinned, wishing she could leave it at that. It could be an easy out for her, especially if he did have someone else. But since she didn't know anything for sure, she was just going to go for broke. Taleah Taylor was a risk taker, but it was not so when it came to her heart.

A hint of mischief danced in her eyes. "You mean to tell me, Lorenz, that a worldly man like yourself hasn't thought of renting a vehicle?"

Lorenz tossed Taleah an engaging smile. "With your brilliant concept in mind, I accept your invitation." As he fell back in step with her, his body brushed slightly against hers. He felt the strong currents of physical attraction down to the core of his essence. It took Lorenz a couple of seconds to regroup and collect his thoughts. Everything about Taleah seemed magical.

"To answer your question about the rental, I hadn't thought of it. Nor did I have a reason to before now." He winked at her. "Thanks for doing my thinking for me. In this case, I don't mind at all." Lorenz didn't know what was happening to him, nor did he believe it was possible for him to stop it. All he could do was pray that whatever had a hold of him would be merciful.

His troubled marriage had been merciless in more ways than one.

In another bold move, Taleah took Lorenz's hand, though she only held on to it briefly. "I promise you I'm not the type of woman who believes it's her right to think for her man. Nor do I think that a man can't make a single decision without his woman's input. I'm glad you accepted. We'll go over the details for your next visit before you leave tomorrow."

The Taylors had breakfast ready by the time Taleah and Lorenz finally arrived. Lynnette and Mark had also showered and changed into fresh clothes. A five-minute walk had taken Taleah and Lorenz nearly thirty minutes. The animated laughter and knowing glances passing between them were a dead giveaway. Something magical was happening for these two.

The Taylors' six-bedroom home was beautiful inside and out. All the walls were painted an antique white and the wall-to-wall carpeting was done in subtle shades of ivory and beige. Soft yet vibrant colors ran rampant throughout the house. Amazing African works of art captured in a variety of magnificent hardwood frames, along with dozens of individual and family portraits, made the Taylors' home look like a mini art gallery. Native artists had created many of the glorious African sculptures and expression-filled paintings.

While everyone held hands, Jack Taylor, as head of his household, passed the blessing in thanksgiving for such a bountiful gift. Jack had prepared most of the delicious-looking breakfast foods, as he was also the head chef. He actually thought of himself as second in command of his household, equal with Allison. God was truly the head and the body of their humble abode.

Communication around the table was easy and relaxed. When Allison asked what the group's plans were for the day, Taleah told her mother a couple of things that had already been mentioned. Lorenz wanted to purchase some of the latest music releases to take back to Japan with him. Taleah had decided to take him to a couple of the smaller, privately owned record stores, which were few in number. Stores like Tower and Wherehouse had practically run all the little guys out of business. Lynette and Mark wanted to hit a couple of the large malls.

Sightseeing wasn't on the agenda since Lorenz wasn't a stranger to California. He had been stationed at Vandenburgh Air Force Base before his second overseas assignment. Lorenz had also been stationed in Korea and numerous other bases throughout his thirteen-year career.

Then Mark announced that several guys he and Lorenz had met at their temporary duty station were coming down later in the evening. The airmen wanted to party L.A. style.

Taleah wasn't too thrilled about clubbing two nights in a row. But being out with Lorenz would make it easier for her to bear. He was such a fun person to be with. He made her laugh, something she hadn't done enough of, as of late. Since Lorenz had made it clear to everyone that he was her date for the entire weekend, she didn't have that to worry about.

It didn't take long for Lorenz to discern that the Taylors were one big happy family. They seemed

very genuine and open in their relationships with
each other. He couldn't help noticing the adoration in Taleah's eyes when she looked at her dad.
It was quite obvious to Lorenz that Jack Taylor was
his youngest daughter's hero, though both sisters
seemed to dote on their mom. He had also gotten
the impression that Taleah and Lynette were not
only siblings, but also the best of friends. How Lorenz would love to have a brother as a best friend
and confidant.

As an only child, Lorenz had always wondered
what it would be like to be from a huge family of
sisters and brothers. While there were plenty of
other relatives in the Hampton clan, he missed
having siblings to bond with and share fun outings, vacations, and secrets with. He had bonded
with one male cousin in particular. Lorenz and his
cousin, Thomas Hampton, were as close as blood
brothers could ever be. Still, they weren't siblings
in the true sense of the word.

Taleah rushed about her bedroom like a chicken
with its head cut off as she prepared herself for the
evening's outing. The group had stayed out shopping much longer than anticipated, which had left
them with very little time to get ready. Lynette and
Mark were getting dressed at her parents' home
since Taleah only had two bathrooms. She had already taken the shortest bubble bath ever, but it
had relaxed her considerably. Lorenz was showering in the guest bathroom while Taleah scoped out
her closet for something appropriate to wear.

The thought of Lorenz standing butt naked in
her shower gave her the absolute shivers.

As Taleah imagined the beads of hot water bounc-
ing off his firm flesh, she closed her eyes, wishing

she could be in the shower with him, lathering him up in more ways than one. Her vision of them entwined together in a compromising embrace was downright erotic. She then imagined Lorenz making wild, passionate love to her under the gentle spray of hot water. Just the thought of his sizzling caresses all over her body had her heated flesh singing his praises.

Taleah moaned with longing as her mind continued to take her to pleasure-invoking places, the kinds of sensual spots it had never treaded onto before. The flaming heat between her legs had rapidly grown tenfold. Her body was on fire. The erotic thoughts of Lorenz had turned her body into a feverish frenzy. How to bring her body temperature back down to normal before leaving the bedroom was her biggest concern. Lorenz just couldn't know what he did to her.

Looking flushed and dazed, Taleah finally shook herself out of one of the best sexual fantasies she'd ever had. Time waited on no one, she reminded herself, as the minutes continued to click off the clock despite her desire for it to slow down. Her heart needed to slow down, too.

Although Taleah knew time wasn't on her side, that she still had to get dressed, she sat down on the side of the bed to try and assess what was happening to her. For a man she hadn't even wanted to meet, Lorenz had undeniably cast a magical spell over her.

Taleah felt utterly bewitched by Technical Sergeant Lorenz Hampton.

How could she have extended an invitation for him to visit with her again? She had to have been suffering from temporary insanity at the time. Their time together wasn't supposed to last past the weekend. But here she had gone and prolonged the in-

evitable. Lorenz would return to Japan and she'd
once again experience personal devastation. Just
the thought of him leaving broke her heart. Taleah
didn't dare call what she felt for Lorenz love, but
her feelings for him seemed to run so deep. What
had Lorenz Hampton done to her to have her feeling this way?

Lorenz more than appreciated the white denim
jeans and the bright red off-the-shoulder, summer-
weight knit sweater Taleah had chosen to wear.
Her look was both casual and sexy. While seated at
a table inside the club L.A. Nights, a little swankier
than the club they'd patronized the night before,
his eyes drank in the smoothness of the bared skin
on her chest and above her breasts: small, round,
and perky. He preferred smaller bustlines. The perfect size was the ones he could fully take into his
mouth. Taleah's pouting breasts reminded him of
perfectly rounded oranges, firm and sweet.

For fear of going crazy with desire, Lorenz
couldn't even allow himself to imagine tasting their
ripened sweetness. After all, he wasn't in private
where he didn't have to worry about his male reac-
tions to Taleah's sexually alluring attributes. Besides
Mark and Lynette, there were three other couples
seated at the conjoined tables. The other three airmen and their dates had met them at the club,
having followed the perfect directions that Mark
had given one of the guys over the phone. The
group of six had rented a van to drive into L.A. for
the evening. The other military men had met their
dates in the same area where they were temporar-
ily stationed.

Taleah tapped Lorenz on the shoulder. "Want
to dance?"

His desire to feel her body next to his was darn near overwhelming. It seemed that she had also read his mind; the same question had been on the tip of his tongue. Lorenz had to laugh when he noticed that no one else was on the dance floor. Taleah had thrown caution to the wind. He was thrilled that it no longer mattered to her that they'd be the only ones on the dance floor.

Just as the couple started for the floor, Taleah turned toward the sound of her name. Her face beamed bright with pleasure. Seeing that her three girlfriends had decided to show up thrilled her. None of the women had wanted to come out to the club without dates, but after hearing Taleah go on and on about Lorenz in a way they hadn't heard her talk about any man, none of them could resist the invite to join their best friend and her guests for the evening.

Drusilla, a master sergeant in the U.S. Army, was stationed at Fort McArthur. She also had conference calling on her phone lines, so all had gotten a chance to hear about Taleah's blind date at the same time. Hearing Taleah squealing like a kid again had made each of them ecstatic.

On the flip side of the coin, that Lorenz was stationed in the Far East had them worried.

The three friends feared that Taleah would get hurt again when Lorenz's TDY was over, since she already seemed so into him. A myth had it that military men had a woman on hold in every corner of the world. As far as male and female relationships went, Taleah hadn't had a lot to gush and coo about in quite a long while. Her fears had so far kept her from moving forward.

Taleah involving herself in a long-distance relationship had all the earmarkings of yet another one that would be short-lived, her friends believed regrettably. Then the rainstorms would return to her lovely eyes. They didn't want to see that happen to their dear friend yet again. Taleah was under the impression that love had to hurt to turn out right. If falling in love meant getting hurt again, she had vowed to live her life without the love of a man.

Taleah warmly embraced Drusilla, Sherra, and Brenda before introducing them to Lorenz. Out of the three women, Brenda and Taleah had been friends the longest. She then presented her girl-friends to the others at the table.

Lynette and Mark were well acquainted with Taleah's female friends. From the look on two of the guys' faces, as they made the acquaintance of the three very attractive sisters, Taleah wondered if they wished they'd shown up solo.

Drusilla Smith had been in a longtime relation-ship with Craig Stanford, but marriage wasn't on the horizon. Brenda Bailey and Sherra Miller were single, but neither of them was the just settling kind. Sherra had once been married, a union that had ended in disaster and heartbreak. She was of the opinion that all men cheated, that all were game-playing dogs. Sherra didn't have high hopes for a future of happily ever after. As a defense attorney, she was around good-looking men all day long, but not a single one had sparked her interest thus far.

Taleah had had the guys connect enough tables to accommodate everyone when they'd first ar-rived. She wasn't sure if her friends would show or not, but she wanted to make sure they had seats at her table. Once the three women were seated, Taleah and Lorenz headed for the floor. The faster song no longer played, which was fine with both of them.

Lorenz slipped his arms around Taleah's waist, looking down into her eyes. "It looks as if your friends rescued you."

Taleah frowned. "From what?"

"Being out on the dance floor alone with me."

Fighting the urge to stand on tiptoes and kiss his inviting lips, Taleah smiled. "I don't see it that way, but it was a bit risky for me. I don't like to be the center of attention. So that should tell you just how bad I wanted to dance with you. Are you okay with that?"

Her statement tugged hard at his heartstrings. Lorenz pulled her in closer, wrapping his arms tighter around her waist. He then gently pressed his lips into her forehead. "You just made my evening, Taleah. I'm more than okay with it."

Taleah reached up and caressed his cheek with the palm of her hand. "You've been making my days and evenings ever since you got here. Spending time with you has been good for me. By the way, do you have someone special waiting for you back in Japan?"

That her question had caught Lorenz off guard was obvious by the surprised look on his face. He took a couple of seconds to regroup. "Taleah, I have to be totally honest with you. I date several women over there, but I do take out one lady more often than I do the others."

Taleah hated herself for asking that question during their first real intimate moment. Now that she knew the truth she felt heartsick. Dating several women at the same time suggested to her that Lorenz was a player. The thought that she also dated a couple of guys a month suddenly came to mind. Since she didn't consider herself a player, why should she assume that about him? But she wasn't involved physically or emotionally with anyone. Did she dare ask Lorenz if he was emotionally involved with the woman he took out more frequently than the others?

Lorenz lifted her chin with two fingers. "Taleah, it's not what you're probably thinking."

Taleah's eyelashes fluttered uncontrollably. "And what am I thinking?"

"That I'm a player."

Taleah had to laugh despite the awful disappointment she felt. "Read my mind, huh?"

"I'd say we're both pretty good at reading each other's mind. I'm not a player, Taleah. My divorce is not final yet so I just try to keep things as simple as possible until then. I don't want to hurt anyone. Everyone involves knows I'm dating other people. They also date other men. However, the one lady that I date the most has come to mean something to me. We've become very close friends. But nothing exclusive is going on with us either. Do you believe me?"

"Does it matter to you whether I do or not?"

He gave her a gently scolding glance. "Of course it matters. A lot."

"Why does it matter to you, Lorenz?"

He eyed her with deep curiosity. "That's a good question—and I have the answer for you. Are you sure you're ready to hear it, Taleah?"

Taleah gulped hard. "I'm not sure I am. But I'm certainly curious enough to listen."

Lorenz lowered his head. "Because I've come to care a lot about you," he whispered in her ear to be heard clearly. "This has been a super weekend. I'm already dreading leaving you tomorrow. To ask the same question you asked me earlier, are you okay with that, Taleah?"

Taleah stood on her tiptoes and briefly pressed her lips onto his. "I'm more than okay with it,

Lorenz," she said, responding with the same answer he'd given her regarding dancing.

Taleah's spontaneous kiss surprised both of them. She was more shocked at her overt behavior than anything, but she had not a single regret. Had he attempted to deepen the kiss Taleah would've gladly opened up her lips to receive it. While it concerned her that he might have something special with one of the women he dated, she wasn't turned off by the possibility. The fact still remained that there wasn't any type of future for her with him due to the distance involved. But that wasn't going to stop her from making the best of the time they did have.

The rest of the evening zoomed by with the speed of lightning. Taleah and Lorenz had practically set up housekeeping on the dance floor. Dancing constantly had given them the opportunity to touch and hold each other intimately close. It was difficult to converse over the loud music, but Taleah and Lorenz managed to get their points across with ease. Body language and heavy eye communication were the mediums they most used for conversing.

Though the other airmen had brought along dates, they also danced with Taleah's friends, who were hardly lacking for male attention. Guys had come from all over the club to ask Drusilla, Sherra, and Brenda to dance. Lynette and Mark, the only married couple present, enjoyed watching the others, but not nearly as much as they enjoyed being alone with each other while everyone was out on the dance floor. Every second of their time together was precious.

Taleah lay in bed, wide-awake. She was alone in the apartment with Lorenz, since Lynette and Mark had decided to go back to the Taylor home for the night. Mark had expected Lorenz to go to the Taylors' with him, but when Taleah had said it was okay for Lorenz to stay there, Mark felt as if he had no choice but to accept the arrangements. Mark also knew that Taleah was perfectly safe with Lorenz. Though Taleah had assured her family that she didn't mind giving up her bedroom another night, they'd remained steadfast in their decision not to deprive her of getting a good night's sleep.

Taleah laughed out loud. She had a good idea as to why her sister and brother-in-law had opted to leave. The walls were much thinner in her apartment than in her parents' home. Besides that, the guest room they always slept in when visiting was downstairs and on the opposite end of the house from where the Taylors' master bedroom was located. Lynette and Mark were crazy in love with each other. They were known for slipping away from the maddening crowds at family dinners and holiday get-togethers. Taleah wouldn't be surprised if they'd gone to a hotel.

A light knock on the door gripped Taleah's attention. It could only be Lorenz on the other side of the entry. Her heart began to race as she looked around for her robe. Finding the soft swatch of peach and green silk at the bottom of the bed, she stretched herself out and reached for it. Instead of yelling for Lorenz to come in, which was her very first thought, she got out of bed. After taking several deep breaths, Taleah opened the door to a handsome, smiling face.

"Hey, Lorenz. What's up?"

Lorenz sighed with relief, happy that he hadn't awakened her. "I'm glad you hadn't fallen asleep yet. If you're not too tired, I'd like you to listen to and give your opinion on a couple of dance cuts off the CDs I purchased yesterday. If you're not up to it, I can just put the headset on. However, I didn't want to touch your stereo equipment without getting your permission first."

You didn't have permission to clean my kitchen, but you did it anyway. Taleah grinned mischievously. "You couldn't come up with a better excuse than that for wanting to spend more time with me?"

Knowing she'd seen right through his pitiful ploy, Lorenz cracked up. "Only if I'd taken more time to think about it instead of acting on impulse. I guess I'm way too obvious at times." His expression suddenly sobered. "Are you really up to joining me, Taleah? If so, I promise not to keep you up too long."

"Sure thing. Let me slip into a pair of sweats. I'll be right out."

"What about some hot tea? I know where the teapot is, since you keep it on top of the stove. And I assume you keep the tea in the canister labeled 'tea.' "

Taleah laughed. "How wise you are. Tea sounds divine. I skipped my nightly ritual so you could get right off to sleep. There are a variety of teas in the canister, but I prefer the Warm Spirit blends. They're soothing herbal teas. No caffeine to keep me awake all night."

The second Taleah closed the door she jumped up and down with joy, ecstatic about spending more time in Lorenz's company. They'd made an early night of it, so it was just a little before midnight. Taleah laughed within, bubbling with excitement, as she thought about the sensuously bewitching things that could happen during the midnight hour.

"Wilson Picket, look out!" Although "In the Midnight Hour" was a song recorded long before her time, her parents still played it enough for her to know it by heart.

Three

As Taleah floated about the pool in her inflated chair, she was highly aware of the time swiftly ticking off the clock. Her time with Lorenz would be up in another few hours. The past evening had been awesome. She and Lorenz had talked about so many things, important things. She'd felt comfortable enough with him to ask about his relationship with his parents, his religious preferences, and his political views. Taleah had really stunned him when she even asked about his credit rating and his overall physical health.

While Taleha hadn't come right out and asked Lorenz if he kept up with his sexual well-being, he had known exactly what she'd meant. All of his answers had pleased her greatly. He had an excellent credit rating and he'd also passed with flying colors all his physical health exams. The air force required each of its members to be in the best possible physical health in order to remain on active duty. That called for routine medical checkups and periodic physical fitness endurance tests. There were many military medical requirements such as seasonal flu shots and other inoculations. Lorenz was fit as a fiddle.

With an amused smile on her face, Taleah watched in awe as Lorenz swam several laps up and down the pool. He had a powerful stroke and had demonstrated a great diving form. Lorenz also looked terribly sexy in his swim trunks. The black and gray spandex swimwear allowed Taleah to see more of his fantastic, barely clothed body. She'd no longer have to wonder about his tight abs and the hairy expanse of his chest. He definitely had it all. He had a powerhouse physique. There was only one fully covered body part of his left for her to fantasize about. Although she could only imagine him totally nude, she blushed at the delicious thought.

A startled Taleah nearly fell out of the floating chair when Lorenz unexpectedly surfaced right in front of her. Her mind had taken her to a sinful elsewhere so she had briefly turned her rapt attention away from his every movement. Lorenz was now staring her right in the face.

Lorenz smiled broadly, showing all of his beautiful white teeth. "Sorry. I didn't mean to startle you, Taleah. Are you okay?"

Taleah stuck her hand in the water and splashed it up in Lorenz's face. "That should answer your question. You scared the dickens out of me, Lorenz." Taleah's silly laughter belied the biting tone of her voice.

Grinning, Lorenz wagged his finger at her in a scolding manner. "That wasn't a nice thing to do, Miss Taleah. Splashing water in a man's face could get you into big trouble, woman. But I'm sure you already knew that."

In response to his remark Taleah splashed him again, knowing exactly what his form of retaliation might be. She then steeled herself for the possibility of him toppling the chair over. Although she'd had a pretty good idea of what might come, she screamed loudly as the chair flew out from under her. Taleah sank deep into the water, her arms flailing wildly about.

It suddenly dawned on Lorenz that Taleah might not know how to swim, since all he'd ever seen her do was float about in the pool in her chair. His heart surged upward into his mouth. Quicker than a flash of lighting, he made a downward arc into the water and grabbed hold of Taleah. He then pulled her toward him, careful not to come into contact with her flailing arms. Her frantic arm movement was another indication to him that she might not be able to swim.

Once Taleah was completely relaxed in his arms, Lorenz turned her around to face him, praying that she was okay. Taleah quickly raised her head and threw her arms around his neck. Before he knew what had hit him, Taleah had kissed him hard on the mouth, surprising the heck out of him. She then squirmed out of his grasp and swam from one end of the pool to the other in an expert fashion. Taleah Taylor could swim like a fish, which made Lorenz feel pretty foolish.

Knowing Taleah had duped him, Lorenz could only laugh. Payback was in store. It was dangerous to play games in the water, but what he had in mind for Taleah wasn't the least bit dangerous; his plan to kiss her until she was breathless made him smile. He would wait until she least expected it. She wasn't the only one who knew how to serve up a plate of raw shock.

Taleah swam several laps before she made her way to the shallow end of the pool, where she seated herself on the steps. Without removing the rubber band from her hair, she twisted her ponytail around her hand and then squeezed out the water.

All smiles, Lorenz joined her, seating himself one step up from the one Taleah sat on. "You're an excellent swimmer. You're also quite a faker."

She nodded. "Drama queen is more like it. Been swimming since I was five. Too bad you're so easy to fool. Maybe you should find out if a person can swim before you topple her into the water. I was only trying to teach you a lesson."

He gave her a wary look. "Is that so? So who's going to come around to teach you not to splash folks with water? Especially on someone's who's a lot bigger than you."

Taleah shrugged with nonchalance. "I knew better, knew exactly how you were going to retaliate. But I did it anyway. Sorry. Hope you're not mad at me. By the way, when are you going to accept that I can read your every thought and know your every movement before you act upon it? I'm all up inside your head, boy!"

Lorenz sobered, his expression growing thoughtful. He wondered if Taleah knew how close she'd come to the truth. They both seemed to know each other's every thought and move. That revelation scared him on one level and intrigued him on another. He wasn't used to anyone being inside his head; or deep in his heart, for that matter. Lorenz had once loved another, but he'd never had the type of spiritual and soulful connection he was now having with Taleah.

Serious compatibility issues had cropped up in his marriage within a week of saying the I-dos. All the joy and passion seemed to fly right out the window when his orders had come down for a permanent change in duty stations. The storms of troubled times had arrived soon after he'd announced his first overseas assignment. His wife simply abhorred the idea of moving to a foreign country and leaving her family behind. Arguments between them had arisen on a daily basis; never were the verbal battles about the real issue. Moving away was the real culprit.

A year into the overseas assignment his wife had packed up and returned to the States, leaving a heartbroken Lorenz behind with nothing more than a legal separation in hand. No promises of "tomorrow" or "when you get back home" had been made. It was over and done.

Lorenz shook off his dark mood, but he didn't know if he'd ever be able to shake loose the pain. Then he looked at Taleah, the beautiful woman sitting there with him. Thinking of her unexpected kiss caused his pain to instantly dissipate. Lorenz laughed inwardly as he focused in on what Taleah had said before he'd so foolishly taken a detour into the dark caverns of the past.

"You might've said that you know my every thought as a joke, but I believe it. As for your weak apology, you don't sound a bit sorry to me, Taleah. That little statement came with way too much sarcasm to be believable."

Taleah nodded. "Yeah, maybe you're right. I couldn't have meant it since I intentionally splashed you. I know that I can be annoying at times. But I can also be adorable." She gave him a great smile. "I'm just a playful person. By the way, you didn't say if you're mad at me or not. And, about your first comment, why do you believe in it?"

He smoothed back her wet hair in a loving gesture. "How can anyone ever get mad at the *adorable* you? Being playfully incorrigible is not a bad thing. And, no, I'm not mad at you. I don't know why I feel the way I do about the other issue. It's very intriguing. We do seem to read each other pretty well. You've said and done some things I was thinking about at the time—and vice versa." He gave her a thoughtful glance. "Do you believe in spiritual connections, Taleah? And what about the ideology of people being soul mates?"

Taleah was caught off guard at such a direct question. However, she did believe that a person's spirit and soul had a way of making connections with others. She also saw it as a rare and beautiful thing to have happen. But at one time she'd also believed in love at first sight; what a myth that had turned out to be. Out of sight, out of mind was more like it. Whenever Taleah was out of Bradley's sight, he'd blown her right out of his mind with his womanizing ways.

"I'd have to say yes to both of your questions." Taleah tilted her head to one side. "It's never happened to me. What about you? Have you experienced those things with someone?"

Only from the very moment I laid eyes on you. Lorenz didn't know if he should just go ahead and tell Taleah how he really felt about her, which would more than likely scare her to death. He truly felt that Taleah was his soul mate, the only one for him. How did he know that for sure? He didn't. Lorenz knew it was crazy, but he couldn't deny his feelings. He'd fallen in love with Taleah Taylor on sight. They had only shared two kisses; an innocent one and the surprise one Taleah had administered to his lips. His deeper feelings for her had nothing to do with the physical, only the spiritual. That didn't mean he didn't want to make love to her, just that he wanted far more than a mere physical relationship with one Taleah Taylor.

How was any of this possible? Although his divorce would be final in a very short while, he was still married. He couldn't offer Taleah any sort of future at the moment. Taleah might not even want a future with him, so those thoughts were pretty presumptuous on his part. Lorenz quickly decided that the best thing for him to do was keep his mouth shut and see what transpired between them during their next planned visit. Since Taleah was still dealing with her own issues, Lorenz didn't want to run the risk of driving her away. She seemed somewhat vulnerable.

For now it was time for him to deliver to her that breathless kiss he'd been anticipating.

The second Lorenz's mouth closed down over Taleah's he began floating on a natural high. The initial surprise in her eyes told him he'd accomplished his mission of payback. Then his eyes closed shut, as he lost himself in the thrilling moment. As the kiss grew more passionate, he felt Taleah relax under the expert manipulation of his mouth and tongue. When her arms went around his neck, he felt instant relief. Taleah kissing him back excited him to no end.

Taleah wanted to be kissed by him as much as he obviously wanted her lips to caress his. She felt herself go completely numb the moment his lips had met with hers. Even if she'd wanted to resist Lorenz, though she had no desire to, she had no strength to do so. His mouth on hers had rendered her helpless. His kiss was so sweet and she wanted it to go on and on. Taleah felt as if she were caught up in a heavenly dream. Being in Lorenz's arms was like floating on a cloud.

As Lorenz's mouth increased the pressure on hers, Taleah's arms wound around and then tightened about his neck. She was surprised that she wasn't the least bit fearful of him. The fear of being hurt again was always somewhere in her thoughts when she was around the opposite sex. The steel bars around Fort Knox had already begun to melt, almost as easily as candle wax. Her fragile heart was slowly but surely being reexposed to the light of day.

Lorenz pulled his head slightly back and looked into Taleah's eyes. "Payback is a dog, huh? It seems that you're all caught up in the element of surprise, just as I was earlier."

Taleah's eyelashes fluttered from a bad case of nerves. She had to will herself to regain calm so as not to show him how much his wonderful kiss had affected her. Daring to continue being as bold as she'd ever been in her life, she reached up and ran her fingers through his close-cut hair. "Ah, so that's what that was. Is payback all that it was?"

His eyes shimmered with passion. "What do you think, Taleah?"

She shrugged. "How would I know?"

"By what you felt."

"Well, it certainly didn't feel like I was being punished, if that was your intent."

"Me, punish you? No, never!" He tossed her a wickedly sexy smile. "I'm glad it didn't feel like a punishment to you. But you still haven't told me how it made you feel."

Taleah put a finger to her temple. "Hmm, it seems that I've forgotten." Taleah brought her lips within a breath of Lorenz's, hoping the slight trembling of her body was noticeable only to her. "Refresh my memory, Lorenz Hampton."

Taleah's heart drummed inside her chest as Lorenz once again claimed her mouth. The gentle undulation of his lips on hers had caused her to go weak in the knees. His kiss was long, passionate, and was nearly her undoing. How was she to recover from such a staggering moment? If the truth was known, Taleah didn't want to recuperate. The soft glow from within her burned warm and bright. The erotic euphoria felt incredible. Her heart loudly rejoiced.

Lorenz ended the passionate kiss, only to kiss her gently on the forehead. His lips possessed a butterfly gentleness. Taleah liked how careful he was with her, as if she were a fragile doll. The warm glow within her had now turned to a fiery sensation. No sooner had she swallowed the lump in her throat than it arose again. Taleah was rapidly becoming a bundle of nerves.

Taleah was speechless. All she could do was stare into the clear blue water. Lorenz and all his charm had taken her completely over. The never-to-fall-in-love-again Taleah Taylor was in love. If it wasn't love she felt, it was certainly something akin to it. Lorenz hadn't ridden up to her on a white steed, nor had he worn a suit of armor, yet he'd rescued her badly broken heart from a very dark and cold dungeon. No longer was her heart imprisoned. Lorenz had set it free. Taleah couldn't help wondering if he'd set her heart free only to imprison it all over again.

Lorenz had claimed her heart, lock, stock, and barrel, but would he really know how to take care of it? Love always seemed to come with a price. Would her loving Lorenz come with too high a price tag, one that she couldn't begin to afford? Time would tell, but they didn't have much of that. Would time prove itself to be a serious enemy? Lorenz was flying back to Japan in a few weeks. That was a given. Taleah could safely bet that time wasn't on her side.

The next few hours flew by. As far as Taleah was concerned, Lynette and Mark had shown up back at her place all too soon. It was time for the guys to hit the highway. Taleah had known that she would hate to see the weekend come to an end; she just hadn't figured on how much she'd hate to see Lorenz leave. Taleah understood perfectly why it bothered her so much to see him go away. She silently prayed that he would come again, just as they'd planned.

Taleah's and Lorenz's bodies brushed against each other as they walked outside.

Lorenz stopped in his tracks and turned to face Taleah. He then took her small hands in his. "Hey, Taleah, I want you to know that I've had a great time. There wasn't a dull moment in your company. Thanks for your hospitality. I'm looking forward to seeing you again next weekend. I'm glad that we all decided to drive down to San Diego and then take a side trip into Mexico. That should be a wild, crazy adventure."

Happy they'd made plans to see each other again too, Taleah smiled. "An exciting one for sure. I'm really only attracted to the shopping. You can still get great bargains south of the border. However, there are some strange going-ons in Tijuana, Mexico. Practicing caution is a must. That seemingly lawless place can get pretty wild."

Lorenz laughed, leaning against the car door. "I bet." Lorenz's eyes suddenly filled with tenderness. "I know I shouldn't kiss you in front of your family, but you have no idea how much I want to do just that. Friday can't come soon enough for me."

"We're definitely on the same page with that, Lorenz. I can't wait either."

Taleah watched as Lynette and Mark got settled into the car. Although their parents' place was only a hop, skip, and a jump away from Taleah's, Mark was going to drive Lynette there before heading out. Before Lorenz could open the back door, Taleah slipped her hand into his. She then knocked on the front passenger window where Lynette was seated.

Lynette rolled down the window. "What's up, Taleah?"

"I forgot to give Lorenz something. We have to go back into the apartment. He'll be right out." Taleah leaned over and hugged her sister. "I'll stop by Mom and Dad's and see you after I get off work tomorrow." Taleah blew Mark a kiss since she'd already said her farewells to him.

The very second the apartment door closed behind them Taleah rushed into Lorenz's arms, surprising him once again. Savoring the sweet taste of his lips, she kissed him thoroughly. Right after Lorenz mentioned not kissing her in front of her family, Taleah's brain had gone to work on how to make it happen. Making up an excuse to get him back into the house hadn't come easy for her, but it was the only reasonable thing that had come to mind. Now she had to think of something to give Lorenz just in case Mark or Lynette asked what it was that she'd forgotten.

Lorenz couldn't keep from smiling all over himself. "Is that what you forgot to give me?"

Taleah looked up at him and smiled. "Sort of. But more importantly, it's what you wouldn't give me in front of my family. Do you have any objections to my clever tactics?"

He brought his face in close to Taleah's. "None whatsoever." While looking deeply into her eyes, Lorenz kissed her passionately. "I like a clever woman."

With a slight wave of his hand, Lorenz turned

away from Taleah and walked toward the door. Before turning the knob, he looked back at her. "I want to call you tonight. Is that okay?"

Taleah threw her head back and laughed. "That's it," she shouted. "You can tell them I forgot to write down my phone number for you, if they ask."

Lorenz chuckled. "Okay, but I don't think they'll buy that one, even if it is true."

Taleah looked perplexed. "What do you mean?"

"Yeah, lady, it is true. You haven't given me your phone number yet."

Smiling broadly, Taleah wasted no time in writing her number down on the message pad next to the telephone. She then ripped the pink paper from the pad and handed it to Lorenz. "I'll be waiting for the call. Make it after eight o'clock. Yours is the last voice I want to hear before I eventually fall to sleep."

Lorenz grinned. "I can make that happen for us. Until later, Taleah."

"Later, Lorenz." Taleah waved her regrettable farewell from outside her doorway.

Loneliness returned the moment Taleah stepped back into her apartment. She felt completely empty inside. Only a short time ago her apartment was filled with laughter and friendly chatter. Her family and Lorenz had been great company. She already missed them being there. Taleah normally wasn't the least bit bothered by being alone in her place, but tonight she felt totally different. In fact, she usually enjoyed spending time with herself. She filled her nonworking hours with reading anything and everything she could get her hands on, as well as working on a host of other little hobbies and projects. Taleah liked to stay busy.

Taleah loved to sew and had recently taken a quilting class. She was very good with her hands.

Piecing together superlarge picture puzzles was also a favorite. Allison had taught her daughters at a young age how to make a variety of both simple and complicated arts and crafts. Taleah was always working on a creative project of some sort. The quilt she was in the process of creating had proved to be quite a challenge for her. Taleah thought that taking the beginning-quilting course all over again and then later embarking on an advanced class would help her out tremendously. She didn't like to give up on anything. Any goal worth setting was worthy of completion in her estimation. Taleah would never be accused of being a quitter.

Taleah suddenly wished she had asked Lynette to spend the night with her. She could use someone to talk to, especially about Lorenz. Her older sisters usually gave Taleah sound advice, but only when she asked for it. Everyone knew that Taleah had to make up her own mind about every little thing, and the not so little things. Though she truly valued the input of her family and friends, the ultimate decision had to be hers, as was the responsibility for her choices.

Taleah felt an overwhelming sadness as she rushed into the bathroom, where she quickly stripped out of her street clothing and pulled off her shoes. After putting the drain plug into place, Taleah turned on the hot water and then drizzled several aromatherapy drops into the tub. Lavender bath salts and liquid bubble bath was added to the water next.

Taleah had also learned from her mother at an early age to take time out for pampering herself. She allotted herself forty-five minutes in the morning and an hour in the evening to execute her self-indulgent ritual. She loved to indulge herself lavishly as she tended to her personal needs. No one could take better care of Taleah Taylor than she could. Taking care of her heart and her spirit was extremely important to her, as was tending to her physical wellness.

Now that the tub was filled with hot water and the relaxing aromatherapy scents were floating through the air, Taleah submerged her petite body into the healing waters. Her spirit needed rejuvenating. Although it was much earlier than the time she normally prepared herself for bed, Taleah felt extreme fatigue. Her body needed the ultimate in relaxation.

Taleah softly voiced a short but meaningful prayer before she rested her head back against the bath pillow and closed her eyes. It was now time for a few minutes of serious reflection. Indulging in deep meditation allowed her constantly speeding mind to also rest.

Of all the goings-on in Taleah's life, meeting Lorenz had been the most exciting one, as of late. Taleah had already begun the process of reinventing and redefining herself when Lorenz was introduced into her busy professional but somewhat socially dull life. She'd been hiding behind her broken heart for far too long. She had made too many inane excuses as to why she wasn't living life to the fullest. While she hadn't become a recluse, the spaces on her social calendar were practically blank. She couldn't even remember the last time she had treated herself to a movie. Taleah had been depriving herself of partaking of the meaningful things in life.

Over the last forty-eight hours she'd seen an even greater need for reassessing her life. *Lorenz?* More than likely, she mused. Although it might seem ridiculous to some, Taleah knew how much Lorenz had already affected her life. Was she foolish in thinking there might be a ghost of a chance for them when there wasn't? But a girl was allowed to wish, hope, and dream. That's what silly girls often did. Lorenz being unobtainable for a romantic liaison didn't stop her mind from creating a beautiful outcome for them. Did it really matter that he might as well be living on another planet? Wasn't love able to transcend all things, like time and distance?

Because her thoughts of them together forever were delightful ones she would continue to indulge in them. Lorenz would soon be gone. Her memories of him could serve her well by lasting forever. Taleah might never speak these things out loud, but she could give her mind a voice and allow her colorful imagination to run wild. She could have Lorenz any way she wanted him within her unruly mind. She could make up any sensuous rendezvous she so desired.

Right now Taleah wanted Lorenz as the leading man in her dreams. With that delicious little scenario in mind, she stood up and rinsed her body off under the shower. In a hurry to get her fantasy on, forgoing the drying-off process, Taleah wrapped herself in a terry cloth robe. She then made a mad dash for the bedroom, where she planned to instantly slip between the cool percale sheets and allow her fantasies to take her completely over.

Taleah hadn't even had a chance to close her eyes when the doorbell pealed. When the incessant ringing first began, she didn't have to put too much thought into whose maniacal fingers were abusing her chimes. One of her best friends lived right in the same building with her and the others lived right across the street. Leaning on each other's doorbell when visiting was par for the course. It could be one or the other or all three of her friends at the door.

After pulling on her robe, Taleah slipped her feet into her worn leather slippers and trudged toward the front door. Regardless of how confident she felt about who was on the other side of the entry, she still practiced precaution by looking through the security window first. If Taleah hadn't been used to her friends' insane but harmless antics, she would've screamed at seeing an eyeball staring right back at her. Nobody but Sherra, she thought, their very own private in-house comedian. Sherra never failed to keep them laughing.

Warm hugs and friendly kisses on the cheeks were exchanged as Brenda, Drusilla, and Sherra entered Taleah's apartment. Everyone followed Taleah into the living room, where they all took a seat. Taleah and her friends had a way of unexpectedly dropping in on each other from time to time. However, more often than not, a phone call occurred first.

Not long after warm hugs were exchanged, Taleah excused herself without offering an explanation. Although no one had asked for refreshments, Taleah was always the perfect host. As she scurried about the kitchen trying to drum up enough goodies to serve her guests, she thought of how lonely her evening would've been had her friends not shown up.

Taleah wasn't surprised when the women all trooped into the kitchen to see what she was up to since she had been gone long enough to arouse their curiosity. Brenda and Sherra sat on the stools at the breakfast nook and Drusilla seated herself at the table.

"What are you putting together, Taleah?" Brenda inquired, picking up an Avon book.

"Just some snack foods," Taleah responded. "I guess I should've asked if you guys have had dinner yet. Have you?"

Sherra laughed at the odd expression on Taleah's face. "No, we actually stopped by here to see if you wanted to join us for a meal out somewhere. But since you've already begun pulling out the goodies, we can eat out another time. Is everyone okay with that?"

The other women agreed by merely nodding.

"In that case, I can do a little more than snacks," Taleah said. "I have more than enough chili-lime chicken wings in the freezer. They're delicious. I can throw them right in the microwave. I also have fresh fixings on hand for a salad—and there are plenty of fresh and canned vegetables in the pantry. Is that cool?"

"All of the above works for me," Brenda offered, getting up from her seat. "I'll put the wings in the oven for us. Are they the ones that I've heard about from COSTCO?"

"Those are the ones. Thanks, Brenda, for helping out. Dru, you can make the salad if you don't mind. I'll take care of the vegetables."

"One tossed salad coming right up," Drusilla replied. Drusilla was the health food nut among them. She liked to have everything she ate to be fresh. No leftovers for her.

"I'll make some iced tea or lemonade," Sherra sang out.

"Iced tea," Brenda shouted.

"I prefer lemonade," Dru quickly tossed out.

Sherra shook her head, laughing. "Why can't we ever agree on anything?"

" 'Cause we're all different people, each with a unique personality. How boring would it be if we were all just alike?" Taleah asked.

"Okay, okay. I see your point. I'll make both drinks," Sherra conceded, laughing softly.

In less than forty-five minutes the women had everything on the table. Each of the women loved their spontaneous get-togethers, which happened pretty regularly. They enjoyed each other's company tremendously. Spats occurred between them, but nothing ever too serious.

Brenda wasn't as spontaneous as she'd like to be. She had the tendency to plan everything out, even her off days. She kept her schedule written down in a day-planner. With a master's degree in special education, working as a special education supervisor in a prestigious school district, Brenda had no choice but to keep a detailed schedule for her work activities.

Sherra, as a defense attorney, also had to keep a detailed account of her private office and court activities schedule. Taleah's job didn't demand her to keep a detailed schedule since very little of her work was done outside the office. As a member of the military, Dru was always on call in her mind whether she was officially on call or not. Taleah worked four ten-hour days.

"So how's your military man?" Dru asked Taleah.

Taleah's eyes grew bright with mist. Just the mention of Lorenz had her heart smiling. "Lorenz couldn't be better. This upcoming weekend will be our second date. I can hardly wait."

"Second? You went out with him two nights in a row this weekend," Brenda remarked.

Taleah giggled. "I know. I just consider both outings as one date, the same as with next weekend. One weekend, one date."

"Gotcha!" Brenda glanced nervously at Taleah. "How are things really progressing with you two, Taleah? You seem so absorbed with him."

Taleah laughed softly. "Way too fast. Sister-friends, I'm afraid I've fallen in love. In fact, I believe it occurred at first sight. Lorenz is in my blood. It feels as if we share the same spirit."

Drusilla looked concerned. "Wow! All of that in such a short time?"

"All of that—and more," Taleah assured Drusilla. "Wow indeed!"

Sherra gave the group a scolding look. "You all need to stay the heck out of Taleah's business. We've all been dying for her to get over the last hurt. Now that it seems she has truly fallen in love, you all looked scared to death for her. She'll be just fine."

"It's just that Lorenz is only going to be here awhile. There's no chance for him to make a commitment to her," Drusilla countered. "He's in the military. I know that life. Remember?"

Taleah lightly struck the table with her fist. "Why does either of us have to commit to anything? That's what's wrong with some of us women. Instead of living in the moment, we're constantly planning out the future and too busy picking out the wedding gown after only a few dates. Just one person rarely decides upon a future between two people. I'm in love. That doesn't mean I'm ready to take a trip down the aisle and up to the altar. Are you all feeling me?"

Brenda shook her head. "We're getting way too serious up in here. Let's put on some banging music and change the mood. We need to lighten things up a bit." Brenda saw how disturbed Taleah looked by the direction of the conversation. That prompted her to try and turn things around. Although Brenda was concerned too, she thought Taleah needed their support right now. She certainly didn't need to be censured for believing she'd fallen in love.

Taleah was a lover of all sorts of music and she had a great collection of various artists, which was one of the many things she and Lorenz had in common.

Thinking Brenda's idea was a good one, Sherra left the room to turn on the stereo. She knew how to get a party started and how to keep it going. The music could be enjoyed from the speakers Taleah's brother Jared had discreetly mounted above the kitchen entry. Rarely pessimistic, Sherra was an eternal optimist and had a great attitude about most things, with the exception of doggish men. Her sharply critical views on men who cheated on their mates never wavered. Despite her jaded views Sherra Miller, attorney at law, wasn't a man-hater.

Sherra loved her wonderful daddy, T.W. Miller, too much to turn into a hater. T.W. was very ill and was not expected to live much longer. The cancer had taken its toll on his fragile body. Getting together with her friends had been a welcome reprieve for Sherra, since almost all of her spare time had been spent by her ailing father's bedside.

Since Drusilla had started in on Taleah, and Taleah was her friend, she felt obligated to spell out for her the rigors of military life. Although Drusilla wasn't a military wife, she'd been around long enough to see the effects that it had on the women with military spouses. She wasn't trying to change Taleah's mind, since military life could be very good, she just wanted her to be informed about the good and the not so good.

Four

Talking among the four friends had ceased once the music and the eating had begun. Taleah loved the chili-lime chicken wings, which fact was evident on her sauce-smeared face. The other women had heard about the spicy wings, but none had tried the delicious delicacy. Taleah was glad to have introduced her friends to one of the best quickie meals she'd ever had the pleasure of preparing. It wasn't KFC, but the chicken sure was finger-licking good.

Taleah could only smile as she affectionately glanced at each of her sister-friends. It was so nice having them living nearby. No matter what time of day or night it might be, if someone was in dire need, the others would come running. How many nights had they sat up with her, nursing her wounds after her devastating breakup? They had been there for her continuously. Each woman was reliable, responsible, and loyal to the others. The four women had a very special relationship. Taleah felt blessed to have each of them in her life.

Brenda turned her warm brown gaze on Taleah. "What plans do you and Lorenz have for the upcoming weekend? I heard mention of Mexico."

"San Diego on Friday evening and Mexico early Saturday morning. Shopping, of course.

Mexico's gotten a little dangerous lately, so we'll be out of there long before sunset. Tijuana is nothing like it used to be. But you all know Mark, with his macho behind. He thinks he can take on the world if he had to. We should have fun, though. Just have to be careful and stay alert."

"It's just as dangerous here. The entire planet is a dangerous place to live. Maybe we should plan a shopping spree to the moon," Sherra joked, laughing at her own silly remark.

"What about shopping for hot bargains on one of the other planets?" Drusilla asked, feeding the silliness coming on. "I bet they got some serious sales going on up on Mars."

Brenda cracked up. "I bet the men on other planets are as fine as men come. I wonder if they even wear clothes way up there in the solar system. I can't even begin to imagine."

"It's rather hot up there from what I've read, especially on Mars. They don't call it the Red Planet for nothing. Nudist colonies are probably all the rage on Mars," Taleah chimed in, laughing hard at their insane conversation. Getting downright crazy wasn't so unusual for these four friends. They loved to have fun chopping it up and being just plain silly.

Taleah fought to get her laughter under control. "Enough of this already. We're acting so stupid right now. But it feels so good. I hope to laugh a whole lot more in the days to come."

"What else is new? It's not as if we haven't acted

sillier than this before. Laughter is the music of the soul. Stupid is good as long as it's done behind closed doors," Brenda offered.

"You got that right! 'Cause when people think you're stupid, they try to take advantage of you," Taleah said with heavy sarcasm. "Bradley thought I was brainless until I kicked his cheating butt to the curb."

"And you kept that expensive diamond ring, to boot!" Sherra shouted out, clapping her hands with enthusiasm. "He sure found out in a hurry how dumb you aren't."

Loud laughter rang out in the room. Sherra always knew how to get her point across in a colorful way. Although a barrel of laughs, she was also one feisty redhead, but so uplifting to everyone. Brenda and Drusilla were not without sharp, comical wits. In fact, there were times when the whole group could benefit greatly from seeking out some serious psychiatric treatment.

Taleah looked unhappy for a brief moment. Then her bright smile came back in full effect. "Will wonders never cease? Mentioning Bradley didn't hurt at all this time. Although I always regret bringing up his name in the same instant it rolls off my tongue, my heart isn't bleeding over it this time. Maybe I'm finally cured. Keeping that huge diamond ring was one of my smarter moves. Maybe I'll one day trade it in on a few other diamond trinkets for myself."

Drusilla patted Taleah's hand in a soothing manner. "Let's hope you're over all of it. But I still have to wonder if you're jumping out of the frying pan and right into the fiery flames. I can see that you're really fired up over Lorenz. Hearing you say you're in love is a little scary for me this soon into the game,

Taleah. It's just not like you to repeat the same old mistakes."

Taleah shrugged. "I see we're back to that. The reprieve sure didn't last long. It's called taking a risk, Dru. If I keep waiting to get hurt again, it's bound to happen, simply because I'm looking for it to. I have come to understand the true meaning of 'seize the moment.' Without worrying where the next one is going to take me, I'm seizing whatever moments I have with Lorenz. They may be short, but they'll be all that we decide to make of them. I've already jumped into the fire—and it's so hot. If I get burned again, I'll just seek first aid. I'm up for a little singeing. The boy is soooo hot to the touch and I'm ready to burn, baby, burn! Okay?"

Sherra held her hand up to Taleah's for a high five. "That's my girl!"

Laughing heartily, Taleah smashed her palm into Sherra's. "Thanks, Sherra. I can always count on you to rescue me from peril. However, I do understand Dru's concern. I really do. But, Dru, since you're in the military, I can get a lot of good advice from you. I promise to ask."

Sherra smiled broadly. "Well, just to take the heat off you, Taleah, I have some interesting news to share with everyone. You guys had better brace yourself for this one."

Sherra licked her lips, as if she could taste on them the secret she was about to reveal. She smiled knowingly. "I met this fine sandy-haired, blue-eyed brother, one that challenged me in a way that I haven't been tested in a while. It happened in the courthouse cafeteria, where I'd joined some of my colleagues for lunch. As I was complaining about life in general, one of my male lawyer friends, John, told me I needed a man. I took out of my wallet the picture of you all know who, Robert, the last sorry guy I dated. I then tore it up. 'All you men at this table are married,' I announced haughtily while ripping the picture into tiny pieces.

"Charlie Brown said to me—that's the blue-eyed wonder's name—'That's not true.' Then I said, 'All men are dogs.' He said, 'That's not true either.' Wanting to have the last word, I said, 'None of you men even know the meaning of commitment.' Charlie countered with, 'Strike three, you're out.' He then left the table. But Charlie later asked one of my friends for my phone number. John told him no way, that he wouldn't be able to get nothing going with me. But once John found out Charlie was really serious, he asked me if he could give him my number."

Sherra started laughing, blushing like crazy. Her smooth, fair, slightly freckled complexion had nearly turned the same color as her fiery, gorgeous red hair. "That all happened a couple of days ago. I'll let you all know if I get that call. You might be surprised to find out that I'm eager to hear from him. So who knows what might happen? Charlie is also a defense attorney. How's that for a change of attitude by the woman who has sworn off men forever?"

Taleah reached over and hugged Sherra. "I think it's a wonderful change of attitude. We can't continue to let our pain and anger feed on our insides. Maybe Charlie Brown will do for you what Lorenz Hampton has done for me. I wish you the best of luck should something special happen with you guys. Wouldn't that be something if we both found true love at the same time?"

Drusilla laughed heartily. "Oh, boy, I can see it now. A double wedding is coming up!"

Both Taleah and Sherra dramatically rolled their eyes at Drusilla.

"Ease up! I'm just kidding, guys. I, for one, can't wait to see what transpires with you two, Sherra. But how come you haven't told us this juicy story before now?" Drusilla asked.

Sherra shrugged. "I had intended to wait to see if he called me before I mentioned it to anyone. But seeing Taleah all misty eyed and joyful made me want to share my news now. We'll just have to wait to see what happens. But, like Taleah, I'm feeling something deep down inside after only five minutes of spirited conversation with Mr. Charlie Brown. I even love his name, though I know next to nothing about him, except that he was once a college football star. His name sounds so freaking American, so down-to-earth. Is all this too crazy?"

Brenda sucked her teeth in a displeasing manner. "*Sick* is what it is. You all are insane." All the eyes, the evil eyes, turned on Brenda, causing her not the least bit of discomfort. "What?"

"What, my foot," Taleah huffed. "As many times as you've been in this very situation, you've got plenty of nerve calling us insane. If that's the case, you're even more insane than the rest of us. I don't know how you even got up the courage to say something stupid like that. Not with all the drama you've had going on in your life. I know you don't want me to start mentioning names up in here this evening. I'd have to go get my long list before I could start."

Everyone else but Brenda cracked up.

"Please, Taleah! You *are* the queen of drama princesses," Brenda countered. "At least I have a list. You've been stuck on one romantic misfortune for over four years now. Get over it!"

Taleah threw a dagger-sharp glance at Brenda,

but there wasn't an ounce of malice in her heart. None of the four women were strangers to these types of huffy exchanges. They normally said what they had to say and then moved on. The bonds of their friendships were strong.

Taleah posted her hands on her hips. "It seems that you haven't been listening, Brenda, as usual, 'cause that's exactly what I've done here. I'm over it. You all don't have to approve of what I do. Lorenz is the man for me. I feel it deep down in my heart—and that's all that matters. One day you all might have to eat your nasty words. So you might want to think about keeping them soft and sweet. I sure don't want to see you end up choking on anything hard and bitter."

Sherra cocked her head back, ready to take a serious defensive stand. "Hey, Taleah, don't include me in that 'you all' stuff. I've been sitting over here championing you from the start," she voiced as a matter of fact. "I believe in you, girl. Go for what you know and feel!"

As she laughed inwardly, Drusilla's eyes darted back and forth between each of the women. She loved their crazy exchanges, but she'd decided to sit this latest one out. She'd said enough already. Her concern for Taleah was born of love, but something was now telling her that Taleah Taylor was going to come out a winner in this situation. Taleah had suddenly changed. Knowing that she could answer most questions that Taleah asked about military life made Drusilla feel better.

Drusilla was aware that her own love life wasn't in the best of shape, but she had a real good man to share her concerns with. Everything in their relationship wasn't the way she wanted it, or the way it needed to be, but she still had high hopes for a bright future with Craig Stanford.

The scowl on Taleah's face softened considerably. "I know you do, Sherra. So does Brenda Faye. She just loves to aggravate us whenever she can. She does it 'cause she can. We usually let her get away with it, since it rarely does any good to hit her with a testy comeback."

Taleah stood up and then reached across the table and hugged each of her friends. "You guys are super-independent AA sisters with supernatural powers, my heroines. I love you to life."

One of Taleah's favorite songs by Beyonce came on and she moved away from the table and began getting her groove on. She had the famous Beyonce rump shaker move down to the letter, although it had already been played out for a while now.

Taleah looked as if she was having so much fun. That caused everyone else to get up and join her. After moving the chairs and table off to the side, the other women began to show off their funky dance steps. While testing her newly sworn vow of living in the moment, making the most of each one, Taleah laughed and laughed as she let her hair all the way down.

Taleah anxiously looked up at the kitchen clock. Lorenz hadn't called yet. While they hadn't set a specific time to talk, she'd told him to make it after eight. It was now nine. Before she could announce her desire to go back to bed, where she was before her company came, Brenda grabbed her purse and said she had to leave. The others then voiced the same sentiment.

Taleah sighed with relief, glad that her friends, and not she, had decided their imminent departure. In being honest with herself, she wouldn't have asked them to leave no matter what she had to do. No man would ever be so important to her for her to hurt her friends' feelings over. These women had been through the fire with her, had seen her through the worst of times. Taking Lorenz's call in the privacy of her bedroom would've been acceptable with her girls.

At the doorway, the four women exchanged parting hugs and promises of getting together sometime during the next week. Once the door was closed behind them, Taleah ran for her bedroom, racing against the message center's set time-response to the sudden ringing of the telephone. *Please let Lorenz be on the other line,* she silently prayed. *Please!*

Holding hands and smiling, Taleah and Lorenz watched after Mark as he drove off. He was on his way to pick up Lynette at the Taylor residence. Their first moments together alone had been awkward after not seeing each other for a week, but it didn't take long for things to heat up. From the moment Lorenz had taken her hand Taleah began to feel that everything between them was just as it should be. His delicate kiss to her forehead had instantly relaxed her. Both of them were feeling confident now and resting easily within their comfort zones.

Taleah entered the apartment and quickly led Lorenz into the living room. She then pointed at the sofa and the chair. "Please have a seat, Lorenz. Make yourself comfortable."

Taleah admired Lorenz's casually attired look, clean, neat, and fashionable. "You look great, Lorenz," she gushed, reaching up to give him a warm hug before he sat down. "I really missed seeing you, Mr. Man. You were such good company."

Since Lorenz had made the first attempt at being affectionate, Taleah hadn't felt the need to hold back. She still wanted to feel this man's arms around her in the worst possible way. Just the thought of being in his arms made Taleah's body go limp. Imagining her body tightly meshed against his while inhaling the manly scent of his cologne sent jolts of pure lust through her.

As if he'd once again read her thoughts, Lorenz put his arms around her and squeezed her tightly. "Same here, Taleah. Talking to you every night has been wonderful, but it wasn't the same as being here with you." Lorenz then seated himself on the sofa, hoping Taleah would join him. His heart leaped for joy when she sat down right next to him. "I missed you, too. How was your week, Miss Taleah?"

"Long and lonely. Just as I said a moment ago, I missed having you around."

"You may've been lonely, but you weren't alone. You were always in my thoughts. Did you play tennis this morning?"

Much to her dismay, Taleah felt herself blushing hotly at his sweet comments. "That was so nice of you to say. Thanks. As for tennis, I did play earlier. Had a great session. I'm getting a little better at it. My instructor is grateful for that. He's not chasing after as many balls as he used to. But I still have a long way to get to where I want my skill level to be. Would you like something to eat or drink, Lorenz? I can make you a nice breakfast since it's not too late."

Lorenz shook his head in the negative, rubbing his hands over his stomach in a circular motion. "No, thanks. Mark and I stopped at a Denny's on the way here. The restaurant's average food has hit the spot for the moment. What about you, Taleah, are you hungry?"

"Not a bit. But that was a smart move on your and Mark's part. That way, I won't be hitting on you guys for food money. Do you think I was tact-less in doing so the last time you were here, when I collected money for the KFC?"

"Quite the contrary. You were just getting your needs met. Why should you have to foot the food bill for all of us? I have a darn good income. I'm also used to paying my own way."

"That was my exact sentiment, Lorenz. I was broke; otherwise I wouldn't have minded treating everyone. I haven't always been careful with my fi-nances, but I've turned over a new leaf in that area. I plan to be debt-free before the year is out. I thank God that I somehow managed not to ruin my credit. Even if I could only pay the bare mini-mum, I have always paid my bills on time. Although I still have a few debts to pay off, my credit rating is very good."

Lorenz gave an acknowledging nod, turning his mouth down at the corners. Taleah's honesty about her credit history and financial mismanagement meant a lot to him. Finances and credit histories were extremely important for couples to discuss openly. It helped to know exactly what to expect in that area. A lot of people didn't realize that they'd inherit the credit history, good or bad, of the per-son they married. Once a couple purchased some-thing together or filed joint income taxes the debts and credit histories merged.

"That's a great goal and a smart one that you've set for yourself, Taleah. I hope you achieve it. I thank God that I've never been bogged down with unmanageable debts."

Curious about his statement, Taleah raised an eyebrow. "How'd you manage that?"

"No plastic whatsoever, Taleah. Living overseas is different from residing in the States. I have no real need for credit cards on the base, though I do have a Star card for the exchange. My housing allowance covers my living quarters and I use base-issue furniture. I let everything of any real value go back with my family. I own a nonexport Japanese car that I paid cash for. I have the best employer-paid benefits anyone could ask for, medical, dental, and optical, just to name a few of them. My DJ salary helps out, too, especially since I get paid in Japanese yen. Military life has allowed me to live comfortably, without getting into financial difficulties. However, that's not true for everyone. Our younger troops struggle a lot at times. I could say much more, but I think you get the big picture."

"Clearly. I've heard from one of my friends that military life is good. Do you agree?"

Lorenz took a brief moment to think about the last thirteen years that he'd served in the United States Air Force. He couldn't help but smile. The vast amount of education and training he'd received, as a member of the armed forces, was invaluable. He'd never once regretted his enlistment. It was the best career move he could've chosen at the time.

"I do agree, for the most part, Taleah. It can be exactly what a person makes of it. Military life can be a piece of cake. But it can also be real hard. That also depends on how each individual handles his or her career. We have strict rules and regulations to abide by and many are really hard to adhere to for some. I've always been extremely disciplined. Everyone has a different experience in this man's military. Mine has been a very positive one, thus far. In seven more years I'll retire from the armed forces. Then I can get on with life, hopefully as a civilian meteorologist. Anything over twenty years in the military would be like working for half pay."

"That's fantastic to be able to retire at such at an

early age and also get paid for the rest of your natural born life for the dedicated service you gave. I'm amazed and impressed. The military has definitely saved a lot of brothers." Taleah looked at Lorenz and smiled. "All I know about the job of a meteorologist is what I see on television. Tell me about your job as a weather forecaster, Lorenz. That is, if you don't mind."

Just anticipating what he'd say to Taleah had Lorenz beaming. He loved his job. It was a fascinating profession to be in. His eyes had a way of lighting up when he talked about what he did for a living. Weather squadrons offered support to the base flying units as well as a host of other integral military operations and missions, making it an exciting field of work. Informing pilots on what to expect in the way of weather patterns was an extremely important mission.

"My job is a great one to have, Miss Taylor. It's also considered a critical career field. Besides my forecasting duties of briefing military pilots on weather conditions, before they take to the wild blue yonder, we forecast weather all over the world by using satellites and other sophisticated means of data acquisitions. I also fly weather reconnaissance missions as a flight crew member. That's one of the more exciting parts of my jobs. I guess I love it so much because it's so unpredictable. A lot of our missions are classified, so I can't go into any detail there. My job is both complex and rewarding. It has been my experience that if you love what you do, you'll do it well and to the best of your ability. I really love what I do."

"I can tell, Lorenz. Your bright smile is one indication."

"What about you, Taleah? How do you feel about your job and what all does it entail?"

"I love what I do, too. I handle lots and lots of paperwork. I take care of the time cards for all the employees, making sure they're turned into the accounting department at the end of the pay period so that we can get paid on time. I set up employee training sessions and schedule outside conferences for the dentists and administrators. I just basically take care of all administrative needs. This job is not my lifetime career choice. I'm considering becoming a dental hygienist. Mom is constantly encouraging me to become a dentist. Easier said than done."

"It can be easy to accomplish if that's what you decide on, Taleah."

"I guess. At any rate, I'm not sure I even want to be a dentist, although I have considered it from time to time. My age could be a factor, but I realize that a lot people go back to school later in life. I'm not so old that I can't completely start over with the education process."

Lorenz stroked his chin thoughtfully. "Dr. Taleah Taylor. Has a nice ring to it."

"Yeah, right! Thanks for the flattery. I have a nice permanent job, and a good part-time gig doing billing for an inhalation therapy company, which I didn't mention before. I work my part-time job from home. Both pay a decent salary. I work with a great bunch of people. I'm content with that for now, Lorenz."

"That's half the battle, Taleah. Getting along with the people we work with and being content in our jobs is so important. So, are you all packed and ready for us to do it up right again this weekend in San Diego and TJ?"

Taleah nodded. "I am so up for it you can't even imagine. All packed and very excited. I haven't been to San Diego or Mexico in a while. It'll take about two and a half hours to get there. With Mark driving it could take a lot less time than that. I'm sure he hasn't shown you any mercy in driving on the freeway. The brother loves to fly low."

Lorenz chuckled. "I know what you mean, but I have no problems speaking up if he gets reckless. I also have a heavy foot. I love putting the pedal to the metal. Do you have a car? I'm only asking because I haven't heard you mention one."

Taleah's eyelids fluttered nervously as she briefly thought about his question. "I don't even have a driver's license, let alone a car. I've never had either. Public transportation works for me. Most of the time, that is."

Both of Lorenz's eyebrows shot up. He couldn't imagine anyone not having a driver's license, especially one living in California. "Why not, Taleah?"

"Driving is just not for me. That I nearly got annihilated in a serious car accident a couple of years ago has a lot to do with it. A coworker was driving several of us back to work from lunch in her car when we were broadsided by a big truck. I couldn't walk for six months. Broken pelvis. After suffering through that, I've had no desire to drive."

"Well, that certainly explains it. I'm sorry you were seriously injured, Taleah."

"Thanks. I had a full recovery, but it was a tough time for me. However, it was truly a blessing that I even survived. And I didn't end up having surgery, because it was a clean break. That was another blessing. My pelvis had to heal on its own. But as you can see, I'm physically fit. I've been back into the swing of things for a long time now. The memories were once nightmarish for me, but I've gotten that under control, too."

Taleah suddenly looked embarrassed. "Back to

our trip. I made the hotel accommodations for us. Same room, two beds. We can go Dutch on the room rate. Okay?"

Lorenz studied her bewildered expression. It seemed to him as if she was seeking his approval for her decision on the two beds. She had it, but she definitely didn't need it. Taleah was free to call all the shots. Regardless of what he might want, her desires would always come first. He had no intention of pushing Taleah into anything she wasn't comfortable with or that which she objected to. Their relationship would go only where she led it. Lorenz Hampton knew what it meant to be a gentleman. His southern-bred parents had raised him very well. He also had character, integrity, and he was very trustworthy.

"Two beds it is. However, I'm paying for the room. This entire trip is on me. I'm your date again this weekend—and I'm not out to catch." *I've already been caught by you.*

They both laughed at that, each remembering the question Taleah had asked Lorenz before their first date had gotten under way. Lorenz would never forget how adorable she'd looked when making her bold inquiry about his intentions.

Lorenz smiled broadly. "Other than that, you are in total control, my lady. You don't have a thing to worry about. I promise you that nothing will ever happen that you don't want to participate in or that you object to. I'm completely safe and you'll always be safe with me."

Taleah felt weak and giddy with relief. Lorenz had released many of her fears with his short-but-to-the-point speech. *If you had any inkling of how totally safe I feel with you, you'd be absolutely amazed.* It was even more amazing to her. "How about a kiss,

Lorenz?" she asked right out of the blue. "I could certainly use one right about now." She wanted to clear the trust issue.

The kiss was riveting, so sweet. Taleah suddenly felt rather shy for someone who had repeatedly displayed such bold aggression toward Lorenz. She hoped he didn't think she was too forceful. It was so unlike her to take the initiative in any intimate contact in a personal relationship. But she was rather enjoying playing the lead role. She didn't want Lorenz to move her too terribly fast, but at the rate he was going a snail would easily beat him to the finish line.

The idea of sharing the same room had more to do with her finances than anything. Since she and Lorenz had shared her living room the week before, without incident, she didn't feel that Lorenz would suddenly change personalities on her. He'd been nothing less than a gentleman.

Lorenz spotted the fancy vase holding a variety of beautiful and colorful wildflowers. It was stationed on the stereo shelving. This floral arrangement was different from the one he'd seen the last time he'd visited Taleah. The others had been all roses, a mixture of red and white ones. The flowers had Lorenz wondering if Taleah had a special someone. She hadn't mentioned anyone to him other than her ex-fiancé. The delicate blooms seemed to suggest otherwise.

Unless, Lorenz mused, Bradley was the sender. If the flowers were from her ex, was he trying to win Taleah back? The thought was downright unnerving for Lorenz. He didn't even have to take time out to wonder why he felt so unsettled deep down inside. Lorenz already knew the answer. Taleah was his soul mate, not someone else's. She was made for him, exclusively, not for someone else. How to make that work for him under the present circumstances was challenging at best. Still, he believed their meeting had all the earmarkings of blessed fate.

"The flowers," Lorenz said, without thinking of the consequences of knowing the truth, "they're just as beautiful as the red and white roses I saw here last week. From a secret admirer?"

The answer to his question just might hurt him if they turned out to be from a man, he considered, hoping they were from her parents or one of her best friends.

"They're from an admirer, someone who loves me dearly, but definitely not a secret one. They're from me." Taleah laughed at the stunned expression on his face. If his jaw dropped any lower, she mused, it would eventually meet up with the floor.

He eyed her with curiosity. "From you? How'd that come to pass?"

Taleah chuckled. "It's one of the ways I show love for myself. I have a standing delivery order at the local florist to have flowers delivered to my apartment every other Friday. The ones you saw here the last time had already been here for a week. Instead of ordering specific flowers, I told them to surprise me each time. They have a dollar amount to work within. When they asked me what I wanted on the card, I expressed my desire for something inspiring. The entire idea to do this came from my sweet-as-pie beautician, Melanie Jeans. She loves herself, too."

Lorenz's eyes shone with his deep admiration for Taleah. "That is really something else. I've never heard of anything like that before. I like the idea. Love for self can't ever be rivaled. You sure know how to keep me inspired, Taleah."

Taleah kissed him lightly on the mouth. "Just as you inspire me. Thanks."

"Since we're not leaving for a while longer, I think I'd like to take you up on your offer of food. I'd like to make a sandwich for both of us. That's if you don't mind me working around in your kitchen. Mark told me you weren't too thrilled about me cleaning it up the last time."

Embarrassed to no end, wishing she could up and disappear, Taleah's right hand flew up to her mouth. "Oh, my goodness! I wish he hadn't told you that. I'm sorry I didn't tell you myself. You washing my dishes just seemed kind of odd to me at the time."

"And intrusive?"

Taleah's skin glowed with her embarrassment. "Mark told you everything I said, didn't he? Wait until I get my hands on him. My brother-in-law has no loyalty whatsoever."

"Trust me, Taleah. You do have his loyalty. Mark also has your back. He has already forewarned me. 'If you don't treat my sister-in-law right, there'll be serious consequences.' He only wanted to make sure that I don't go over the line with you. He's been assured of that."

Taleah sighed with relief. "Mark can be such a macho man. Not to worry, though. His bark is much worse than his bite. Your last remarks just saved his butt. Now, let's talk about that sandwich. I've somehow worked up an appetite by doing absolutely nothing. I'd love you to make mine with three slices of smoked turkey and lots of brown deli mustard. Hold the lettuce. You can also put two dill spears and a couple of sliced tomatoes on the side of the plate."

Lorenz smiled as he got to his feet. "You don't ask for much, do you?" He leaned over and kissed her gently on the mouth. "I'm here to deliver whatever you want. Two of the world's best made-to-

order smoked turkey sandwiches coming right
up!"

"You might have to make that a to-go order,
Lorenz. Lynette and Mark are probably on the way
here by now. If that happens, there's plenty of Saran
Wrap and aluminum foil on the lower shelf of the
pantry. The pack of brown lunch bags are also on
the same shelf."

"Your request is hereby granted," he joked, laughing softly, happy to fulfill all of Taleah's orders. If
Taleah only knew how much Lorenz aimed to please
her, she'd be either thrilled to death or absolutely
terrified.

Taleah felt a little funny about being in a hotel
room with Lorenz. She hadn't expected to feel too
much different from how she'd felt with them spending the night together at her place, but she did.
Dragonflies had invaded her stomach. There was
too much nervous carrying on for them to be considered butterflies. There was nothing soft and
fluttering about what she felt inside. Taleah began
to think that perhaps she had pushed the envelope with this one.

On the other hand, Taleah couldn't help noticing how totally relaxed Lorenz looked. He didn't
seem to be aware of her inner turmoil either, as he
glanced over his Mexican bargains. Since it had still
been very early by the time the foursome reached
San Diego, they had decided to go on over into
Mexico, as opposed to waiting until the next day.
They were now going to use all of Saturday to ex-
plore San Diego.

Lorenz hadn't made any purchases for himself
since he didn't have a lot of extra luggage space.
The Mexican serape was for his mother and the

colorful sombrero was for his dad. However, he'd
mentioned to Taleah that the hat would more than
likely end up on one of the den walls as a decora-
tor item in his parents' Connecticut home. He had
also picked up several T-shirts bearing a colorful
imprinted map of the Mexican coastline. The
shirts were for friends.

Lorenz had also insisted on purchasing for Taleah
a bottle of Jungle Gardenia perfume and a beautiful vase for her home. To complement the large
gold vase Talaeah had bought a varied arrangement of beautiful ivory and white silk flowers to fill
the ceramic container.

In her anguish Taleah wrung her hands together.
Now that she was tired and wanted to go to sleep,
Taleah's dilemma had her feeling nervous as a cat.
As she thought about what Lorenz had said about
her being safe with him, she began to relax, realizing she was making way too much of this thing.
*Just take your nightclothes into the bathroom, shower,
and then put them on. Dry off, and then come back out
and get into bed.* Taleah laughed out loud at herself.

Lorenz looked over at her. "What's so funny,
Taleah? You seem to be having a good laugh at a
private joke. Am I right?"

"Pay me no mind. I'm alone so much that I
laugh at anything funny that comes to mind and I
talk to myself all the time. Don't worry. I'm not too
crazy."

Lorenz chuckled. "It sounds to me like you have
a great relationship with yourself, that you really
enjoy your own company. That's rare, you know.
Most people are scared to be alone with themselves,
scared that their demons might go on the attack.
There are times when being alone is good. It helps
you to keep in touch with self. I talk to myself, too."

"Do you also answer yourself? 'Cause I sure do. Talking out loud helps me to really hear what I'm saying. There are some things that come out of my mouth that make me glad I said them while alone and not around anyone. I'm never downright cruel, but there are times when my tongue grows a few sharp edges." Taleah grabbed her overnighter. "I'm going to shower and get ready for bed. We've had a really long day and we still have to get through tomorrow."

"Try to save some hot water for me."

Taleah laughed inwardly, wondering if Lorenz's comment was a hint of some sort for him to join her in the shower. *Not tonight, baby boy,* she mused, at the same time wishing it could be different for them. He was definitely the man of her dreams. His hand under her elbow, the light kisses on her cheeks and on the lips, his hand gently on her back, and the smoothing of her hair away from her face were all the little ways he showered her with intimacy and care. Things weren't any different with them, so she'd just have to keep on dreaming about how it might've been if the circumstances were changed.

Taleah passed Lorenz as she came out of the bathroom. He was on his way in. Lorenz did a quick turnaround as he caught a whiff of her tantalizing scent. "What did you bathe yourself in, Taleah? It sure smells wonderful."

"I didn't bathe in it. Just sprayed a little on my pulse points. It's the Jungle Gardenia you bought for me. I thought you smelled it before you purchased it."

"I did, but I don't remember it smelling like that. Maybe it's one of those perfumes that mingle with your body chemistry so that it smells differently on everyone. Well, it sure smells great on you. I'm glad I bought it despite your softly voiced objections."

"I'm glad, too, especially since you like it so much. Thanks again."

His eyes glowed with joy. "You're welcome again. I hope you don't fall asleep before I get back to you. I'll rush through my shower."

"Can't make any promises, Lorenz. This girl is completely fagged out." Taleah yawned to make her point.

Smiling broadly, Lorenz backed out of the bathroom and stopped in front of Taleah. He then took her in his arms and kissed her passionately. "That was my way of saying good night to you just in case you can't stay awake. Good night, Taleah Taylor. Sleep tight."

Now how in the world did Lorenz expect her to get to sleep after that passionate kiss? After that intimate a kiss she might never fall asleep again. She'd meet him in her dreams, for sure. Lorenz had only been starring in her fantasies every night since she first laid eyes on him.

The moment Lorenz closed the bathroom door Taleah slipped out of her robe, pulled the covers back, and climbed into bed. Feeling self-conscious about what little night attire she was wearing, she pulled the spread up around her neck. Lorenz had seen her in her nightclothes before, but Lynette and Mark had been around then. Tonight they were all in the same hotel but in different rooms. Lynette and Mark's room was two floors below theirs.

Although Taleah felt safe with Lorenz, she was alone in a hotel room with him. She hated to admit that it was herself that she didn't trust. She had daydreamed too many times about him making mad, passionate love to her for her to try and say she didn't desire him physically.

Remembering that she'd brought along a book to read, Taleah quickly jumped up and retrieved it from her overnighter. She realized that getting the book was just an excuse for her to attempt to stay awake until Lorenz returned. How could she even think of sleep with a fine, exciting man lying in the bed right next to hers?

Taleah was certain that nothing physical would happen between them, but she didn't think of it as the worst thing that could occur. In fact, making love to Lorenz would fill her up in every way. It would definitely rid her of all her pent-up frustration. "It's not going to happen," she whispered. "It can't happen. Go to sleep and stop the agony of thinking of the ecstasy."

Taleah quickly closed her eyes when she heard the bathroom door open. She listened intently for the sounds of his every movement. Would he just go to bed if he thought she was asleep? Maybe he'd turn on the television. The hotel did have cable. Her heart nearly stopped when she felt his weight on her bed. He was seated on the side of her mattress. What was he about to do? Taleah fought hard to remain calm, but her heart was already thumping erratically.

Lorenz leaned over and kissed her forehead. "I guess you just couldn't hang on. Sleep tight, precious angel." He then kissed each of her eyelids as he smoothed back her silky hair.

Taleah dared to breathe after he'd moved away from her bed. After a couple of minutes had passed, she turned her back and faced the wall. As she thought about his gentleness, tears slipped from her eyes. Taleah knew without a shadow of a doubt that she loved him, loved him like crazy. What was a girl to do when the man she'd fallen hard for would up and disappear from her life within the next couple of weeks? If anyone had the answer, she wished they'd share it with her. Being in love at a distance couldn't possibly be easy.

Taleah sank her teeth into her lower lip. Ignoring Lorenz's presence just wasn't working for her. They were both adults. Nothing would happen that she didn't want. Lorenz was trustworthy, but was she? Would her love-starved body betray her? She hoped not.

Taleah sat straight up in the bed and stretched her arms high above her head. "How about watching a movie, Lorenz? Are you up to it? I can't sleep, but if you're too tired, I understand."

Grinning with satisfaction, as if a prayer had just been answered, Lorenz picked up the remote and turned on the television. "Let's see what's on. I'm up for anything you're up to." Lorenz got up from his bed and came over to Taleah's. "Mind if I lie down with you to watch the movie? All I want to do is hold you, Taleah."

Without comment, her heart racing at top speed, Taleah moved over to the center of her bed. She then picked up and positioned one of the pillows between them. "Make yourself comfortable, Lorenz. You're safe with me, Mr. Man."

Locking his dark gaze into hers, he laughed softly. Lorenz then lay down next to Taleah. After removing the pillow from between them, he placed it partially on his chest. While drawing her head down onto the pillow, Lorenz kissed her lightly on the mouth. "I've never felt safer than I do with you, Taleah. My virtue feels safe, too." He and Taleah both laughed.

Five

Time had been fleet for Taleah and Lorenz during their last weekend. The wonderful trip to San Diego and Mexico had passed by quickly and everyone had had loads of fun while sightseeing and shopping for great bargains. While Taleah and Lorenz had talked on the phone every night in between his visits to L.A., another one was now upon them—and it was nearly over already. Lorenz had a few days of leave now that his TDY was over. The couple had spent the latter part of the evening with friends and family at yet another L.A. hot spot. Dinner in a popular intimate eatery in Hollywood had preceded the trip to the nightclub.

Lorenz had come down with Mark early afternoon on Friday, but he and Taleah had opted to spend that evening in her apartment. They'd shared in preparing an easy but delicious meal of baked chicken, roasted red potatoes, steamed cabbage, and a fresh garden salad.

As this was Lorenz's last days to spend with Taleah, she felt so saddened by his upcoming departure. She just couldn't get over how quickly their time together had passed. Lorenz was leaving for Connecticut in a couple of days, where he was to spend a few days with his loving parents, Cynthia and Edward Hampton. He would then fly back to Japan and resume his regular military duties on Yokota Air Base. His flight to Tokyo was out of San Francisco, which meant he'd come to California again but not back to Los Angeles.

Both Taleah and Lorenz had been extremely quiet on the ride back to her apartment. It was well after midnight and each of them was tired from dancing the night away. While Mark and Lynette had chatted away in the front seat, the restless couple in the backseat had had very little to contribute to the conversation.

Taleah and Lorenz were simply feeling the draining effects of thinking about his imminent departure. Neither of them was eager to see their visits finally come to an abrupt end.

Inside her apartment Taleah kicked off her shoes and dropped tiredly down on the sofa. Her roller-coaster-like emotions had just about worn her out. She couldn't help glancing at the clock again, something she'd done all evening long. Taleah had lost count of the times she'd consulted her wristwatch a good while back. Time had refused to stand still. No matter how hard she prayed for it to at least slow down a bit, the seconds had continued to tick away.

Lorenz dropped down next to Taleah. Frowning slightly, he made direct eye contact with his beautiful hostess. "Hey, why are you so quiet? Aren't you feeling well?"

Taleah smiled weakly. "I'm not the only quiet one. Neither of us has had much to say, especially the last couple of hours. Physically, I'm fine. I'm just not dealing too well emotionally with you leav-

ing pretty soon. Yet I know you have to go. Is that
also why you're so quiet?"

Lorenz nodded. "Miserably so. This is a tough
situation for us to be in. I wish I could make a commitment to you, but we both know I can't. My personal life is full of uncertainties."

Taleah sighed, fighting hard to hide her disappointment over his statement. "I'm not asking you
to make a commitment to me. I never expected
such a thing to happen, anyway."

"I know that, Taleah. I just thought I'd be up
front with my feelings. That you don't expect anything from me blows my mind. You haven't made a
single demand. You're a rare, precious gem. I hope
I've successfully conveyed that sentiment to you."

"You have, Lorenz." As Taleah got to her feet,
she sighed hard again. Her tears were going to
give her true feelings away if she didn't get out of
the room right away. No, she didn't expect a thing
from him. Had she hoped for more? Without a
doubt, but only after she'd come to know him as a
person. No matter the outcome for them as a couple, Taleah loved Lorenz Hampton with all her
heart. The memories of their time together would
stay with her forever.

"Excuse me, Lorenz. I'm going outside for a minute. Out by the pool."

Lorenz scowled hard. "It's almost one o'clock in
the morning, Taleah. Are you sure that's such a
good idea?"

Taleah didn't answer him. Her voice would crack
if she did. With as much dignity as she could muster,
Taleah held her head high as she exited the room.
She then left the apartment wearing her shattered
heart on her sleeve.

The chill in the air was instantly felt by Taleah,
making her wished she'd slipped on a heavier sweat-

er or a lightweight jacket. She briefly looked back at her apartment door. Instead of turning around, she proceeded toward the complex's patio/ pool area. Upon reaching her destination, she unfolded one of the chaise longues and lowered herself down onto it.

The sadness welling up in Taleah was darn near tangible. She had once again given her heart to someone who couldn't receive it, someone unavailable to her. Although the two situations were as different as day and night, there were similarities. Bradley hadn't been committed to her, though he'd vowed to be. Lorenz couldn't commit to her; he was already obligated to his estranged wife. That is, until the divorce was final. He was also dedicated to the United States Air Force, which Lorenz considered one of the highest callings in the land.

Taleah didn't bother to wipe away her tears. Although there were many times she'd felt like losing it altogether, she hadn't cried this hard over her dilemma until now. She had avoided falling apart so she could savor the joyous emotional highs she felt when she was with Lorenz.

No matter what happened, no matter the outcome, Taleah knew that she was a much better person for having met the incomparable Lorenz Hampton. He had been such a positive force in her life. If nothing else, though there was plenty of goodness in this situation, she had to be grateful for at least that. Lorenz had helped her to see that she needed to move on with her life, that she could feel again—and love anew.

Deciding not to waste any more time out of Lorenz's company, Taleah stood, folded the chaise longue, and put it away. She then started the short trek back to her apartment, hoping Lorenz was still up. They should be together and continue to talk. All night if need be.

Taleah's heart leaped with joy the second her eyes connected with Lorenz's. Thrilled that he hadn't gone to bed while she was outside, Taleah felt her heart dancing with glee. However, Lorenz looked a little sad to her. That caused her heart to empathize with him. But she understood his somewhat dark mood since she felt the same way he appeared to feel.

Lorenz had immediately noticed the redness of her eyes and nose. Had she been crying? Or had it just been too cold for her outside? "Want some tea to warm you up, Taleah?"

"Thanks, Lorenz. I would. Do you want some, too?"

He nodded. "Come, sit down and get relaxed. I'll take care of the tea. Or maybe you might want to put on your nightclothes while I'm getting things ready."

Taleah smiled sweetly. "Your suggestions keep on getting better. Dressing for bed now will allow me to just jump in when I'm ready to go to sleep. Be back in a few minutes."

"Before you go, I was wondering if you'd like to try some of my delicious cinnamon toast. I have to warn you, though. I make a mean slice. You might become addicted."

Taleah laughed at his tempting expression. "Just go lightly on the sugar. Sounds like I'm in for a real treat." After blowing Lorenz a kiss, Taleah practically floated from the room.

* * *

After a thorough washing up, Taleah dressed herself in a lovely pair of pink silk pajamas and a matching robe. She then brushed her hair out and sprayed on a touch of Jungle Gardenia. Lorenz truly loved his choice for her in perfume. In thinking that the robe might be a tad too thin for entertaining a male, Taleah kept it on and slipped a heavier one on over it. Satisfied that she looked morally decent and still presentable, Taleah made a hasty retreat, heading for the kitchen.

Lorenz was just setting the hot mugs of tea on the table when Taleah entered the room. The toast smelled heavenly to her. He looked over at her and smiled. Before pulling out a chair for her, Lorenz raised her hand and kissed the back of it. "You look beautiful in pink."

Taleah blushed, feeling deeply the sensuousness in his simple kiss to her hand. "Thanks."

While sipping on the hot tea, Taleah and Lorenz chatted about their previous weekend in San Diego and Tijuana, stressing how much fun it had been. They also talked about all the fun and happenings from earlier in the evening. Lorenz raved about the delectable restaurant meal.

Only minutes into their conversation Lorenz grew noticeably quiet. He suddenly seemed lost in his thoughts. The expressions crossing his face were troubled. His bright smile had gone completely away. There was nothing in his demeanor to lead Taleah to believe that he was happy and content. In fact, he looked downright unhappy and discontent. His easily discernable body language showed how restless he was.

Taleah took a deep breath. She didn't want to intrude upon his strange mood, but she was surely worried about the drastic change in him. The fact that he'd stopped talking in midsentence had her wondering what he might be going through. She couldn't get a read on the exact expression in his eyes, but there was a definite sadness there.

Lorenz finally looked up. He then trained his eyes on Taleah. "I want you to come to Japan and live with me, Miss Taleah."

Taleah instantly felt crushed. What was it about her that made men think she was downright stupid? She'd never live with any man, lover or not. And she surely wouldn't go ten thousand miles away from home to do it. Taleah gave Lorenz a pensive glance. "I think you've gotten a very wrong impression of me. I don't cohabit with the opposite sex. Going all the way to Japan to live with you is absolutely out of the question, Lorenz. That's not who I am."

Lorenz's dark eyes held a mysterious glint. "I'm not asking you just to live with me. I want you to live with me as my wife, Taleah. As in 'let's get married.' "

Taleah's heart was off to the races. Her hands were suddenly sweaty and her brain felt nauseously numb. As his wife? Had he really said that? She was completely dumbfounded.

Lorenz chuckled. "I know what you're thinking. That I already have a wife. My divorce is nearly final, Taleah. You probably think it's crazy of me to want to get married again so soon after a divorce, since I've been alone a long time. But the truth of the matter is I'm crazy about you. If you say no, I'll have to go through life without you. But know this. I don't want to."

Taleah shook her head from side to side, having a hard time believing how this conversation was going. "Earlier you said you couldn't make a commitment to me. What has changed in less than a half hour, Lorenz? It hasn't been too much longer than that."

He looked her dead in the eye. "The thought of losing you. When you went outside, I perceived that move as you walking out on me. It was the same way I felt the night you jumped up and ran out on me in the nightclub. Your absence left me feeling pretty empty inside. If you can just wait until my divorce is final, I'd love to marry you. I believe that you're my destiny."

Taleah was at a total loss for words. She didn't have a clue what to say, but his expression told her he was expecting her to say something. Her heart was screaming, *Yes, marry him,* but her head was doing an altogether different number on her, logically so. She didn't know how she knew it, but Taleah somehow felt absolutely positive that Lorenz would take very good care of her fragile heart. He didn't seem to be a user and an abuser of women. Still . . .

This was the most insane position Taleah had ever found herself in. Well, she thought, her engagement to Bradley had definitely topped the insanity charts. If this moment was so insane, why did it feel so darn wonderful? Lorenz asking her to be his wife wasn't something she would ever have expected, not under the current circumstances, not in a million years. That she wanted desperately to accept his proposal of marriage was the most insane of all. She could hardly believe that she was even considering the idea of marrying him after only three weeks.

The voice of sanity was still vying to be heard, but she simply wasn't listening.

Taleah wanted to rush into Lorenz's arms, but

now was not the time for her to come off too needy. This moment was very surreal for her. What if she was only dreaming? She reached down and discreetly pinched herself hard. The fleeting pain confirmed the reality of the situation.

"Taleah, are you going to give me an answer? I want to marry you. Don't ask me how I know what I know. I just know that you're the one for me, without reservation. You and I are meant to be together as one. Destined. Talk to me, Taleah. Tell me what's on your mind."

As Taleah battled with her welling emotions, she sighed hard. She still couldn't get over his proposal. "I feel the same spiritual connection that you feel between us. I've felt it from the very first moment we met." She closed her eyes for a very brief respite. "Lorenz, my heart wants to accept your proposal, but I can't help thinking of how I rushed into an engagement before. I couldn't bear the pain of a second failure if you later change your mind. I know this isn't the answer you're looking for, but I need to give your proposal a lot of serious thought."

Lorenz felt weak with relief. She hadn't turned him down flat. That had to count for something. He was ecstatic to know that her heart felt the same wonderful things his did. Unable to keep his distance from her for another second, Lorenz stood up. He then brought Taleah up from her chair and into his arms. "We don't have to rush into this serious decision, Taleah. That you've decided to at least consider it is enough for me right now."

Taleah looked up into his eyes. "Are you willing to talk to my dad about your intentions? I know I'm grown, but I value my parents' opinions. I deeply regret that I didn't listen to them before. They turned out to be one hundred percent right about the last situation I made a mess of. Is talking with my father too much to ask of you?"

"Is tomorrow soon enough for me to talk with him? It's way too late to do it now."

Taleah's heart warmed even more toward Lorenz. That he didn't back away from talking to her parents showed what type of man he was. Her mother and father might have a problem with the fact that his divorce wasn't final, but they'd be fair in their assessment. While she respected her parents and valued their advice, the final decision to marry him or not was hers.

As Lorenz reseated himself, he drew Taleah down onto his lap and nuzzled her neck. "I'm sorry I didn't create a more romantic setting to ask you to marry me in. The truth is I hadn't planned out this proposal. It was strictly spontaneous. I was as surprised by my question as you appeared to be. But I know it's exactly what I want, Taleah. Nothing would make me happier."

Taleah giggled. "I could tell that by the bewildered look on your face, Lorenz. I wish I could've been just as spontaneous with my answer to your proposal, but I just couldn't do that without thinking about it. This may not be the most romantic moment between us, but it is nonetheless a very special moment in time for me. Neither one of us has spoken of loving each other. But I need you to know that I do love you, Lorenz. Otherwise I wouldn't be considering your proposal of marriage. And I am seriously considering it. I fell in love with you on sight."

He drew in a shaky breath. "It seems that we fell in love with each other in the very same instant. I love you, too, Taleah. Your heart will always be safe with me. After we get all the issues out in the open

in front of your family, I'm going to ask you to
marry me all over again. The next time will be so
different from this one. I can promise you way
more romance."

Taleah touched her lips to his for a brief moment. "You keep me intrigued, Lorenz. Us falling
in love so quickly will seem crazy to everyone but
us. Your asking me to marry you will be right at the
top of their list of the craziest things they've ever
heard of. I can assure you that my friends are going
to think I've completely lost my mind. They'll be
right, 'cause I'm truly insane over you. And I look
forward to all the promising things that are yet to
come."

"Wonderful things, Taleah! I'm looking forward
to one day having a bright future with you. I hope
your eventual answer will be yes." Lorenz didn't
think he could deal with a no as the answer. To
have a genuine woman like Taleah as his wife
would be a dream come true.

Hoping and praying for the same outcome,
Taleah put her arms around Lorenz and hugged
him something fierce. Everything had changed in
an instant. He had proposed marriage to her. Her
heart was joyous. Taleah believed wholeheartedly
that a yes was in their future, but she was determined not to jump the gun. Haste most always re-
sulted in waste.

To take her mind off the mind-blowing subject
of marriage, Taleah picked up a second slice of
cinnamon toast. She then ate every bite of it before raving to Lorenz about how good it was. He
had gone light on the sugar, just as she'd requested.
The sweet-tasting bread was so much better than
good. The description "utterly delightful" worked
best for her. Full and totally relaxed now, Taleah
was ready to settle in for the rest of the night and

get her mind wrapped around other matters. She felt happy and content in letting tomorrow take care of tomorrow.

As she sat in her living room looking nervous and unsure of herself, Taleah saw that she had no fingernails left to chew on. She'd only been nibbling on them for the past two hours, ever since Lorenz had left to go meet with her father. Taleah had expected the meeting to last awhile, but never had she thought it might run for two hours. What were they talking about? Lorenz's life history? It certainly shouldn't be taking Lorenz that long to tell Jack Taylor his intentions toward his youngest daughter.

The doorbell rang just as Taleah completed her last thought. It had to be Lorenz. Ready to fire at him every question in the book, Taleah jumped up from the sofa and ran to the door. Her heart dropped the same moment she saw Lorenz's long, unhappy face. What had gone down in her parents' home? What had her father said to Lorenz to make him look so pitiful and sad?

Taleah reached for Lorenz's hand, gripping it tightly. "You look as if it didn't go too well with my dad, which is a total surprise to me. What did he say to have you looking so upset?"

Lorenz squeezed Taleah's hand. "I think we should go and sit down first, Taleah."

Taleah looked worried. "That bad, huh?" Was it really that bad? "What did he say?"

Lorenz shook his head from side to side as they moved on into the apartment. "It was worse than bad. It was brutal. Are you sure you want to hear what your dad had to say?"

Taleah shrugged. "By the look on your face, I'm not sure I do. But I guess I should know. Otherwise, I'll probably lose my mind if I don't find out. This is so unreal."

Lorenz waited until Taleah was seated before he sat down next to her on the sofa. In a loving gesture, he ran his thumb across her lower lip. Lorenz then stared at Taleah for several eternal seconds. She was so stunning. Fear and uncertainty about their future had suddenly given her beautiful golden brown eyes even more depth. Seeing her looking so eager to hear him out excited him in a strange kind of way. He also saw in her eyes the look of the sheer love that she'd confessed to. She was on the edge of her seat. This was also a very heady moment for him. Lorenz could only pray that he'd see the look of love in Taleah's eyes for the rest of their lives.

In the next moment Lorenz was on his knees in front of Taleah. After cupping her face between his two hands, he kissed her sensuously. "I love you, Taleah. I love you with all the passion and emotion I'm capable of. Will you marry me? Make me one of the happiest men alive. Please marry me, Taleah. Love is ours for the taking. We have your parents' blessings."

Taleah toppled Lorenz over when she leaped from the sofa and flew right into his arms. "You're the one for me, Lorenz. I knew it from the start. I'll marry you, Lorenz, today, tomorrow, whenever. You name it." In all her joy, tears falling, Taleah began to whoop it up.

Lorenz gave Taleah a staggering kiss to make the engagement official. Taleah had agreed to marry him. He was astounded and couldn't be more thrilled. *Taleah Hampton. Taleah Taylor-Hampton,* he mentally corrected himself. Miss Taleah Taylor was a new-millennium woman. She would no doubt want to keep her surname, her loving daddy's name.

Lorenz then slipped a beautiful emerald-cut diamond ring onto Taleah's finger. Taleah began to cry harder as she looked down at the incredible ring. This sparkling gem belonged to her very own mother, she now realized. Taleah stared openly at the ring for several seconds. She then turned her questioning gaze on Lorenz, her body shaking from the impact on her emotions.

While stroking her arms, in hopes of calming her down, Lorenz kissed Taleah's tears away. "Your mom was kind enough to loan me her diamond for this amazing occasion. It came at your dad's incredible suggestion. You'll have your own diamond soon, Taleah. I promise."

Thrilled by her parents' loving gestures of kindness and support, Taleah kissed him on the mouth. She knew without a shadow of doubt that it was the heart of this fantastic man that had won them completely over. "I already have my highly polished diamond in you, Lorenz. I can't imagine you ever having been just a gem in the rough. You're always so real, so down-to-earth."

Taleah drew her head back and settled her tear-filled gaze deeply into Lorenz's dark eyes. "Are we officially engaged now, Lorenz?"

Lorenz's incredible smile dazzled Taleah. "I asked you to marry me—and you did say yes, so I guess that makes it official." He looked a bit chagrined. "Perhaps you're referring to the absence of an engagement ring chosen just for you. Is that the case, Taleah?"

Taleah's expression was thoughtful. "A ring isn't important to me. As I just said, you are my precious

gem. I asked that question for a different reason,
Lorenz. Totally different."

Lorenz gently brushed his knuckles down the
side of her face. "Care to let me in on it?"

Blushing hotly, Taleah felt the heat of her embarrassment all over her body. "Well, I thought that
if we were officially engaged now, we could make
love to each other, Lorenz. Can we? I desperately
want to make love to you."

Lorenz was astounded by her question. He never
would've guessed at what had been on her mind.
Taleah wanted him to make love to her, wanted to
make love to him. *Amazing!*

The right response just wasn't coming to him.
Why couldn't he think of something to say? Even
something clever might work in this instance. He
felt the magical moment slipping away, so how
did he save it? *Make love to her. Make her your
woman. Let her know that you're her man, the only
man for her, her husband-to-be,* his foolish head
sounded off.

You're not completely divorced, came the calming
voice of reason. *It wouldn't be fair to her until your
past is behind you. Your future with Taleah Taylor can't
begin until then. This relationship has to be an honest
and fair one. You just can't make love to her right now.*

How to convey his sentiments to Taleah without
hurting her feelings was impossible. Still, he had
to try, had to give it his best shot. Honesty was important in determining their future.

Lorenz sat back on the sofa and put his arm
around her shoulder. "Taleah, making love to you
would make this moment in time complete." He
continued to grope for the right things to say to
her while his frustration showed in his eyes. He
had the kind of eyes that revealed the soul.

Fearful of his thoughts, Taleah took his hand in hers. "I sense a but. But what?"

He grimaced. "It's the timing, Taleah. The timing is all wrong. I don't want to spoil this incredible moment with unattractive facts. But the truth is this: we have to wait. I want to be totally free when we make love for the very first time. I want to be exclusively yours. Our magic moment should only include us. Do you understand what I'm trying to say here, Taleah?"

Taleah's eyes instantly filled with tears.

He held her tighter. "Taleah, please. Please don't cry. I'm not rejecting you."

Lifting his hand to her face, Taleah wiped her tears with his fingers. She then dried his fingers in her hair. "No, no, it's okay. I *do* understand. I'm just a bit overwhelmed by your thoughtfulness. I can always count on you to keep it real. Making love to you is what I want, desperately so. But under the circumstances, and after hearing what you've had to say, I think we should wait. I totally agree with you. I'll wait with bated breath for our magic moment."

Lorenz hugged and kissed her. He then held her at arm's length. "When we do come together in our physical love, it will be awesome for both of us. I promise you that."

Highly aware of the certain powers women had over men, Taleah had the thought of seducing Lorenz into surrendering to her, convinced as she was that he'd give in to what she had in mind. That wouldn't be very nice of her, she considered. Waiting would build the excitement to fever pitch. When they did come together, Taleah had a pretty good idea of what it might be like for them. Just as Lorenz said it would be, utterly awesome, magical. Waiting on the physical side of love did have fringe benefits, she finally concluded. But how long a wait would they have?

Lorenz gently stroked Taleah's arms, loving how she made him feel all over. He would also be waiting with bated breath. Like Taleah, he, too, wondered how long. "Since our future is now looking a lot brighter, are you happy with the way things now stand, Miss Taleah?"

"Ecstatic, Sergeant Hampton!"

Unable to get his fill of her sweetness, he kissed her again. Lorenz then adjusted his body so that he faced her. "I have a couple of things that should be said, Taleah. I don't want you to anticipate our marriage with blinders on. The life of a military member can sometimes be hard on a spouse. Everyone is not cut out to be a military wife or husband. There are instances where our lifestyle is totally unpredictable. We can be in one place today and in another one by tomorrow. Duty can place us at installations all around the world. We can also be sent on assignments to remote and sometimes dangerous places that our spouses can't go to. When duty calls, a military member has to respond without hesitation or reservation. Taleah, simply spoken, military wives have to have *fearless hearts*, just like the fearless hearts of their military men."

Taleah laughed. "Was that speech meant to deter me in some way, Sergeant Hampton?"

He rubbed her shoulders. "Not at all, Taleah. I just believe in telling it like it is. If I don't tell you that it's not the easiest lifestyle to manage, then I'd be remiss in my responsibility to enlighten you. There are many military members who may never see combat and then there are those who are never assigned an overseas duty station. No one can ever say for sure what might happen. Again, a lot of it hinges on what the individual member makes of it and wants from it. There are so many great benefits in serving your country. We can also travel the world on-duty or off-duty, compliments of Uncle Sam. I could go on and on."

"That sounds exciting to me. My sisters don't seem to have any problems with being military wives. If so, I've never heard one of them complain. At least I have them to talk with about the lifestyle if I needed to. To travel all over the world would be like a dream come true for me. I'm very adventurous, Lorenz. And I do believe that I possess a fearless heart. That is, in some cases. Where our love is concerned, you can rest assured that my heart is fearless."

"I have that feeling about you, Taleah. I think you'll do just fine as a military spouse. However, there are parts of the world that we'd rather not find ourselves in, like the situations we've found ourselves in with Iraq. But if duty calls we have to be ready at a moment's notice. I also need you to know that I'm the acting first sergeant in my squadron. The *first shirt,* as some members refer to the position, administrates services for the enlisted, which includes a vast array of duties. In other words, he's the organization's go-to man in representing the enlisted. The numerous duties in that position can also be quite harrowing at times. Our unit is not big enough to have an official first sergeant, which is an actual career in itself. I acquired the position because I'm the ranking NCO in my squadron. Otherwise, I wouldn't be on flying status."

Taleah laid her head on his chest. "Sounds like you have a full plate there, Sergeant. I can only imagine how wonderful you are at all your duties. Otherwise, I don't think you'd have so many important responsibilities. As long as you tend to your duties where our marriage is concerned, we'll be just fine. I promise to wear your stripes as proudly as you do."

Lorenz cracked up. "You're already starting to sound like a military wife. You can't imagine how many women wear their husbands' stripes, sometimes better than they do. Officers' wives are no different. A woman doesn't ever have to wear her man's rank, but she does have to represent it as proudly as he does. Pride in one's country is a must, even when you may not agree with some of the things that are said and done by the powers that be."

Taleah heard somewhat of a strain in his voice and an underlying current in his statement. She eyed him curiously. "Are you at odds with the stance our country has taken the last couple of years? The bombing of the WTC and the horrible things with Iraq are still unsettling to me."

He shrugged. "If I were, I'd never give a voice to it. I have to do as I'm ordered. I came into this man's military with a full understanding of what was expected of me. Serving one's country is an honor and a privilege. I took a vow to preserve the honor of my country and to die for it if necessary. I carry out my duties accordingly. I do it with extreme pride and dignity."

Taleah had clearly gotten the message he'd conveyed; he'd never dishonor his beloved country by speaking out against it, no matter how he felt. It was easy to see that Lorenz Hampton was a diehard military man, one that she was tremendously proud to be the fiancée of. The thought of him dying for his country scared her, but she silently vowed to conquer that fear, too.

Fearless hearts! She would continuously remind herself of what was expected of her.

Taleah put her arms around Lorenz's neck. "Now that we have all that out of the way, what about getting on with the celebration of our engagement?"

Lorenz's bright smile bowled Taleah completely over. "Sounds like a wonderful plan!"

His eyes captured hers; her breath quickened at the passion she saw in his. His hands caressed her body, making her flesh come alive. She licked at the moisture on her mouth, wishing it were Lorenz tasting the dew from her moist lips. Their mouths met and hers parted receptively. Taleah's heart fluttered at the provocative way his tongue searched for hers.

Lorenz's kiss kept deepening, so much so that Taleah felt as if there'd be no end to it. Her breathing became shallow, but she didn't dare to attempt to come up for air. His kiss was sweeter than any forbidden temptation. She found herself hoping it would never end; praying all the while that his kiss would forever belong to her.

Taleah finally pulled back, but only slightly. She looked into his eyes. "Are you sure we have to wait, Lorenz? I desperately want you to make love to me. I need you so much."

Unable to find his voice, Lorenz fervently crushed his lips against hers.

Six

Standing at the door of Taleah's apartment, Lorenz wiped away Taleah's tears of farewell with the pads of his fingers. She looked so beautiful to him, even in distress. It had been her outer beauty that he'd been first attracted to, but the soulful connection between them had come in the next instant. Her spirit had reached out to his from the very start. It was over for him at the first glimpse inside her heart. Over the past month this amazing woman had shown her wonderful heart to him in every light imaginable. Taleah possessed a fragile heart made of gold. The heavy precious metal surrounding it had allowed her easy-to-break heart to withstand the cruel pain and emotional abuse inflicted upon her by the hand of another.

His eyes anxiously scanned her lovely face. "Are you going to be okay, Taleah?"

Taleah nodded, though she felt everything but okay. "I'm just a little emotional right now, but I'll soon be fine." She looked into his eyes. "I'm going to miss you. I wish you didn't have to go, Lorenz. I need you here with me."

"I know, Taleah. Three months away from you is going to seem like an eternity. But I have to look at it this way. It's June now. I'll be back in September. Shortly after I return to the States we're getting married. The next time I leave California I'll be taking you with me. We've had an incredible beginning. Engaged on the third date and getting married three months later is a remarkable feat to pull off in just a short time. I know there are doubters, but as long as we don't doubt ourselves on the decision we've made to be together forever, nothing can stop us. It may seem crazy to most, but both you and I know better. We fell in love instantly, the moment our spirits met. Together, with God leading our paths, we're invincible, Taleah. I love you."

"Yeah, we did fall hard, at first sight. It seems as if we've found our soul mate in each other. I love you, too, Lorenz. As for God, I know He's always in control. If He sees fit to bless this union, we *will* be together forever. That we both believe in and love God is a tremendous way to start out in a new relationship. With God leading, we can't go wrong, not if we follow His directions. It's also a powerful testimony for the way He has healed our broken hearts."

While fighting off a new wave of tears, Taleah allowed Lorenz to draw her in closer to him. As a godly man himself, he was glad that he and Taleah had the love of God in common. Out of all the wonderful attributes that he saw in her, her love for God was the most important.

The final good-bye kisses were sensuous and wonderful, but they only made Taleah even sadder. This was the end of the road for them. *Only for now,* she reminded herself.

He'll be back and I'll be right here waiting for him.

Lorenz gently kissed both of her eyelids. "Three months, Taleha. We'll be back together in three months." He lifted her hand and kissed the brilliant oval-shaped diamond ring he'd given her last evening. "I can hear wedding bells already. I can't wait for you to become Mrs. Lorenz Hampton. In the meantime, I promise to write you every single day."

"Every day," she reiterated. "I plan to stalk the mailman until he delivers the first one."

With her heart breaking over his departure, Taleah melted her lips against his for a brief kiss. Every second counted, as did every smile, kiss, and caress. Each gesture of love was so special. Taleah was recording every precious memory for later retrieval. Her memories of their love would be all she'd have for months to come. She shuddered at the thought of his absence.

As Taleah pulled back, Lorenz brought her back to him for another kiss. "Please don't get discouraged, Taleah. Please wait for me. I am coming back for you. Make no mistake about it."

Taleah looked up at him and smiled. "Not to worry, Lorenz. I'll be right here waiting for you. Just please hurry back, Sergeant Lorenz Hampton."

"As quickly as I can, Miss Taleah Taylor. Fearless hearts! Remember?"

"I'll never forget what you told me. Military wives have to have fearless hearts, just like the fearless hearts of their brave military men."

He stole one last kiss. "Our combined hearts are indeed fearless, Taleah. Our spirits are linked together forever. Our love has no boundaries to keep it from blossoming. I love you."

With more tears falling, Taleah watched after her fiancé as he settled into Mark's car. This was the first time she'd ever seen Lorenz in uniform. He looked magnificently scrumptious in his full air force dress blues. He wore his uniform so well, so proudly. There was just something about a man in a uniform that had always turned her on. Lorenz was more than just a man in a uniform. He was her man, her soon-to-be husband. *Praise God!*

With no desire whatsoever to take on the outside world, Taleah propped herself up in bed so that she could read awhile. She had to do something to keep her mind off Lorenz's departure. Although she'd cried in front of him before he'd left, Lorenz would never know how many tears she'd cried once back inside her apartment. Watching him drive off with Mark had caused the dam to break. Anyone in close proximity to her would've been threatened by the flooding.

Taleah stole a quick glance at the clock radio. Lorenz's flight to Connecticut had taken off at nine-thirty A.M. Since he hadn't called yet, Taleah wasn't sure if he'd arrived safely. Since it was already six-thirty in the evening in L.A., that meant it was nine-thirty on the East Coast. Taleah closed her eyes and said a silent prayer.

Her mind had seriously strayed from the novel. Thoughts of Lorenz were always close at hand, never in the back of her mind, always at the forefront. Thoughts of him constantly filled her head both day and night. Their last night together had played out in her head at least a thousand times already. It was hard to concentrate on anything other than her memories of him.

Although Lorenz had gently denied Taleah's request for him to make love to her a couple of nights back, Lorenz had set about making her feel as though he'd made sweet love to her. The feelings of euphoria that he'd left her with were nothing short of amazing. That one night of utter passion would have to burn brightly in her memory until the real thing happened between them. Waiting for that to occur would be the hardest part of all since she had an idea of what to expect.

The sudden jingle of the phone startled Taleah. As she bolted upright and reached for it, she felt that it was Lorenz on the other end even before she'd heard his voice. Her heart began to race, just like it always did whenever she was around him or talking to him on the telephone. He had a way of making her heart do all sorts of crazy leaps and daring dives.

Her smile couldn't have grown any wider. Hearing her man's voice on the line had perked her right up. "Hey! I knew it was you, Lorenz. God answered my prayer. And it didn't take long for Him to respond to me, since I just got through praying that you'd call soon."

Lorenz chuckled. "God is always right on time, Taleah. He's never late. I had plans to call much sooner than this, but I was immediately whisked away by my mother. I've been to every single relative's as well as friend's house in this area. All I could think of, especially during many of the most boring visits, was getting back to the house to call you, worrying about how you might be worried about me. I'm safe and sound, baby. How are you?"

"Missing you. Boy, your absence is being felt in spades. Other than that, I'm fine."

"I know the feeling. I already miss looking into your eyes and holding you in my arms. I hated to see you cry. Leaving you in emotional distress was pure agony for me."

Oh, boy, if you only knew. All you saw were a few tears.

The actual waterfall might've scared you speechless. Surely it would've had you doubting my fearless heart.

"I love you, Taleah."

Taleah closed her eyes to savor the sweet sound of his confession. "I love you right back, Lorenz. So, your mom and dad are good?"

"Real good. Thanks for asking. I've told them all about you. They hope to meet you one day soon. I don't know if they'll make it to our wedding but they'll be there in spirit."

Lorenz didn't have the heart to tell her that his mother was completely opposed to them getting married. She couldn't see him jumping into another marriage so soon after getting out of the previous one. Lorenz loved his mother dearly, but he had no intentions of taking her advice in this matter. "Wait a year or so," she'd told him. Lorenz didn't need to wait a year or more to know that Taleah was the right one for him. The bond between them was stronger than any power that they each possessed.

This spiritual coming together had been predestined by the greatest power of all.

"Wedding! We haven't even decided on a date yet, Lorenz."

"Yes, we have. September twelfth, exactly three months from now. I'm going to secure my leave around that date as soon as I get back to the base. We also met on the twelfth of the month and we'll be together until the twelfth of never. I've been consulting my calendar—and we're getting married on that date, Taleah. I think it's a good omen. It also falls on a Saturday."

Taleah looked totally dazed. *The twelfth of never!* What a beautiful analogy he'd come up with. Lorenz taking the initiative on setting their wedding date had impressed the heck out of her. It also sounded as if he'd gone to great lengths to achieve it. "Oh, gosh. I really hadn't thought that far ahead yet. You are too sweet. Do you want a big wedding, Lorenz?"

"I want what you want. You get to call all the shots for our big day."

"Thanks. In that case, we're going to a wedding chapel. Our guest list will be miniscule, only extremely close friends and our families. As soon as possible, please send me your guest list with the appropriate addresses so I can send invitations to your close friends and family."

"I won't be inviting anyone, Taleah. You can't always find time to foster close relationships when you're constantly moving around the country and the world. I have made some great friends, but I couldn't tell you where most of them are right now."

"No really close friends?" His revelation saddened Taleah.

"I do have a real good mentor, but he's in Germany now. From what I've heard from talking to the guys in my squadron, Zurich Kingdom, whom I attended Buckley Academy with, might be coming to Japan to assume command of our unit. He just made lieutenant colonel. He also just got married about a year ago to a former NCO, Hailey Hamilton, which could've been a disaster for both their careers had the affair been discovered before the marriage. But she's now a second lieutenant. The military frowns on fraternization between officers and NCOs, but with good reason. I'll tell you all about the Kingdoms when we have more time, Taleah. Sad to say, Zurich probably won't be able to come to our wedding. I also have dear friends in Houston, Texas, R.C. Robinson and his wife, Linda, but I can't imagine them being able to get away since they also have very busy careers."

"I'm sorry that no one will be there for you. As for your friends, wouldn't you want to just send them invitations, anyway? You never know what might result from it."

"We can do that if you'd like. I'll see that you get the information."

"Perhaps Mark will be able to come back for our wedding. If not, do you mind if I ask my brother Jared to stand up with you? You already know how close he and I are. I can't wait for him to get back home next week, though we talk on the phone all the time. He's been gone for two months now. But he's only up in San Francisco with our older brother, Joshua. They're starting a business together, a spa and physical fitness center. I don't know if I mentioned it or not, but both of them are personal trainers."

Lorenz chuckled softly. "You've mentioned Jared and what he does for a living a dozen times or more. In fact, I've heard more about Jared than anyone else. I feel as if I know him."

Taleah had to laugh, too, knowing Lorenz was right on the money. She talked about Jared all the time, not that she didn't love Joshua just as much. But she and Jared had always had a very special bond, and it had even deepened considerably when Taleah was seriously hurt in the car accident. Jared had stood beside her every step of the way, had been there for her at every waking moment. She truly believed in her heart that if Jared had not held her feet to the fire she might never have walked again. Not once had he allowed her to give up on herself.

"Whatever arrangements you can make with Mark or Jared will be fine with me, Taleah. I'd be honored to have any member of your family stand up for me."

"Okay, then. I'm glad that's settled. But I'm going to keep our wedding plans small and simple. By the way, Lorenz, I'm a low-maintenance woman. I don't require much."

Lorenz cracked up. "That's an interesting statement, sweetheart. However, regardless of how little you may require, I plan to move heaven and earth to try and give you everything your heart desires. You want the Taj Mahal? I'll make a bid on it for you. You want an island in the Caribbean sun? I'll put a down payment on one right away. But if you want the moon and the stars, I'll consult God on your behalf. Just as the cattle on a thousand hills belong to Him, so do the moon and the stars. But, our being His children, He wants us to have them, and so much more. So it's my understanding that all the brilliant light in the skies already belongs to both you and me."

Along with Taleah, Lorenz had to laugh at his own foolishness. But his mention of God had humbled each of them. Their belief in God was strong.

"Your love and respect and for you to always be honest and forthcoming with me are my heart's desires. If it's only material trappings that I want, I can get most of that for myself if I want it bad enough. It's you that I want, Lorenz, you and your heart. I want our united spirits to always dance in tune to the romantic music of our hearts."

"Your optimism is one of the things I love so much about you. We're going to be great together. I love you, sweetie, and I miss you so much. To address your wants, you're in business, Taleah, because you already have each and every one of your desires. Our spirits *will* continuously dance, through the good and the bad. As laughter is the music of the soul, we will always find something to laugh about, no matter how difficult life becomes."

* * *

Taleah felt so sleepy but she had too much on her mind to rest. Lorenz had left her with so much to think about. Although she knew he'd return in three months, preparations for a wedding hadn't crossed her mind. Her mind had stayed on him leaving her behind, which hadn't given her much time to think about anything else. Now she'd have nothing but time to sort out all these incredible events of the past month. She and Lorenz had given a new meaning to "whirlwind relationship" by taking things to the maximum level in hardly any time at all.

The three-month waiting period was scary for her, she finally had to admit to herself after giving it some real thought. Her fears weren't because she didn't believe in what they had; she did. The fact that she'd surrendered her heart to Lorenz on sight was more than a little frightening. While she knew her love for him was strong, she couldn't help wondering if a three-month separation might change his mind. After all, he was a worldly man, yet she hadn't gotten the impression that he had worldly ways.

Taleah then thought about the woman Lorenz said he'd grown closer to than anyone else. This woman was going to lose a great guy. She had no doubt that his close friend might very well put up a fierce fight to keep him. Would he be able to resist her? Would his memories of the time he'd spent with her there in Japan cause him to have a change of heart? Was she Asian or black? Would he dare to have a last rendezvous with her for old times' sake? She cringed at the thought. Taleah suddenly realized that she didn't even know the name of the woman she silently rivaled with for Lorenz's love and affection. He'd never once called his friend by name.

Conquering any and all fears that she had over their relationship was a must for Taleah. Otherwise, she couldn't prove to Lorenz that she had a fearless heart. He needed a strong woman, not someone who worried about what might or might not happen. Negative thoughts like those could end up driving her insane. Living in the moment should take care of that.

Instead of entertaining things that might never occur, Taleah promised herself to deal with only those issues right before her. Lorenz had pledged his love to her and had asked her to marry him. She looked down at the brilliant fireworks on her ring finger and smiled. If that wasn't an indication of his honorable intentions, she didn't know what was. No more negative thoughts, she told herself. No more looking into the future or stepping back into the past.

Living for today and in the moment was the remedy to what ailed her.

The Sophisticated Lady Boutique was a unique place to shop. The African-American-owned business loved to cater to its customers. Inside the quaint little shop patrons could enjoy themselves before, during, and after their shopping sprees. Sipping on hot or cold drinks, feasting on a variety of freshly baked pastries and deli-fresh sandwiches, all specially made to order at the boutique's café bar, was a favorite pastime of many of the regular customers. All genres of music could be heard coming out of the surround-sound speakers located throughout the store.

The Sophisticated Lady stocked some of the most beautiful dresses ever fashioned, many of them one-of-a-kind designer originals, but the special one for

Taleah's wedding had yet to be discovered. With a look of utter disappointment on her face, Taleah shoved another lovely dress aside. "This is looking downright impossible. I usually can find exactly what I want in here."

"Another one bites the dust. That's number twenty-five," Brenda said, laughing. "This is getting old real fast, Taleah. I'm starting to see spots and swatches of colors before my eyes."

Sherra pulled a face. "Maybe you should just elope, Taleah. It might be easier on you. You look ready to drop, girl."

"I'd still need a wedding dress, Sherra. Maybe not one that's too elaborate, but a dress nonetheless. I have an idea." Taleah glanced at her watch. "Why don't we go have lunch in the café? Then we can try a few more stores afterward. We've been at this since this shop first opened at ten A.M. It's now one o'clock. Besides that, my feet hurt. Lunch, everyone?"

"Lunch sounds like a plan, but I don't know if I'm up for any more shopping today. I have to be well rested this evening and looking my very best. I have a date with gorgeous Charlie Brown, attorney at law," Sherra announced excitedly.

Taleah, Drusilla, and Brenda eyed Sherra with curiosity, each of them burning to know when all of this had happened. It wasn't like Sherra to keep them in the dark. But she did have a lot on her plate right now. Her dad was still critically ill.

Taleah sucked her teeth. "This'll never do, Sherra. Looks like you've gotten into keeping secrets from your girls. Let's get to the café. Can't wait to hear all the juicy details."

* * *

Once everyone had ordered their choices in deli sandwiches and garden salads, and the moment after the waiter left the table, all curious eyes turned on Sherra. She didn't need further prompting from her friends, because Sherra was extremely eager to spill her good news.

"Charlie called me to see how my father was when he learned that T.W. was ill. That was sweet of him. We have talked and talked over the past week, staying on the phone all hours of the night. He's great to converse with. We have a lot in common. Sister-friends, I have found myself hanging on to his every word. I am smitten. No doubt about it. Our first date is tonight."

Taleah leaned over and hugged Sherra. "This is great, girl! I'm so excited for you."

Brenda and Drusilla also voiced their joy for the bubbling-over Sherra. Champagne didn't have nearly as many bubbles as Sherra appeared to have at the moment. Her smile was effervescent. If anyone deserved to find happiness, Sherra was the one. She was the kind of woman who always brought cheer along and spread goodwill wherever she happened to go.

Taleah had a great set of friends in these three women. Their spirits had immediately connected also, just as hers had instantly connected with Lorenz's. The women were all caring and very giving individuals, not a selfish bone in their bodies. Each was a complement to the others.

"Keep us posted, Sherra. No more holding out," Taleah warned, smiling softly.

Sherra laughed. "I hear you, Taleah. I promised to keep you all updated. We'll even do a conference call after the date tonight. I hope I have a lot of juicy stuff to tell you."

Everyone laughed at that comment.

The waiter appeared and set each food order in front of the appropriate patron. After refilling their water and iced-tea glasses, the server took his leave. Taleah then led the group in a heartfelt prayer of thanksgiving.

"Everything looks and smells divine," Taleah commented. "I want a taste of something off of each your plates. You all know the routine. And you know you can help yourself to any food on my plate whenever you feel like it."

"As hungry as I am, you might get your fingers and your feelings hurt if you mess with anything on mine. If I were you, Taelah, I'd keep your hands over there," Drusilla menaced playfully, knowing Taleah could have a taste of anything on her plate. "I'm not sharing any of this with you. Not this time around."

Taleah turned her lips down at the corners. "Okay! Be selfish and reap what you sow, Dru. I'm not mad at you, girlfriend."

"What I'm going to reap is all that's on my plate right now. Where'd you get that weird habit, anyway? I never knew anyone that had to have something off everyone's plate. Most normal people don't share their man, their money, or their food."

Taleah cracked up. "Who said I was normal? I used to be the one to eat all the leftovers at the table, after the meal was over. Mom rarely had anything left to put away for later. Also, when Jared didn't want something on his plate, he put it on mine, making sure no one was looking. During the times when our parents took us out to eat, everyone ended up giving me something off their plate. I don't know why that was, maybe because I was the youngest child. I don't know, but they always did it. And I always ate it. So I guess that's how it got started." Taleah pointed at the door. "Oh, Dru, look. There's Craig."

Just as Drusilla looked toward the entry, Taleah took a morsel off her plate and popped it into her mouth. The others began laughing heartily. Drusilla figured out what had happened before anyone had a chance to say anything. Taleah looked guilty of wrongdoing and it was obvious to Drusilla that her dear friend was doing her best to keep from laughing.

Drusilla scolded Taleah with a mere look. "You are such a spoiled brat!" Drusilla started laughing, too. "You tricked me this time, T. I'm usually sharper than that. You'd just better be glad you got your thieving little fingers away before I had a chance to stick 'em good with my fork. You can be so darn bad."

Taleah blew Drusilla a kiss. "I'm sorry but I just couldn't resist. I also knew you didn't mean a word of what you'd said, though you tried to sound so adamant. I've been eating off your plates forever. I guess it is a bad habit. But I now know that I can break it."

"How's that?" Brenda asked, raising an eyebrow.

"Although I was tempted, not once did I ask Lorenz for anything off his plate. Nor did I eat anything off of Lynnette's plate while he was around. I guess you can say I was putting on airs. So I *am* aware of it being an unusual practice. Even Lynnette mentioned how surprised she was that I'd practiced good table manners in front of Lorenz."

"Thank goodness for that," Dru smarted off. "He probably would've been embarrassed."

Taleah suddenly looked as if she were having a lightbulb moment. "Ladies, you all should've seen my man in uniform. He looked so darn good. Too, too fine is he. It was all I could do to keep from gushing out loud. I'm so glad he's all mine. The last few weeks have been incredible." Taleah looked down at her diamond. "Can you all believe I'm actually engaged?"

"As a matter of fact, I really can't," Dru remarked, frowning slightly. "I'm worried. Lorenz seems like a wonderful guy, but you guys got engaged after only three dates. What worries me the most is that he's not all yours, Taleah. The man is still married."

Although they'd known this conversation was going to eventually take place, Sherra and Brenda exchanged nervous glances. Drusilla rarely bit her tongue, so for them to intervene wasn't likely to change the course she was on, both Sherra and Brenda knew. It was probably best to let things play out since everyone did have concerns over the engagement. It was better to get each of their issues out in the open and then put everything behind them.

Taleah might get huffy for a minute, but she didn't expect her friends not to play the devil's advocate. And they really didn't expect her to change her mind. Taleah would do what she thought was best for her despite what everyone else thought.

Taleah sighed hard. "You're not the only one saying that, Dru. There are also those who think exactly what you're saying but won't dare to confront me on it. Please know that I'm not worried. Maybe I should be, but I'm not. I can't explain it, yet I know Lorenz is the man for me. Our spirits became entwined the same moment our eyes locked for the very first time. We both felt the instant connection. I know it sounds silly, but we fell in love on sight. As for him being married, he won't be when it comes time to marry me. What else can I say?"

Despite her own concerns for her dear friend,

Sherra gave Taleah a high five. "Hello! You certainly have the look of a woman in love. I've never seen you glow like this. You are radiant, Taleah Taylor! You need to share some of that light with me."

Sherra had to laugh. She and Charlie had had pretty much the same sort of connection, so she understood, but she was still worried. Had she and Taleah gotten involved too deeply too soon? Charlie kept Sherra grinning from ear to ear. Although they hadn't had a date yet, she often saw him, with his fine self, lurking around the halls of justice.

"I know, huh! I feel radiant. Lorenz is so sweet. You guys just didn't get to know him like I did. I can't wait to marry him."

Drusilla looked Taleah in the eye. "I don't want to continue to be the pessimist here, but as always I feel that I have to play the devil's advocate. I understand that this is your life and that you have to run it the way you see best. But you're leaving your family and friends behind to go ten thousand miles away with a virtual stranger. Aren't you the least bit frightened? What if he turns out to be the world's worst husband?"

Not the least bit rattled, Taleah shook her head. "It's not going to happen. I feel his spirit. It's a darn good one. Nothing evil lurks within him. If I turn out to be wrong, they do have return flights from Japan. He's in the military. You know that certain protections come with that gig."

Drusilla scowled hard, knowing of all the stories she'd read and heard about domestic violence on the military installations. As a member, she often thought it seemed as if the military protected their own more so than the civilian spouse. She couldn't help thinking about the several military men who had killed their wives on a base somewhere in the

South. Drusilla knew firsthand that military families had the same sort of problematic issues to deal with as civilian ones, if not more. Separation of the military spouse from his or her family was an everyday occurrence and often posed a huge problem. Drusilla lived the military life and it wasn't always easy.

While Drusilla certainly didn't want to see any harm come to Taleah, she also knew that Taleah had her mind made up. Still, she had to voice her opinion, anyway, and let the chips fall where may. Drusilla cleared her throat before continuing to weigh in on the issue.

Once Taleah had heard everything her friends had to say, having listened intently, with an open mind, and a receptive heart, she hugged each of them. "Guys, just try and be happy for me. I'm really going to be fine. I appreciate all the love you're showing me, but I've got to do this my way. I can darn near guarantee you it's going to be all good. Lorenz and I have a deep understanding of what we need to give and receive from each other. We've both been hurt before and we don't want to be hurt again. Therefore we've promised to safeguard each other's hearts. Twenty years from now we'll all be laughing over this conversation. You just wait and see."

The other three women had tears in their eyes by the time Taleah finished her speech.

Accepting her decision to move forward with her wedding plans, her friends gave Taleah their heartfelt congratulations, prepared to help her in any way they could to make her wedding day a memorable one. The aura surrounding Taleah was more of a peaceful one, which wasn't lost on a single soul. Turmoil no longer seemed to be her constant companion. Taleah appeared genuinely elated within her heart, happy with herself, and totally comfortable with and undoubtedly confident in her decision to marry Lorenz. Loving Taleah as they did, her friends announced to her that they'd support her in every way possible. She had finally convinced them that she was in control of her destiny. No one wanted to see her take another nasty fall, God forbid, but they all vowed to be there for Taleah no matter the circumstance.

Smiling lovingly at her wonderful girlfriends, Taleah pulled a list from her purse. "Is it okay if we go over the list of things we have to do?"

"Sure," Brenda responded. "What is on the agenda for after we get the dress?"

"Well, once I get the dress, I can shop for the shoes. Since beige or off-white is the color I've chosen for the dress, we can always have the shoes dyed to match. I don't seem to be feeling the dress today, so perhaps we should go on over to the florist shop. Since my mother has already secured the Ivy House Chapel in Inglewood for the ceremony, we don't have that to worry about. Our appointment for the caterer isn't until next week."

Drusilla turned up her nose. "Caterer! I'm the only caterer you're going to need, with the exception of ordering the wedding cake from a reputable bakery. I can do everything a professional can do, perhaps even better in some instances. With me doing it all, you only have to pay for the cost of the food. I will donate many of the delicacies, of course. Am I hired?"

Taleah laughed, slapping her open palm down on the table. "Hired! I wanted to ask you if you'd mind helping in that area, but I know how busy you are, Dru. Thanks a million."

"I want to order all your flowers for you. I also want to do the centerpieces and the decorations for the chapel and the reception," Brenda chimed in. She was a pro in this area.

"As artistic and creative as you are with your hands, I have no qualms about that," Taleah said. "I've seen so many of your creative works, so I know you're going to hook me up right. What about going downtown to the flower market to purchase the flowers?"

Brenda chuckled. "We're a little ahead of ourselves, but you can rest assured that I'll take care of everything in that area when the time comes. The flowers I'm going to use for the decorations are a last-minute purchase for freshness. However, we do have to order the wedding party flowers well in advance of the date."

Sherra threw up her hands. "I've been sitting over here thinking of where I can throw my help, but I'm not a creative person. The best thing I can do for you, Taleah, is to give you some good legal advice."

Taleah looked horrified. "As in divorce information?"

Sherra threw her head back and laughed. "Not even. I'm referring to your assets and your personal belongings and such. Anything that you don't want to become community property I can tell you how to handle it. California is a community property state. What's yours also becomes the property of whomever you marry. I may be a defense attorney, but I know a little something something about finances and such."

"A little something," Dru exclaimed. "Girl, you're an expert at it. You sure got my butt in gear to start investing. I'd probably be broke today if you hadn't stepped in and showed me what I was doing wrong."

"Don't leave me out. I'm almost debt-free because of you. So I'm ready to listen to all the legal

advice you have to offer. And for free! You can't
beat that deal with a stick," Taleah said.

"Who said it was free?" Sherra joked. "All of you
owe me half of what's in your savings accounts.
You, too, Miss Brenda, sitting all quiet over there,
not wanting to give me my props."

"I haven't had a chance to, so hush your face. I
can only add to the singing praises, which you're
sitting over there just lapping up. But I have no
problem admitting that the great tips you gave me
on refinancing my mom's house were invaluable.
Mama owes you, too, 'cause she's sure much better
off financially than she was. Your advice to her
about taking some equity out of her house helped
her out tremendously. If she were here, she'd be
bowing down to you also."

Brenda got down on her knees and bowed down
to Sherra, causing everyone to crack up.

"Oh, stop it, already! My head is already big
enough as it is. You guys are going on and on about
something that should come naturally to everyone.
We are all the same way with each other and with
others. Helping people as we all do also helps us. I
love the feeling I get. Helping out with some good
advice is the least I can do for my best friends."

"Yeah, but some of your advice outright sucks,"
Taleah charged, rolling her eyes.

"Like what?" Sherra inquired haughtily, positioning a hand on one hip.

"Like that last boring lawyer friend you introduced me to. 'Ray will be good for you, Taleah. Just
someone nice to talk with and to go out with from
time to time. It doesn't have to be a love connection. You need to have some male friends to call
on when you're lonely.' Not!"

Knowing exactly whom and what Taleah was referring to, the others cracked up. Sherra's friend

had latched on to Taleah like a leech—and she'd had a hard time getting rid of him. The fact that he was boring as all get out hadn't helped the situation one iota. He was definitely not the bad-boy type like Bradley, but Taleah hadn't been able to find a thing in common with him.

The four women continued to lightly banter with each other until it became apparent that time was ticking away rather rapidly. In the interest of time, everyone decided to wait till the first part of the week to call on the florist. No one wanted Sherra to be exhausted or late for her date.

Seven

After a good hot soak in the tub, where she'd spent plenty of time pampering her aching feet, Taleah had quickly dressed for bed. Since Lorenz was no longer her houseguest, she'd opted to wear shortie pajamas and no robe. It was only six o'clock in the evening, but the all-day shopping trip with her friends had worn her out completely. She was now stretched out on the living room sofa talking to Lorenz on the telephone, looking happy as a lark.

"Are you serious, Lorenz?" Taleah couldn't believe she was going to see Lorenz again so soon. He had invited her to meet him in San Francisco, where his connecting flight would take off from, headed for Tokyo, Japan.

"Of course I am. I'm going to leave Connecticut on Friday as opposed to Sunday. My flight will get into San Francisco around noon. I'd like to set your flight up to arrive about the same time as mine. All you have to do is give me the okay and I'll make the arrangements."

Lorenz's flight was still scheduled for the same

Sunday departure time, but he had shortened his stay in Connecticut by two days so he could spend another weekend with Taleah. He was supposed to arrive in San Francisco on Friday with a layover until Sunday. Military personnel could change their flights around without penalty on many of the major airlines. Besides, the government had paid for Lorenz's trip, since he'd come to the States on official business. Any type of training or temporary duty was taken at the expense of Uncle Sam.

"By all means, Lorenz. But I can make my own airline reservations, though I'll need your flight number and exact arrival time and the terminal number so I'll know what I'm doing."

"I'll take care of it, Taleah. This is something I want to do for you, for us."

"I know how to accept a blessing, 'cause seeing you again so soon is definitely a blessing, Lorenz." Taleah couldn't wait to see her military man. This trip wasn't something she would ever have expected from Lorenz, but she was glad that the opportunity had presented itself.

"That you're off on Fridays makes this setup easy enough to do. I wouldn't want you to miss work on my account."

"Huh! I would've called in sick had Friday not been my normal day off. Another couple of days with you is well worth the risk. I guess we'll have to meet in the baggage claim area with all the security issues that still surround the airports."

"Not necessarily. If we fly into the same terminal, we're already cleared through security. I can then wait for you at your arrival gate. I'd like to have your flight land after mine so I'll already be there when you get in. But I'll check all that when I make the travel plans."

"That's a great idea. Since you'll already be in

the terminal, security won't be an issue. When are you going to make the reservations?"

"In the next few minutes. I'll call you back once everything is confirmed. Oh, what about your tennis lesson, Taleah?"

"I do that early in the morning. If you're setting me up for a noon arrival, I'll have plenty of time to take my lesson and still make my flight. However, I need to ask Dad if he can take me to the airport. I don't like to take his time for granted. I try to see what his schedule is like first, before I spring anything on him. Being retired doesn't mean that you don't have a life."

"That's very thoughtful of you, Taleah. If he's busy, I'll set up a round-trip door-to-door shuttle reservation. You don't have to worry about a thing, my lady. I got you covered."

Taleah giggled. "You're spoiling me."

"Intentionally so. Are you sure you're okay with everything?"

"Positive, Lorenz. I can't wait to see you."

"In that case, give me about an hour to do my thing. I'll call you back as soon as I have everything arranged. Ring you later, sweetheart. Love you."

"Okay. Talk to you then. Love you, too." Taleah disconnected the phone line. She then kicked her feet up and down on the sofa. Laughing like crazy, she was beside herself with excitement, and thrilled to death over seeing Lorenz again sooner than she'd ever thought was possible. This was just another major blessing from above.

Taleah tried her best to get her excitement under control as she dialed Jared's cell phone number. With both her brothers being in San Francisco, she thought it would be a perfect time for them to meet Lorenz. Since time was so short, they could at least have coffee together. As she waited for Jared to answer, Taleah hoped Lorenz would be okay with meeting them.

"Hey, little sister, what can I do you for?"

Taleah smiled at the handsome image of her tall, powerfully built, cocoa-complexioned brother. "I'm coming to San Francisco this weekend, man. Think you can find some time to have coffee with me?"

Jared laughed. "I think we can do a little more than coffee, baby girl. What's bringing you up to San Francisco, anyway? I know you're not missing me that much. So what's up?"

"I'm coming to the Bay Area to meet up with my fiancé." Knowing the fireworks were coming, Taleah held her breath. Jared would not be pleased by her news. She had planned to wait until he came home to tell him, but she didn't want him to miss out on the opportunity to meet and assess Lorenz for himself. Just like it was with her parents, she valued Jared's opinion.

"Your what?"

"You heard me, boy, and I know it. So don't even try to pretend otherwise."

"I know you're not back with Bradley. Not after the way that brother disrespected you."

"It's not Bradley."

"Then who, Taleah? Stop messing with me, girl. Who the heck are you talking about?"

"The guy Mark introduced me to."

"The guy you've only had three dates with?"

"One and the same."

"Girl, I know you have lost your darn mind! Why haven't you told me this before now? Mom and Dad haven't mentioned it either. Do they even know?"

"Calm down, Jared. Everyone but you and Joshua

know about the engagement. I wanted to wait until you came home to tell you, 'cause I knew you'd react this way. Lorenz is a great guy, Jared. You'll really like him."

"You said the same thing about Bradley when you first started dating him, and look what a mess he made out of your life." There was a moment of deafening silence. "Whoa, whoa, wait a minute here, girl. Doesn't this guy live in Japan, Taleah? If so, how's that going to work?"

"I'm going to live in Japan with him. He *will* be my husband, you know."

Jared felt his muscles constrict from the onrush of unexpected tension. He couldn't believe Taleah had gotten herself engaged to someone she barely knew. The thought of his sister being emotionally devastated again by yet another man made him cringe inwardly. Taleah was too vulnerable with men, especially slick-tongued devils like Bradley. He could only pray that she hadn't gotten herself involved with the same kind of guy. But past behaviors were a strong predictor of future behaviors. How many times had he heard Dr. Phil say that?

"Taleah, I'm not so sure about this. Japan! Do you realize how far away that is? It's also on another continent, baby girl."

"Both Lynette and Marsha have lived overseas. You didn't carry on with them like that."

"Please! This is not the same deal, and you know it. Those guys all dated forever before they got married. How can you agree to marry someone after only three dates? It's insane, Taleah. What are Mom and Dad saying about all this?"

"We have their blessings, Jared. I wish I could get yours."

He sucked his teeth hard. "What drugs have they gotten hooked on since I left home? Offering my blessing wouldn't be a problem if you were going into this with a clear head. Somebody has to think for you. It looks like it has to be me, since everybody else's mind in the family has deserted them, too. It's painfully clear to me that your brain cells are all fogged up. What are your girlfriends saying? If I know them, they must be hard on your case, too. Something is terribly wrong with both you and your fiancé if you ask me."

"Nobody asked you, so there." Taleah regretted the foolish remark. "Listen, Jared, just agree to meet him before you castrate him. We're not getting married for three months. His divorce won't be final for another few weeks." Just another remark instantly regretted by her. She covered her ears in anticipation of a loud verbal assault.

"Divorced! Ah, hell no. This ain't happening, Taleah." Jared's laugh was filled with cynicism. "I can't believe my baby sister is engaged to someone who's already married. If that don't take the cake, nothing will. Are you listening to yourself? If so, doesn't all this sound just a little crazy to you? What *are* you thinking, Taleah Taylor?"

"That you're overreacting to this. You've always been so fair and nonjudgmental. Where's that sense of fair play now?"

Jared let out a huge gust of breath. Hearing the pain in his sister's voice sobered him. The last thing he wanted to do was alienate her. She needed all the support she could get from him, and then some. "I pray this isn't hopeless. I see that I can't reason with you right now, at least not over the phone. I'll meet your new guy, Taleah, only because I want to see what he's like for myself. After that, you know I won't pull any punches with you. I wish you could've talked this over with me first. It's so unlike you not to do so. We share practically everything. I can already tell that this engagement is changing you. I don't want it to come between us, Taleah."

"No, Jared, it's not like that at all. Nothing can come between us. We're family. I just can't explain the kind of spiritual connection Lorenz and I have. That Dad thinks he's a great guy should count for something. And I know you'll think so, too. Some things are just destined. Please hold out on making any rush in judgment. Once you meet him, I promise to listen to everything you have to say. But that doesn't mean I'm going to agree with you."

"Oh, yeah, as if I ever thought that for a second. I don't expect that part of you to ever change, Taleah. You're much too strong-willed for that. At any rate, let's form the plan for getting together in Frisco. Let's at least have lunch instead of just coffee. Is Joshua going to be in on this little meeting of the minds, too?"

"I don't think I have a choice in this instance. He is the oldest sibling. Consulting him is a must. But let me call him and break the news first. That's the only fair thing to do. I don't anticipate having an easy time with him either, but I don't expect him to go completely off on me like you just did. But I understand your concerns, Jared. I love you, big brother."

"I love you, too, little sister."

Taleah snatched up the phone when it rang. It was way over the hour that Lorenz had said he'd call back within. She hoped that this was her man on the other end as she gave her normal greeting. Her heart nearly stopped at the sound of an old familiar voice, one that used to make her weep with joy. Taleah couldn't believe that Bradley Fields had the nerve to dial her number.

Taleah prayed for courage as she listened to what Bradley had to say. Her first thought had been to hang up on him, but she wasn't into allowing people to dictate her actions. Rudeness wouldn't come without consequences. She had to take control of herself and this situation. Taleah knew that she was totally responsible for how she acted upon an instance or how she reacted to it. Handling things in a positive or negative manner was strictly her choice to make. The devil couldn't make her do anything she didn't want to be a party to.

"I'm fine, Bradley, but can you get right to the point as to why you're calling?" she said as softly and as politely as she could manage. "I'm really rather busy at the moment."

"I miss you, Taleah. I want to see you so that I can apologize to you face-to-face. I know I hurt you badly, but I just wasn't thinking clearly. You're the best thing that ever happened to me. In short, T, I want you back."

Taleah cringed at the name he'd often called her by. It no longer sounded endearing to her ears, seeming more as an insult. "Your thinking wasn't the problem. It was your actions. Your total disrespect and blatant disregard for me and my feelings are what got us to where we are. I may've been the best thing for you, but our relationship was the worst thing I've ever gotten myself into. About getting together with you, not possible, Bradley. I'm engaged."

Taleah didn't know if she'd told him about her engagement to shock him or hurt him. It didn't take her long to realize that it was probably a bit of both. It galled her that he could even suggest getting together with her. Hearing his voice and not swooning to it told her that she had become immune to his sweet but lying come-ons and his false charm.

"Engaged! To who?"

"That's not important, Bradley. You wouldn't know who he was if I told you. It's been four years since we broke up and we haven't spoken in over two. I find it interesting that you want me back after all this time. How'd you reach that decision?"

"Correction. Four years since *you* broke us up. I continually tried to patch things up with you. I never wanted the breakup, T. Remember?"

"Yeah, I do, vividly. You just wanted to have me right along with all the other sisters you had managed to keep on the side throughout our relationship. I deserved better than that. It had to be over, Bradley. Nothing in that relationship was worth salvaging, not even our friendship. You were never much of a friend to me, anyway. I've moved on, Brad. And I was sure you'd already moved through several other victims by now. Perhaps that's why you're back to me. I won't be your victim again. You'll never be able to throw that kind of party up in my life again."

"Are you trying to tell me there's no chance for us to get back together, Taleah?"

"You're finally hearing what I'm saying after all this time. Bravo! No chance whatsoever. Now I've got to run, Bradley. I have to pack for a weekend trip."

"With your new man?"

"That's really none of your business. But since you asked, I'm meeting my fiancé in San Francisco. Got to run."

Taleah disconnected the lines without giving Bradley the opportunity to say another word. Although her voice had remained syrupy sweet and cotton soft, the rage she still felt from within had her somewhat worried. It was rude of her to have hung up on him, and she was in no doubt that she'd pay for it later, but it had felt darn good to her at the time.

Bradley Fields had more nerve than he should ever dare to own up to.

After deciding that she had to give a few more minutes of thought to what had just occurred, Taleah stretched out on the bed. Although sure that she was completely over Bradley, she had to wonder why he could still make her so darn angry. Anger was also considered a sign of passion toward something or someone. People just didn't get angry with those they no longer cared about or things they didn't care about. Wouldn't all the issues between them cease to matter once a person was truly over someone? Taleah didn't have the answers at the moment, but she vowed to delve deeper into the questions that intrigued and frustrated her at the same time.

The short flight from Los Angeles to San Francisco had been smooth and without incident. Although a few years had passed since 9/11, Taleah was still a little nervous about flying. She wouldn't even allow herself to think about the long flight to Japan. Fifteen hours in a plane was sure to be a maniacal nail-biting kind of experience.

Taleah's insides trembled with eager anticipation as she gathered her belongings and prepared to deplane. Her thoughts had stayed on Lorenz the entire flight. Every detail of their time together was etched in her brain. She couldn't count the times she'd gone over each thrilling moment. Lorenz had managed to leave Los Angeles without making love to her, but if she had her way all that would change. They were engaged now and soon to be married. San Francisco wasn't where she'd lost her heart, but it would hopefully be where they would first make love.

Lorenz might see things differently, Taleah considered. If he was still on the opposing side, she had a few devilish ideas to help him change his mind. Lorenz was a mere flesh-and-blood man regardless of his disciplined mind-set and the tight control he had on himself. Taleah knew she shouldn't think like that, but she couldn't seem to help it. She wanted him in the worst way, wanted him to want her, too, in the same feverish way.

As promised, Lorenz was right there waiting for Taleah when she stepped out of the passenger gateway at San Francisco International Airport. Taleah's eyes lit up the moment she saw him. Lorenz's loving smile caused her heart to swoon. It was all she could do to keep from racing to him and flinging herself into his arms. *Cool down,* she told herself. *Just chill.*

This fine brother had turned her life upside down, inside and out, and all around. Lorenz was a gift to her from God. No one could make her believe differently. His love had worked miracles on her. Becoming Lorenz's wife would make her the happiest woman in the universe. They would soon have it all. Their marriage would be the beginning of forever after. *Love at first sight.* Who would ever have thought it could happen to her, especially after she'd suffered such a terrible defeat in her last relationship? She certainly hadn't thought it could ever happen.

It *had* happened for her—and that's what made their union nothing short of miraculous.

As soon as Taleah reached her husband-to-be,

Lorenz lifted her up and swung her around, their laughter joyous. The numerous passionate kisses and hugs came next. Neither seemed embarrassed by their public display of affection. Passersby stared but only smiled.

Taleah knew she had missed Lorenz something awful, but that seemed like an understatement now that she was reunited with him. Mourning his absence was a more accurate description of what it had felt like for her without him. What had seemed like an eternity to her had only been five days in reality. Their two days together would go by quickly, as time always did when you were having fun. Taleah planned to make the most of their every second.

Meeting with Taleah's two brothers was the first thing on their agenda, after getting checked in at one of the airport hotels. Jared had told them to take the Bart train down to Ghirardelli Square, where they were to meet up. The rest of the weekend was theirs to spend alone. Taleah's flight back to Los Angeles on Sunday was scheduled to leave an hour and fifteen minutes before Lorenz's flight back to Japan. Lorenz had taken care of every minute detail.

Lorenz hadn't been the least bit put off about spending time with Jared and Joshua when Taleah first presented the idea to him. That came as a huge relief for her. She saw it as a plus for Lorenz to meet the majority of her family before the wedding. The oldest sister, Marsha, would be the only one left for him to meet. Marsha and Miles had already promised to come for Taleah's wedding if all systems remained on go. Military life was unpredictable from day to day.

Mark and Lynette were ecstatic for the couple. They both thought that Taleah had made a great choice for a husband despite the short courtship.

Of course, Mark was taking all the credit for bringing them together. Since Mark had already put in for another overseas assignment, they weren't sure if they'd be in the States. Mark had told Taleah he'd be proud to stand with Lorenz.

It was becoming more and more apparent to Taleah that Lorenz was a take-charge kind of man. As she watched him retrieving with ease their bags from the baggage carousel, her heart filled with pride. There seemed to be no end to his capabilities, no end to the things he had been willing to do to please her. This man had cut his home visit short just to be with her for another couple of days. That meant a lot to her and it also told her a lot more about him.

Taleah smiled as she remembered something her mother had told her and her sisters a long time ago, right before they each began dating.

"The amount of time a man spends with you when he's going with you is the same amount of time he'll spend with you after he's married to you. If he's frequently absent and hard to locate during the courtship, he'll be just as hard to find and equally as absent once you've married him. A good man is truly hard to find but so easy to keep if you treat him as good as he treats you."

How true the absent-and-hard-to-find part turned out to be with Bradley, Taleah mused.

Taleah could only hope that she'd be as loving and accommodating to Lorenz as a wife as he had already shown himself to be with her as just her fiancé. Everything about him suggested to her that he was a very good man, one that she definitely wanted to keep. She was truly blessed to have a man like Lorenz in her life, a man very much like her beloved daddy, Jack Taylor.

* * *

Taleah spotted her tall, fine-looking brothers the second she and Lorenz entered the quaint little authentic Chinese restaurant her family had chosen. The site was near Ghirardelli Square, a world-famous San Francisco landmark.

While Jared had cocoa-brown skin, Joshua had a mocha-coffee complexion. Each had dark, curly hair, hazel eyes, and keen features. Although they didn't look exactly alike, at a glance you could tell they were closely related.

The Taylor brothers were equal in height, standing right at six feet. As personal athletic trainers, both Jared and Joshua had bodies that were a walking advertisement for their line of business. Their marvelous fine-tuned physiques were a surefire testimony to what working out could do for a body. Jared was twenty-nine and Joshua was thirty-three, yet neither brother had ever been married. Neither one was currently in a committed relationship.

Taleah hugged both of the brothers, but her and Jared's embrace lasted a lot longer. Taleah wasn't as close to Joshua as she was to Jared simply because Joshua hadn't spent a lot of time with her when she was younger. Joshua had also been rather mean and impatient with her, something she had yet to get over. Her older sisters and Joshua were not as close as Taleah was with Jared. Joshua was a hard person to get close to. For whatever reason, he had always set himself apart from his siblings. Joshua's aloofness bothered Taleah more than it did the others.

Taleah and Jared were also much closer in age and had been each other's constant companion and playmate as little children. The family often said that the two of them were joined at the hip. As her fierce protector and strongest supporter, Jared adored his baby sister.

Taleah took a hold of Lorenz's hand before sitting down. "Guys, this is Lorenz Hampton, my fiancé. Lorenz, Jared and Joshua," Taleah said, sounding a bit nervous. She sighed with relief as she took the chair closest to Jared.

Lorenz shook each of the extended hands before he seated himself next to Taleah. "Nice to meet you both. I feel like I already know you. Taleah talks about you all the time."

Joshua chuckled. "It's great to meet you, too, Lorenz. But I doubt that Taleah talks about me very often. I'm the mean brother, the big brother who never had any time for her. I'm afraid I saw her as a royal pain in the butt when she was little. I deeply regret the awful way I often treated her, but I don't think she's ever going to forgive me. Isn't that right, pint size?"

Taleah glared at Joshua, hating that he fronted her like that, especially with Lorenz present. "Those cutting remarks certainly aren't going to get you forgiven, Joshua Taylor. The *pint size* title was okay way back in childhood, but would you mind losing it? Permanently?"

Joshua reached over and ruffled Taleah's hair. He then turned to Lorenz. "You see what I mean, man? My baby sister has it in for me. The problem is she's been spoiled rotten."

Lorenz felt uncomfortable with what was happening at Taleah's expense, surprised that something like this was happening at all. "She hasn't mentioned a thing to me about it, so I think she's forgiven you. Haven't you, Taleah?" Lorenz lovingly stroked her cheek with his finger, disturbed by the pain in her eyes. He could tell this situation had totally unnerved her.

"Since you've brought it up, why did you treat me the way you did, Josh?"

Joshua shrugged, smiling sheepishly. "Like I said, you were a real pain. You're pretty cool now, now that you're all grown up and sophisticated. You're no longer that spoiled rotten little girl that everyone always doted on."

Joshua laughed at his own crude comments, but Taleah's eyes quickly filled with tears. She wasn't spoiled, not in the ugly way Joshua had meant it. Taleah didn't have a selfish bone in her body. She was actually selfless, always putting others before herself. To have her brother continue to refer to her as spoiled deeply hurt her feelings. He was too old to be jealous of her, but that seemed to be the case. There were several siblings that had come before her, so it wasn't an issue of her moving him out of his only-child position with Mom and Dad.

Jared's arm instantly went around Taleah's shoulders, meeting up with Lorenz's in the process. Both men had been quick to come to her aid. That both guys felt it necessary to try and shield her from Joshua made her feel even more animosity toward her oldest brother. Taleah saw the fleeting glance of admiration that Jared had leveled on Lorenz.

Unable to believe that Taleah still took him so seriously, Joshua gathered her into his arms and hugged her tightly. He then held her at arm's length. "I'm sorry, sweetheart. I hurt you again without intending to." Joshua kissed Taleah's forehead. "Are you okay?"

Embarrassed by the whole terrible scene and mortified that Joshua had started this unfair attack on her character, Taleah pushed Joshua away. "I'm fine. Thank you." Her tone was curt and unforgiving. She then stared at Joshua, her eyes turning much softer. "I'm sorry I was so short, Josh. I just hate that this ugliness has happened."

Taleah turned to Lorenz. "I apologize to you,

too. Sorry you had to see this unattractive exchange." She leaned over and kissed Lorenz on the mouth. "Now you know the truth of why I'm not as close to Joshua as I'd like to be. It wasn't an attempt to deceive you. I just don't like talking about it. But this is not what we're here for, so we should change the subject. How's the business deal coming along, guys?"

Joshua felt that he just couldn't leave things unresolved like this. He had behaved badly and he desperately wanted to make it up to Taleah. He took his sister's hand and wrapped it up in his. "I'm sorry for embarrassing you like this, Taleah. There's no excuse for it. I know you're due to fly back to L.A. on Sunday, but I'd like you to stay over until the late evening. I'll take care of the airline penalties. I want us to talk and get everything out in the open so we can become closer. I do love you despite the fact that I probably don't make you feel as if I do."

Wishing they could become closer, Taleah smiled gently. "I'd like that, Joshua. Thanks for wanting us to work things out. It's important to me."

Joshua squeezed Taleah's hand in a comforting way and then let go of it.

Jared gave Taleah a reassuring wink, hating what had gone down. Joshua had also been no less than cruel to his younger brother, but Jared had learned at an early age to ignore his arrogant older brother. Their relationship was so close today because Jared had refused to allow Joshua to intimidate him. Joshua had changed a lot in recent years, but he'd become frustrated with Taleah because he felt that she wasn't even trying to accept the changes in him. Taleah was cool to her older brother because she wasn't sure the changes in him were permanent.

"To get back to your question about the business deal, Taleah," Jared said, "we should be fully funded by the beginning of next week. Looks like I'll be moving to San Fran for good, at least until the business is up and running at full speed. We hope to open another fitness center in L.A. within the next two years."

"Congratulations!" Taleah sang out. "I'm proud of you both." Taleah hugged each of her brothers, embracing Joshua with the same amount of warmth she'd given to Jared. "Are we all ready to order now? I'm starving."

"We can go ahead and order lunch," Jared responded, summoning the waitress. "I'm as hungry as you are, baby girl."

The meals were ordered and then delivered in a timely manner. It was during the ordering process that Taleah had learned that Lorenz didn't eat pork or shellfish. They had the no-pork diet in common, but Taleah loved shrimp, lobster, and crab, which made her curried shrimp, sautéed vegetables, and steamed rice an easy choice to make from the menu. Lorenz had ordered chop suey, his favorite Chinese dish, accompanied by hot and sour soup and vegetable egg rolls.

Taleah kept a watchful eye on how Lorenz and her brothers interacted. It seemed that Jared and Joshua were warming to him rather effortlessly, but Taleah wasn't in any doubt that the pointed questions were soon to come.

Her concerns were more about Jared than Joshua. Jared hadn't been able to stand most of the guys she'd dated. It seemed that no one was good enough for Taleah, which he made clear quite often. Joshua had never cared about Taleah's personal relationships one way or the other. His indifference to the events in the life of his siblings was also a bone of contention for Taleah.

As for Bradley, Jared had distrusted him from the start. The family had had a hard time talking Jared out of confronting Bradley in a threatening manner. Jared had readily put on the armor and was ready to go to battle for his sister's honor. Bradley ended up with only a stern warning from her brother, but it had been strong enough to make Bradley take heed to all that Jared had had to say. Getting into a brawl with a muscle-bound fitness trainer wasn't a smart thing for anyone to do. Jared had also been a champion wrestler in high school and in college.

Jared laid down his fork and made direct eye contact with Lorenz. "I know my sister is a great woman, Lorenz, but what else made you ask her to marry you after only three dates?"

Lorenz showed no signs of nervousness, as he looked Jared in the eye. "If I could answer that with an in-depth response, I would. But I'm afraid that I can't. There is an undeniable attraction and an unexplainable spiritual connection happening here. Our spirits connected instantaneously. Taleah is a sensitive woman with an incredible heart of gold. She's honest and respectable. She's the kind of woman a man marries. It didn't take me long to see these wonderful characteristics in her. She also loves herself. One moment I was telling her I couldn't make a commitment to her. Almost in the next instant, I was asking her to marry me."

"So I've heard," Joshua tossed out without the slightest hint of sarcasm. "But you have to know that we're deeply concerned about this engagement, especially since you're not yet divorced from your current wife. How can you assure us that

Taleah is not getting into something with you that she can't handle? We do not want to see her get hurt."

"Taleah is the only person I will ever try to make any assurances to. However, I can try to shed some light on the current circumstances. Without going into a lot of detail regarding the issues in my marriage, I've been estranged from my wife for four years."

"Then why haven't you divorced before now?" Jared inquired.

"Our marriage has been over for a long time, just not on paper. The emotional attachment for us has been over for quite a while also. Our marriage has been a casualty of a set of unfortunate circumstances. The separation is not something I wanted, but we sometimes have to play out the hand dealt to us regardless of how lousy we think it is. You can't make a person's heart feel what it doesn't or even what you want it to. I can't place blame on either of us. These sorts of things can occur regardless of how hard you work to avoid them."

Lorenz pulled Taleah closer to him. Looking deeply into her eyes, with love aglow on his face, he kissed the tip of her nose. "All I can tell you is that I plan to be extremely good to your sister. I'm a good man, an honorable one, but not without flaws. No man is perfect. As it stands, life doesn't come with any guarantees. So I can't guarantee forever for us, yet I'm going into this marriage with a *happily ever after* and *until death do us part* mindset. I promise to be the best friend and husband that I can be to her. That's all I can offer you guys in the way of letting you know my intentions toward Miss Taleah. What I feel for her is different than anything I've ever felt. There's calmness and a serene aura about our spiritual connection, yet the storms of passion are there also. I don't use the word *love* loosely, but what's going on between us goes so much deeper than what that one big word can be defined as. Our feelings actually defy description."

Taleah sat there speechless. The way Lorenz had defined their relationship was exactly how she saw it. They'd confessed to loving each other, but he was right, their feelings were so much stronger than love, more powerful than either of them could adequately explain. Taleah could tell that her brothers were also in awe of his eloquent response.

Although satisfied with Lorenz's initial responses, the brothers continued to ask the hard questions. Lorenz had no problem in giving it to them straight. He wasn't the type to offer lip service. He meant every word that came out of his mouth and could back them all up in action.

Taleah laughed nervously. "Guys, can you lighten up a bit? His intentions are honorable."

"They'd better be," Jared boomed, softening his sharp command with a smile.

Lorenz ran his fingers through the length of Taleah's hair. "It's okay, Taleah. If I had a sister, I'd be doing the same thing, more so under these conditions. Big brothers are supposed to be protectors. You're blessed to have siblings who care about you the way they obviously do. Whatever Taleah wants that's within my power to give, she'll have it. But the most important thing of all, we've vowed to take care of each other's hearts."

Smiling broadly, Jared extended his hand to Lorenz. "I don't think we can ask for anything more than you've given us, man. We don't like the idea of her moving so far away, but I'm thrilled for her opportunity to see the world. Exploring the Far East has been a dream of hers since junior high school. Starting out in Japan with someone you love isn't too shabby a beginning." Jared hugged his sister warmly and he then embraced Lorenz.

Joshua was the next to shake Lorenz's hand, warmly, firmly. "I'm behind you, brother. You two have my blessings. Just know that we'll also be keeping a close eye on you, Lorenz. I don't know what it is, but I'm also feeling the special connection you two seem to have. It's radiating all over this place. The look on your faces says a lot about how much you care for each other. Congratulations, Taleah and Lorenz!" Joshua leaned over and kissed his sister. Surprising his siblings, he also hugged Lorenz. Joshua wasn't known for being affectionate or sentimental.

Taleah loved how all her guys had fallen into an easy camaraderie in such a short time. Lorenz was going to make an awesome addition to their family. She could feel it.

Taleah laughed, sighing with relief. "Thank you all for not making the seat too hot for Lorenz." She eyed her fiancé with genuine pride. "I admire the way you handled these two brothers who pride themselves on being tough guys. You were eloquent, your honesty is so refreshing. Love you." Something Taleah normally wouldn't do in front of her brothers, she practically leveled Lorenz with a very passionate kiss.

Lorenz's response to her overdisplay of affection was no less fervent. "Love you, too."

Although there were two beds in their sedately decorated hotel room, Taleah's stomach began that nervous fluttering known as anticipation. She couldn't help wondering if Lorenz would change his mind about making love to her. Her insides fluttered even more at just the thought of it. Taleah moaned while thinking of the long three months she might have to wait for their physical love. Lorenz had been adamant about waiting, which she had to admire. If she had her way, the wait would be over within the next few minutes. Why was it so important to her for them to make love before he left? she had to ask herself. After only a few seconds of thought, she simply chalked it up as knowing exactly what she wanted.

At the moment, Taleah Taylor wanted Lorenz Hampton, all of him.

Not long after a quick shower and dressing herself for bed, Taleah, sharing the same bed with Lorenz, lay perfectly still in his arms. He held her tightly against him, thrilled for the opportunity to be with her again. Her being stretched out next to him, dressed in the softest of black silk, felt so right. While Taleah hadn't outright broached the subject of them making love, she'd been making hinting references to such from the moment they'd left her brothers. He wanted desperately to have that ultimate experience with her, but he still felt the timing was wrong. Lorenz did not want Taleah to feel cheated or for her to have any delayed regrets.

Taleah raised and propped herself up on her elbow, looking down into Lorenz's face. "Thanks for making this happen, Lorenz. Being here like this with you is so unbelievable. Being apart three months is ingrained in my mind. I try not to think about the long separation but it seems impossible to do. I'm glad we're here together, happy for the extra bonus time."

While she cooed softly, the kisses Taleah rained down on Lorenz's face were tissue-soft. She then lowered her head and outlined his ear with the tip of her tongue, hoping he could feel her heat burning hotly for him. Moaning against his lips, she kissed him softly on the mouth. Her tongue then took another journey around his outer ear before flicking around in his inner ear. Slowly her hands snaked up under his silk T-shirt, where she gently stroked his rock-hard abs.

These wild feelings were hard for Lorenz to fight, but not nearly as hard as was his attempt to keep his manhood in check. That Taleah had made up her mind to seduce him hadn't come as a complete surprise; the way she was now setting him up for utter surrender was a bit shocking. This mesmerizing woman had his body feeling good all over. He could get up right now and move over into the other bed or succumb to Taleah's thrilling seduction of his entire being. The latter was so much more appealing to him. Either way he chose, he was in big trouble.

Deciding to take her seduction of Lorenz to the next level, Taleah lifted his shirt and then circled his nipple with her tongue. Her finger lazed a line down the center of his chest and all the way down to the waistband of his boxers. The desire to go farther caused her fingers to itch.

Taleah brought her mouth close to his ear, tasting it once again. "Why don't we pretend we're already married, that this is our wedding night? What delicious things would you do to me if we were on our honeymoon, Lorenz?"

The softness of Taleah's sweet whispers of wantonness went straight through him. He stifled what would've been a loud moan. Lorenz had to swallow hard to try and locate his voice. Taleah's bewitching fingers dancing with wild abandon over his body had his anatomy on fire. If he could talk, what would he say to her? He didn't consider himself a devil, but she had him hotter than Hades. How could he go back on his word after being so adamant about waiting? The next heated caress from Taleah, which had his body shuddering uncontrollably, completely stripped away his ability to reason this out. His thought processes had gone up in smoke.

Lifting his head, Lorenz captured Taleah's lips in a sensuous kiss. "You are flirting with the devil and arousing more than temptation."

Taleah's mouth closed over his again. "Since the devil is red hot, I think we should attempt to douse the flames. Don't you?"

"You have a three-alarm fire going on up in here, Miss Taleah. Getting these flames under control is going to be hard since I'm a weatherman, not a fireman. Come here, baby." He brought her body flush with his. "Let me show you how a weatherman gets all sorts of weather-related storms started."

Smiling sweetly, she looked over at him. "I'm all for that, but is the weatherman going to be able to put out the raging flames? My body temperature has already surpassed the degrees on regular thermometers. Are you able to bring my temperature down and save the day?"

His grin was devilish, flirtatious. "I guess you'll have to wait and see. But I promise not to let your sweet, creamy flesh burn to a crisp. This forecaster has been known to deliver the fire-quenching rainstorms right on time, but only with the assistance of the *Man* upstairs."

Lorenz pulled Taleah on top him. As a man who loved to use a slow hand, he began stoking her gently yet fervently, to further stir up the fires of her passion. Hungrily, his mouth sought out hers, again and again, kissing her until they were both breathless. Excited beyond her wildest imagination, Taleah moaned and cooed at his slow, gentle, fiery caresses. Smiling softly, hopeful of him taking her on a trip to seventh heaven, she closed her eyes.

Lorenz didn't know how far things were going to go on this last night of them being together, but he could hardly wait to find out. Thoughts of being inside Taleah ruled his head; his hopelessly in love heart could never, ever deny her whatever were her wants and needs.

Eight

Taleah's fingers trembled as she ripped open the first letter from Lorenz. This letter had been a long time coming. With no communication from him since he'd left eleven days ago, apprehension had already paid many invasive visits to Taleah's serenity. That he had changed his mind was her biggest fear. That is, when she allowed her head to play twenty questions with her heart. For Lorenz to back out of their plans would absolutely devastate her.

Fearful of what the letter might contain, Taleah sat down on the sofa, slowly unfolding the sheets as if she expected them to blow up in her face. *Please, God, please don't let this letter reveal a change of heart by Lorenz. I don't want to become a Dear Jane.*

The first sentence put a huge smile on Taleah's face. She then relaxed her head against the sofa back. The words *I love you, miss you terribly, can't wait to be in your arms again* put her at total ease. That he hadn't had a change of heart had her heart singing. Taleah kissed her small oval solitaire diamond. He still wanted to marry her.

Thoughts of their last night together blew softly into her mind. That had been their best night yet. While he hadn't completely surrendered to her blatant acts of seduction, the passion between them had been flying at an all-time high. They'd come so close to answering their physical needs in the ultimate way. Lorenz had definitely put out the raging fires of her desire, but he'd taken care of her in his own unique way. No matter how she summed it up, their relationship had been consummated in a very special and deeply satisfying way.

Taleah couldn't stop smiling through the reading of the rest of the letter. Lorenz had written all the things she needed to be reassured of. The reassurance hadn't come a moment too soon. As Taleah put the letter back in the envelope, she noticed another sheet of paper. When she unfolded it, a document of some sort floated to the floor. Upon picking it up, Taleah recognized it as a U.S. postal money order for two hundred and fifty dollars.

While recalling that she'd jokingly asked Lorenz if he was going to start taking care of her now that they were engaged, Taleah had to laugh. They'd had a good laugh over the idea of her becoming a kept woman. A kept woman she wasn't. His woman; she was definitely that.

The decision to deposit the money came quickly. She wasn't going to spend any money that Lorenz sent her. She'd save it until after they were married. In case the marriage didn't happen, God forbid, she'd still have the money to send back. But their union *was* going to happen. Besides that, she and Lorenz were going to take care of each other, had promised to take care of each other's hearts. Their marriage would be a fifty-fifty deal—and a huge success story.

After getting up from the sofa, Taleah walked into the spare bedroom and turned on the computer. Writing Lorenz back right away would keep the letters flowing at a steady pace. She had practically lived for the first one to arrive. Now that she'd received it she could hardly wait for the next one to be delivered. Getting mail from overseas had taken a lot longer than she'd anticipated. The overseas mail seemed to move much slower than the stateside U.S. postal system, yet Lorenz had an APO San Francisco address. That was something she could ask him about in her return letter. She would have to learn how the military mail system worked.

Taleah started her letter by telling Lorenz that she loved and missed him, too. After all the gooey mush was out of the way, she wished him luck on his next softball game. She then told him how her job was going and how things were shaping up for their wedding day. Taleah also mentioned in her letter that she had no idea of how much stuff she'd have to get rid of before she could even clear the apartment. She had accumulated a lot of things over the years.

The last few paragraphs of Taleah's letter revealed to Lorenz how much she loved and missed him. She talked of the loneliness she constantly felt and how she was counting the hours until his return. She asked for pictures of him so that she could have them professionally framed. In fact, she wanted one for each room of the house, including her bathroom. The guest bathroom was exempt. Despite the fact she'd be moving to Japan in a short while, she still wanted to have the photos. Taleah had given him a large picture of her before he'd left Los Angeles.

A neatly printed I LOVE YOU in large block-style

letters was used in the closure. Before sealing the correspondence, Taleah sprayed it with a light spritz of the Jungle Gardenia perfume that Lorenz had purchased for her in Mexico. *That should give him a gentle reminder.*

Finished with her computer, Taleah shut it down and then went into her bedroom.

In order to save a little money Taleah had decided to move in with her parents until after the wedding. She had planned to move right away, before the first of the month, but she'd now have to give that more thought. There was no way she could get everything taken care of by then. Her privacy was also an issue that she hadn't initially thought of, which made her entertain the idea of keeping the apartment up until about a month before Lorenz was due back. But that didn't mean she couldn't start getting rid of the smaller items. She had a huge task in front of her. One step at a time was the attitude she'd have to adopt to see her way clear.

A coworker had already expressed an interest in purchasing Taleah's bedroom furniture. The Taylors were going to take in the living room set since it was fairly new. Allison planned to put the sofa and two chairs in her retreat/sewing room. The furnishings would be kept there for Taleah should she want them back one day.

Cringing inwardly, Taleah stood in front of her closet door, feeling guilty. In her opinion it was a sin for one person to have so many clothes and to wear less than half of them. She began to mentally thumb through all the churches and charities with clothes closets always waiting to be filled with giveaways. Packing everything up and getting the boxes to the proper places within the next couple of weeks should be a snap, Taleah considered. Too tired to start tackling the job at the moment, she thought it best if she began early in the morning.

Taleah looked at her newly acquired driver's license and smiled. The photo of her didn't look half bad compared to some of the pictures she'd seen on other licenses. Taleah couldn't believe she had actually taken a driver's test to obtain her license a couple of weeks back. It had just arrived in the mail and she was ecstatic. For someone so fearful of cars, she had managed to conquer one of the many fears she still had to work on in order to even take the test.

In one of his letters to her Lorenz had convinced her that she should try for her license. Although she'd passed the written part but failed the driving test the first time out, she'd gotten right back in line to retest at her dad's prompting. Taleah felt that she'd done worse on the driving portion the second time around, but the new instructor had passed her. Taleah believed he might've passed her because she told him she'd be moving to Japan.

That Lorenz had been able to talk her into getting the license in the first place still amazed her. He thought it was important for her to have it while living abroad, but that didn't mean she had to use it. One terrible car accident was enough for her. God forbid that she'd be the one to cause a serious mishap. Her driver's license would more than likely be just another addition to her wallet.

Me, living in Tokyo, Japan, she mused, another miracle among so many miracles that God had sent her way. It looked as if the dream in her youth was about to come through. What she'd seen on film in geography class would soon become a reality. Taleah laughed heartily as she imagined herself dressed up in a red, black, and gold kimono made of fine silk. She could also see her hair done up in the beautiful traditional style, entwined with delicate ornaments.

Taleah then wondered if there were still geisha girls and samurai soldiers in Japan. The thought of seeing a real live sumo wrestler tickled her funny bone. Seeing one of those big guys in person would probably scare her silly, since they weighed hundreds of pounds. She had read that the Japanese wrestlers began training for the sport on special farms at a very young age.

Visions of beautiful Japanese gardens and wooden bridges danced into Taleah's mind. Pagodas and intricately designed oriental archways were such a thing of beauty. Unusually shaped bonsai trees, colorful dragons on silk banners, and hustling street vendors were all a part of the mesmerizing landscape of the Far East. Sampling the native foods should also be a delightful culinary experience. It seemed to Taleah as if she hadn't forgotten a single sight that her teacher had caught on film.

Flashing pictures of Mount Fuji, tall and majestic, covered with crystal-white snow, made Taleah smile. In concluding her visions of life in Japan, she had to admit that being married to Lorenz would be the most adventurous of all. Exploring these exciting places with him would be divine. Taleah could hardly wait to land in Tokyo, Japan, another world, far, far from home.

The sound of the doorbell chimed in Taleah's ear. Not expecting anyone, she wondered who had come to visit so late. Her friends were all otherwise occupied for the evening, so she didn't know whom to expect. Taleah looked down at her disheveled state of dress. She had put on the wrinkled sweats as soon as she'd gotten home from work. As the doorbell pealed again, Taleah ran for the front of the house, prepared to make an excuse for her messy-looking attire. Whoever was at the door would just have to accept her as is, since they hadn't bothered to call.

A look through the security-viewing window revealed the face of her handsome ex-fiancé, Bradley Fields. The boy's athletic body was still in top form. His light brown eyes looked a little tired, but outside of that Bradley looked as good as ever. The boy always dressed to the nines and what he'd chosen to wear this evening was no exception to the rule.

Taleah's heart skipped several beats before anxiety grabbed a tight hold of her stomach. What was she to do? Would letting him come in be a mistake? After quickly deciding that she had to find out if she was as immune to him as she believed— and that now was as good a time as any—Taleah opened the door.

The tantalizing scent of his cologne was the first thing to have an effect on her. She used to love the way it smelled on him, fresh and provocative. Taleah would be willing to bet that Bradley had purposely worn the same type of cologne that she'd given him for Christmas their first year together. He knew how much she'd once loved it. He was there to try and win her back.

His light brown eyes roved over her body like the warm, slow hand of a lover. "Hey, Taleah, sorry for dropping in on you without calling first, but we both know what would've happened if I had phoned. I need to talk with you. It's urgent."

Taleah eyed him curiously. "Calling would've been nice, Brad. But since you've never been the least bit considerate of me, I don't know why I should expect you to start now. What is it that you so urgently need to discuss?"

"Can we at least sit down first?"

Taleah gestured toward the living room. "Don't make yourself comfortable, 'cause I don't plan for you to be here that long."

Bradley gave her an impatient look as he seated himself on the sofa. He watched Taleah closely as she took the chair opposite him. His eyes on her made her nervous. Bradley conversed with his eyes, so Taleah often knew what was on his mind before he said it. What was on his mind right now was how good she looked despite her rumpled clothes. She could tell his thoughts by the appreciative gleam in his eyes.

"You look darn good, Taleah. It's nice to see you looking so well and rested. How are things going for you? What about on your job?"

Taleah smiled inwardly at his predictability. She then stiffened, wishing she had the nerve to slap his smug face. That Bradley would dare to try and make his unannounced visit a social call galled her to no end. "Bradley Fields, I did not let you in my place so we could sit here and chitchat. You claimed urgent business. Let's hear it so I can get on with my evening."

Bradley raised an eyebrow, looking slightly injured. "When did you become so hard and cold, T? Your tone is as frosty as a subzero-degree winter."

"When you decided to trample all over my heart and treat me with disrespect, that's when! How do you expect me to warm up to something as cruel as that, Brad? You're the one who was cold and calculating. So you need to rethink your accusations and then place the blame squarely where it belongs. On your shoulders, not mine."

"For someone who's supposed to be engaged, why does what happened in the past still bother you so much? That was four years ago. Could it be that you still have feelings for me?"

Bradley had caught Taleah off guard and he knew it. His eyes revealed such.

Taleah swallowed hard, wishing she could zap him right off that sofa with just the wiggle of her nose. She didn't like him at all asking the same questions she'd been asking herself lately. Why indeed was she so bothered by it still? In that instant she knew the answer.

Taleah got up and walked over to the sofa where Bradley was seated and sat down very close to him. For several seconds she only stared at him, though she was already quite familiar with every minute feature on his pretty face. "So you think I still have feelings for you, huh? What makes you think that, Brad?"

Bradley was now the one caught unaware. Taleah sitting down so close to him had shocked him senseless. She'd only been keeping her distance from him for four long years. Now all of a sudden she was close enough for him to feel her uneven breath. "How could you not still have feelings for me, T? We were in love."

"If I'm not mistaken, *were* can be considered as past tense for *was*. You think?"

"What are you getting at? Everything but the answer to my question is what's going on here, Taleah. You're trying to confuse the issue because you don't want the truth to be known."

Taleah leveled an inquiring eye on him. "And what is the truth that I'm trying to hide, Bradley? I'm not sure what you mean since you have yet to tell me why you think I still have feelings for you. It *was* the first question I asked."

Bradley put his arm around her shoulder. When she didn't flinch or try to move away, he dared to turn her face to him and try to kiss her to show her why he thought what he did. She backed her head slightly away from that, but Taleah didn't move the position of her body.

Bradley threw up his hands in frustration. "Okay, I can see this is going nowhere. Taleah, you *do* care about me, a lot. You're just too stubborn to admit it. You still feel me, girl. Why don't we just get over the past and move on into the future? We belong together."

Taleah smiled sweetly. "I do feel for you, Brad. Sorry for you is the only thing that I feel. That you can bring your arrogant behind up in my house and talk trash to me is just another thing for me to add to the dozens of reasons why I kicked your cheating, lying butt to the curb. I don't have any feelings left for you, Brad, not the kind you think I do. Taking you back would make me dumber than dumb. However, I'm glad that you forced this showdown. It gave me a chance to compare what I once had with you to what I have now. No comparison! You were right, though. I did have questions about my feelings for you, but everything has become crystal clear. I now know the difference between true love and blinding infatuation. You haven't changed one bit and I don't see you ever changing. I'm happy and *truly* in love now. Try to be happy for me."

Anger was written all over Bradley's face. "Yeah, T, you think you're over me, but . . ."

Taleah waved her forefinger back and forth. "Uh, uh, uh! Let's not go there, Bradley," she said in a sweet yet condescending tone. "We want to keep things civil between us." Taleah then wrinkled her nose, fluttering her fingers in a waving gesture of dismissal. "Let me see you to the door now, Mr. Fields. This game of truth or dare is over."

* * *

As she dressed for bed, Taleah felt smugly satisfied with herself and with the way she'd handled Bradley. He had forced the issues and had set her heart and mind free in the process. She was way over him. His selfishness and disregard for others had never been more apparent than it had been tonight. The truth had been staring her in the face all along, but she hadn't been able to recognize it for what it was.

All she ever could've felt for Bradley was deep infatuation. There was nothing about him that brought on feelings of love. His good looks and his effervescent but false charm were the things that had swept her away. Being blinded by infatuation was what had kept Taleah from seeing the real Bradley, although he had shown his true colors more often than not. Taleah couldn't help humming a few bars to "Amazing Grace." No longer blind; now she could see. Clearly so.

The dozens and dozens of letters from Lorenz that Taleah kept in shoe boxes were the last items she stored in the trunk of her father's car. All of the things she treasured would be put in safekeeping at her parents' home. The rest of her things had been either sold or given to an organization that would put them to good use. The apartment was all cleared now. Her wedding was only ten days away. Lorenz was expected back two days before the nuptials were to take place. He would also be a welcomed guest in the Taylors' home.

Taleah felt like crying as she locked the apartment door for the last time. She had loved living there. The owner of the building, Mrs. Beakman, who also lived on the property, had taken Taleah under her wing when she'd first moved in. They had bonded in a very special way. Taleah would miss the elderly lady, though she planned to stay in close touch with her. The apartment keys would be turned in to the property manager the next day since it was the weekend and the office was closed.

While it wasn't necessarily considered a bachelorette party, Taleah and her best friends were meeting up for an evening out on the town. They planned to hit several hot spots during the course of the evening. Sherra also had some special news to share with the group. Taleah couldn't wait to hear it, assuming it had to do with Sherra's new love interest, Charlie Brown.

Smiling, while dressing for the evening's activities, Taleah gently fingered the delicate gold heart-shaped locket Lorenz had sent to her. Inside the locket he had placed the little white piece of paper found inside the fortune cookie they'd broken open at the Chinese restaurant in San Francisco. *You will soon find eternal happiness* was what the fortune had revealed.

While neither of them put a lot of stock in fortune cookies, the message seemed so appropriate and timely for their particular situation. That Lorenz had managed to think up something so special to do with the small piece of white paper had her ecstatic. She loved his romantic and adventurous spirit. So romantic were they, his letters always left her on cloud nine. He'd only called a couple of times, as it was expensive continent to continent, but the daily letters more than made up for the lack of phone communication.

Lorenz was also full of wonderful surprises. Although there were times when it seemed to drag on and on, the three months had gone by relatively quickly. It was hard to believe that she'd be getting married fairly soon.

Taleah looked at the clock and then stepped up her pace. Drusilla was due to pick her up in less than an hour. After taking from the guest bedroom closet a simple but elegant black pantsuit, Taleah removed the protective plastic covering. Instead of the white shell she'd normally wear with this suit, Taleah selected a red silk one. She then pulled out her red shoes and bag. Being out of her own place made her feel as if she were living out of a suitcase, though her parents' residence was very much home for her. But this would all be over very soon, she told herself. In a matter of just days she'd be living with her husband in the home he'd provide for her. She was excited about living on base in the three-bedroom garden home he'd written to her about. From his descriptions of the place, Taleah was sure she'd love it as much as Lorenz did.

Taleah and her other two friends were still in total shock an hour after the informal get-together had begun. Sherra had shown up at the club with Charlie Brown in tow, her brand-new husband of two days. Sherra and Charlie had been married at the courthouse by one of the judges, a friend to both. While it was just supposed to be the two of them, Sherra's law partner had spread the word in the cafeteria of the upcoming nuptials to take place at noon, so many of their colleagues had filed into the chamber to witness the marriage. Sherra and Charlie had only known each other six weeks. They had grown close while working on a case together, a divorce case, no less. Charlie had taken himself off the case once they'd gotten romantically involved.

Sherra and Charlie's marriage had turned into somewhat of a surprise wedding, since they'd had no idea that their colleagues would show up. According to Sherra's description, the ceremony had certainly been unique, sounding like a one-of-a-kind experience. They had chosen this quickie route because of Sherra's father's illness. Many other important matters were also piled high on their plates, so getting married right at the courthouse during business hours was what had worked best for the couple.

Seeing the golden glow on Sherra's face made it hard for her girlfriends to be upset with them. Several of Charlie and Sherra's lawyer friends and a few of their family members had also shown up at the club, which meant there was now a double celebration going on.

Beaming like a morning ray of sunshine, Sherra dropped her arm around Taleah's shoulders and pulled her head close to her own. "Looks like I beat you to the altar, hey, kid? I hope you're not upset with me. I wasn't trying to upstage you, you know."

Taleah hugged Sherra's neck. "Girl, that never even crossed my mind. All I'm sitting here thinking about is how you managed to pull this whole thing off without uttering a word to any of us. For a woman who talks her butt off for a living, you sure kept this big secret inside. Just tell me one thing. Are you happy?"

Tears came to Sherra's eyes. "I can't begin to tell you how happy, Taleah. Charlie does it for me in every way imaginable. I know exactly what happened between you and Lorenz, because the same wonderful thing happened to Charlie and me, instantaneously. We can't explain it either—and we're not even going to try. If people don't understand it or don't want to accept it, that's too darn bad. That's their problem. We're now just going to bask in our feelings for each other. There will be no looking back. We love each other, Taleah. There's nothing more to say. Our marriage is going to work because we plan to work it."

Taleah smiled knowingly. "I know exactly what you mean. The introductions, Sherra, when are you going to introduce us to Charlie? We're all dying to meet him," Taleah enthused.

Laughing, Sherra slapped her forehead with an open palm. "You all must think I'm crazy. In all my craziness and euphoria, I forgot to introduce my handsome, blue-eyed husband to my best friends. Be right back." Everyone watched Sherra floating on air as she made her way across the room to where Charlie was chatting with a couple of guys

Taleah laughed heartily, feeling extremely ex-cited over Sherra's recent nuptials. "Close your mouth, Dru and Brenda. And you all thought I was rushing to the altar!" Taleah shook her head from side to side. "I love anyone who sees what they want and wastes no time going after it. Dru, you weren't too far off the mark when you mentioned a double wedding. They won't happen at the same time, but there will definitely be two marriages. If I weren't a party to it all, I wouldn't believe this jubilant mad-ness myself."

Sherra held on to Charlie's hand tightly as she introduced him to Taleah, Brenda, and Drusilla. Taleah thought Charlie was even better looking up close. He had a nice smile and his blue eyes were like bright-as-star sapphires. The adoration he held for Sherra was apparent in the way in which he looked at her. Although he seemed a little shy,

Charlie was both sweet and friendly. Sherra had obviously found herself a precious gem. They made a striking couple.

The remainder of the evening had passed by rather quickly. Toasts had been made repeatedly; many of them were for Taleah and Lorenz's happiness, making Taleah wish he were there with her. In a matter of days he would be, and she could barely wait.

Taleah looked over at Drusilla, who was intent on maneuvering her brand-new SUV through the crazy freeway traffic. "Dru, you've been the most vocal in your objections to my marrying someone I haven't known for very long. After finding out that Sherra has married someone she barely knows, and then seeing her so happy, do you still feel the same way about my situation with Lorenz?"

Drusilla took her eyes off the road for a quick second to glance over at Taleah. "It's not important what I feel, Taleah. This is all about how you feel about your situation. I never should've said that people couldn't fall in love so quickly. I shouldn't have questioned your decision, period. My opinion can be high-handed at times. I wish you and Sherra nothing but the best."

"Since you've been a soldier for a long time, do you think I'm cut out to be a military wife? Do I have what it takes to survive in that world, a military environment?"

Drusilla reached across the seat and briefly touched Taleah's hand. "You're one spunky sister, Taleah, and you're very strong-willed. I've never lied to you before and I'm not going to start now. As I've already said, military life can be hard. But

knowing you as I do, I think you can handle it—
and anything else that comes your way. I haven't
gotten to observe you with Lorenz for any length
of time, but I see how you glow when you talk about
him. I have to believe in love at first sight after seeing what's happened for you and Sherra. Taleah,
you're going to be okay. You'll make Lorenz a fine
military wife."

"Thanks. I worry so much about it. I've talked
with my sisters, and they assured me that their lifestyle is not that tough. They mentioned that there
were differences in the way army wives lived versus
air force wives. Why do you think there's a difference, if there is?"

"Soldiers are out in the field way more than airmen, which means they're away from home more
often, leaving their women in charge of the family.
Soldiers are tough, hard-nosed blue-collar workers
and airmen are white-collar, high-tech workers.
That doesn't mean they don't work equally as hard
at their jobs. Each branch of the service plays an
important role in executing the multitude of missions of this man's country, often coming together
to do so."

"I can't imagine one branch working harder than
the other, including the wives."

"Soldiers fight hard on the ground and airmen
fight hard in the air; both are thoroughly trained
in all aspects of modern technology. Army wives
often work harder at maintaining their families in
the frequent absences of their men. Navy wives
have the same experience when their men are out
to sea. Regardless of what branch of the service
their men are in, military wives have to be strong
and they have to be able to stand up against anything. I know you can stand up and be counted

among them. Stop worrying yourself to death about this, Taleah. The love you and Lorenz share between you will get you through the best and worst of times."

"I certainly agree with you on that. We really do have something very special. One of the things that is so interesting about our relationship is that I really didn't want to meet Lorenz to begin with. I was sort of hoodwinked into it by Mark. With my sister being here, Mom thought I should go on the date for Lynnette's sake. I wasn't looking for love but it seems that love was looking for me. How come these sorts of things happen when you least expect them?"

"It's the unexpected that holds the most intrigue. It's your time, Taleah. Is Lorenz's divorce final yet? I guess it would have to be with the wedding right around the corner."

"I would think so, too, but he hasn't even mentioned it, and I haven't asked about it. He's the one who set the wedding date. I'm sure he wouldn't have done that if the divorce weren't going to be final by then. What do you think about him marrying within such a short time of being divorced?"

"I'd be really concerned if there wasn't already such a long separation between him and his former spouse. If they haven't been together in four years, I can see how easy it would be for him to move on. I don't think any marriage could survive a four-year separation."

"Speaking of separations, when a military man or woman is separated from a spouse because of duty, what's the normal length of time for them being away?"

"Most unaccompanied tours are for a year, but there are some that are longer. It all depends on the situation. An unaccompanied tour is when the member is sent to a duty station where spouses can't go. There is also a TDY, temporary duty, which is much shorter than a tour of duty, but it can last for weeks. Lorenz was TDY when he came here. You'll get used to all the military terms and jargon once you're living the life. Just keep in mind that Lorenz has been in the service for a while so he gets to pretty much call a lot of the shots pertaining to his career, unlike someone just coming into the military. He's at the point where he can darn near pick and choose his own assignments. His rank affords him many other privileges. Everything will be okay, Taleah. The military can be a great way of life."

Drusilla pulled her red SUV into the driveway of the Taylor home. "I got you home safe and sound, kid." Drusilla's smiling expression quickly sobered. "You know, I wish I had what you and Sherra have found. Craig and I seem to be at a standstill. Our relationship isn't moving forward or backward. We're both in the military and are subject to being separated with only a moment's notice, especially since we're not married. Marriage is one subject that we've never discussed despite the fact we've been seeing each other for over three years. I don't know how to bring it up and he's probably scared to. I guess we'll go on like we are until the issue is forced through separation or some other entity. I would like to get married one day."

Drusilla leaned over the seat and hugged Taleah. "Be happy, Taleah. You deserve it."

Taleah squeezed Drusilla's hand. "You deserve happiness, too. It'll come, when you least expect it. Just like it came for me. Love you, girl. Thanks for the ride. We'll talk tomorrow. Be careful getting into the apartment. You and I both know that the streets of L.A. are some of the meanest in the country. In fact, call me and let me know you made it inside, okay?"

Linda Hudson-Smith

Drusilla laughed. "Okay, but you know this tough-as-nails soldier can handle herself quite well. Good night, Taleah."

"Good night, Dru."

Nine

The Ivy House, a quaint little white-steepled chapel, had been the chosen venue for Taleah's small wedding. The romantic garden setting was the backdrop in which Taleah and Lorenz would exchange vows. Fresh white and beige flowers filled the outdoor chapel. Brenda, as she'd promised, had taken care of all the beautiful floral arrangements.

Lorenz Hampton looked utterly divine in his full military dress blues. His uniform was immaculate, all the way down to his spit-shined black patent shoes. All the colorful and meaningful ribbons he wore on his uniform were indicative of his many accomplishments in the service. Waiting to marry the woman of his dreams, Lorenz stood tall and proud at the altar.

Jared Taylor looked extremely handsome in a dark blue Dior dress suit. He was a gorgeous vision for the roving eyes of all the single ladies, as he stood next to his soon-to-be brother-in-law, proud of the role he played in his sister's wedding. Mark hadn't been able to make the wedding. His overseas assignment had come through at the eleventh hour. Miles and Marsha had made it into town for the wedding; each had taken an immediate shine to Lorenz.

Brenda, Drusilla, Sherra, and Taleah's sister Marsha were the first to come down the aisle, each escorted by the men in their lives, with the exception of Brenda, who was escorted by Joshua Taylor, Taleah's oldest brother. The men immediately took seats down front once the women were at the altar; they weren't official members of the wedding party.

Floating down the aisle on her handsome father's arm, Taleah Denise Taylor looked like a fairy-tale princess all dressed up in a stunning ivory-beige Victorian-style gown fashioned from guipure lace and silky smooth satin. The designer original matched her timeless beauty. Styled in large cascading ringlets, her shiny hair hung loose about her shoulders. A single layer of fresh flowers circled her head. Taleah's smile was radiant as she floated toward the man of her dreams.

Once Pastor Charles Wilkes, the presiding minister at Taleah's home church, asked the question as to who gave this woman away, Jack Taylor gently placed his daughter's hand into Lorenz's. Jack then stepped back, taking a seat on the front row alongside Allison, his daughter Marsha, and his son-in-law Miles.

Praying that her tears wouldn't come too soon, Taleah smiled at Lorenz. Love shone brightly in her eyes. Standing at the altar ready to be united in holy matrimony seemed so dreamlike to her. The man standing toe-to-toe with her would become her husband within the next few minutes. Since she was dying to kiss Lorenz breathless, she could hardly wait for the pastor to pronounce them husband and wife. Happily ever after was their ultimate goal.

Lorenz had to choke back a gut-wrenching sob the moment his gaze fell upon his bride-to-be. Taleah couldn't look more beautiful to him than she did right now. It was hard for him to believe that he had actually found true love after all these years. Lorenz was the type of man who desperately needed to belong to someone who loved him and could appreciate him for who he was. He had finally found that someone. Taleah Taylor did love him, loved him for who and what he was—and she had already shown him over and over again how much she appreciated him. Taleah would soon join the ranks of the millions of proud and fearless military wives.

The look of love floated in Lorenz's eyes as he looked into Taleah's, repeating the vows that would make her his dearly beloved wife. An eternity wasn't long enough for them to be together. He wanted past eternity with her, past forever. "Till death us do part," he vowed.

Into Lorenz's arms Taleah came, crying, laughing, and hugging him tight. She then kissed him deeply to seal their sacred wedding vows. That Lorenz loved her like crazy, Taleah was in no doubt. He had done everything he'd promised to do— and then some. From the moment he'd promised to take care of her heart he'd never stopped.

Two hearts now beat as one. Their love-filled hearts would remain united for today, tomorrow, and forever.

Pastor Wilkes stepped forth. "What God hath joined together let no man put asunder. I now present to you the happy couple, Sergeant and Mrs. Lorenz Hampton!"

The reception was a happy, lively event, as Taleah and Lorenz made the rounds, greeting each of their guests personally. Though it was only a small group of folks, they'd heard enough sincerely voiced congratulations to last them a lifetime, which was exactly how long they planned to stay in love.

Lorenz and Taleah wouldn't have the luxury of a honeymoon since their flight to Tokyo had been scheduled for two days after the wedding. He regretted not being able to take her away to some exotic place for a week or two, but he had to get back to duty. However, Lorenz had booked the honeymoon suite in a plush hotel in Hollywood. He'd also promised Taleah that she'd have a proper honeymoon as soon as it was possible for him to take more leave.

Taleah saw things totally differently than how Lorenz did. Being able to live in Japan with the man she loved was the honeymoon of all honeymoons. Lorenz was her honey and he kept her on the moon. Just living with him every single day was all the honeymoon she'd ever need.

Lorenz pulled Taleah out of earshot of everyone, quickly wrapping her up in a loving embrace. "I love you, Mrs. Hampton," he whispered, pressing his lips into her right temple.

"Love you, too, Sergeant Hampton. We're finally married, baby. We did it, Lorenz," she squealed with delight, briefly resting her cheek again his.

Lorenz kissed the tip of her nose. "We did, didn't we? Not that we have anything to prove, but all the naysayers are going to have to eat their words at our twenty-fifth anniversary celebration. We'll retake our vows then, too."

Taleah laughed heartily, holding her hand over her heart. "Twenty-five! Don't you think we should get through year number one first?"

He hugged her tightly. "We will, baby, one day at

a time. On our twenty-fifth I'm going to remind you of this very conversation, Mrs. Hampton."

Happier than she'd ever been in her entire life, Taleah smiled brilliantly. "You won't have to, my darling husband. I can't imagine me ever forgetting a single moment of this glorious day, our wedding day." Her lips found his once again.

Before Taleah and Lorenz could pull apart to rejoin their celebratory reception, Drusilla walked up and practically dragged the happy couple to the middle of the dance floor, where they joined together in their first dance as husband and wife.

Taleah looked over at her parents and smiled when she heard the beginning of the selection "Look at Me, I'm in Love" by the Moments. This was the same song her parents had had their first married couple dance to on their wedding day thirty-five years ago. Earlier, as Taleah and Lorenz walked the aisle as the happy husband and wife, "The Wedding Song" from the *Quiet Storm* album recorded by Smokey Robinson was the special selection Taleah had requested. This song had also been played at her parents' wedding.

Taleah then danced with her adoring father. Father and daughter moved smoothly over the dance floor to Beyonce Knowles's song "Daddy." This incredible song said everything that Taleah felt about Jack Taylor. Through God's blessing and His divine intervention, Taleah felt that she'd truly been blessed with a wonderful man, a man just like her daddy. Lorenz was so much like her daddy it wasn't even funny. The two men had been cut from the same cloth but different molds, because each of God's children was one of a kind.

Lorenz Hampton and Jack Taylor were two honorable men who possessed an amazing strength of character. Jack Taylor was a good husband and father. Lorenz would be both as well.

Taleah and Lorenz ended up dancing with practically every one of their guests. Cutting of the beautiful, multiflavored five-tiered cake came next. Taleah and Lorenz couldn't stop laughing while feeding each other a slice of the butter-cream-iced confection. Right after more pictures were taken of the wedding party, the music was once again cued up.

While seated at the head table, Taleah nudged Lorenz when she saw Joshua leading Brenda to the dance floor. "I wonder what's up with that. He's never paid any of my friends an ounce of attention. He'd sooner shoot one of them than give them the time of day. They all think he's arrogant beyond imagination. Drusilla positively can't stand him."

Lorenz shrugged. "Well, he was Brenda's escort down the aisle. You put the two of them together, so I don't see why you're so surprised that he'd ask her to dance."

"I didn't do that. Mom did. It's just that Joshua hasn't always been a nice person."

Lorenz gripped Taleah's hand. "I thought you two worked your differences out."

"We did. He promised to treat me with more respect and to always consider my feelings. We had a great meeting of the minds. But the jury is still out. The believing is in the seeing for me. Joshua asking Brenda to dance is certainly a change for the better. I'm giving him the benefit of the doubt. I can see that he's trying to be more cordial and easier to approach. I'm impressed."

"Glad to hear it. When are we going to blow this gig? We have a marriage to consummate. I can't wait much longer, Taleah Taylor-Hampton."

Taleah giggled, blushing like the new bride she

was. "I like the sound of that, Lorenz, also the utterly divine sound of my new name. Taylor-Hampton sounds exotic. We can start making our farewell rounds now. Everyone knows the deal, at least the adults do. Every newly married couple lives for their wedding night, especially if they haven't ever made love." She nudged him playfully after that comment. "Hint, hint."

"I know what you're getting at, Miss Taleah. None of your hints have been subtle. But we're about to make our wedding night real interesting."

"Off the hook is more like it. I understand there's an age gap going on here, especially with how we express ourselves, but we'll make up for that too."

Laughing, Lorenz nudged Taleah back. "I get the feeling you're calling me old, Taleah. Haven't you heard that older men are more experienced, baby? They know just what to do to please their women and how to keep them satisfied and content. Speaking of expressing oneself, many of us old guys are known as masters in the art of physical expression. You'll get to see firsthand what I'm talking about in a little while. Just try to be patient, sweetheart. I know how bad you want it."

Laughing, Taleah bumped Lorenz hard. "I can't believe you went there. And quit tooting your own horn, boy. I'm the one who's going to decide if you're a master or not. As for how badly I want it, don't start writing a script that you can't possibly perform the starring role in."

Lorenz had to crack up at the comment. He couldn't have made a better point, but he wasn't going to concede that to Taleah. "Baby, what are you talking about? I'm star quality, leading man material! You'll see soon enough."

Joshua interrupted the playful exchange between

Taleah and Lorenz when he came and asked his sister to dance. As much as she wanted to stick to her husband like glue, this was one request Taleah couldn't turn down. Unlike her and Jared, who'd always taken turns teaching each other all the latest dance steps, Taleah couldn't remember ever dancing with Joshua. This was a thrilling moment. Dancing with her big brother seemed like an awesome thing to do.

Joshua took Taleah by the hand and led her out to the dance floor. After taking her in his arms, he planted a sweet brotherly kiss on her lips. "You look absolutely beautiful, sweetheart. Congratulations on both your wedding day and for picking out a great guy like Lorenz. I really like him, Taleah. He seems to be a good man. I can clearly see that he's in love with you."

Taleah pulled her head back and stared at Joshua. She had an odd look in her eyes. She found it so hard to believe that Joshua and the man talking to her were one and the same person. None of what he'd said sounded like something her brother would ever say. She'd never heard him pay compliments to anyone. Either he had changed or he was pulling off an Oscar-winning performance. The transformation in Joshua Taylor was an amazing one to her.

Taleah pecked her brother on the cheek. "Thank you. I can't believe how sweet you've been to me, Joshua. I'm really happy we're getting along so well. I love the way we're now able to interact so freely with each other. I can't thank you enough for helping to get us to that point. Lorenz *is* a great guy. I'm thrilled that you've noticed, too."

"The entire family has noticed Lorenz's genuineness, Taleah. You can't fake a pure spirit like that. About us getting along, I promised to make the necessary changes. Although I'm still a work in progress, I plan to continue in my quest for personal change." Joshua cleared his throat, as if he was nervous. "Your friend Brenda, is she in a serious relationship with anyone?"

Taleah could only stare at Joshua again. His question had her speechless. Was he romantically interested in Brenda? If not, why would he care about her personal life one way or the other? Taleah felt her laughter bubbling inside at the possibilities. "No, she's not." Instead of probing into his intentions, which might or might not be anything, Taleah thought it best just to answer his question. Letting Joshua lead his way into this was the only way to handle it.

"Do you think I've changed enough to ask her out? Or do I need to do more work?"

Taleah couldn't hold her laughter, but she prayed Joshua wouldn't think she was laughing at him. Taleah's laughter came from hysterical disbelief of Joshua asking her for advice.

Joshua scowled hard. "I'm that bad, huh? I'm glad I consulted with you first. I could've gotten my feelings hurt. I don't think Brenda likes me, anyway. When I asked her to dance, the look she gave me seemed to suggest that I was the last person she'd want to dance with. I guess accepting my offer was the only polite thing for her to do under the circumstances."

"Not at all, Joshua. I wasn't laughing at you. It just struck me funny that you'd even ask something like that. You're a very private person, you know. I think you've changed a lot, but you're the only one who knows if you've changed enough to ask Brenda out. The girl has very high standards. So if your intentions are anything but honorable, you don't want to go there. Besides that, you're all the way up there in San Fran."

"I can assure you that they're honorable, Taleah. Living in San Franciso is only a temporary stay. It only takes forty-five minutes to fly to L.A. So, with all that in mind, do you think you can hook your older brother up with one of your best girls, namely Brenda Bailey?"

"I'm glad you added that last part. For a minute it sounded like any one of them would do. Sherra got married a short time ago. Her husband, Charlie, was the one that escorted her down the aisle. So she's also a newlywed, completely off the singles market. She has known her husband less time than I've known Lorenz. Everybody ain't fickle, Mr. Man. When you think you've found the one, you just have to go after what you want. Sherra and I did just that."

"You two didn't waste no time at all. Grass wouldn't have stood a chance at growing under you two sisters' feet. I'll have to congratulate Sherra before she gets away from here. Now what about that hookup?"

Taleah frowned. "I don't think I should get involved in that. You're a fully grown man. If you want to get to know her, you should just go ahead and do it. I suggest that you continue to dance and talk with her. But don't use the smooth, devil-may-care brother approach. She just might start to like you if you keep it real."

"So it's true, she doesn't like me."

"I didn't want to go there, but since you've mentioned it, here goes. No, none of my girlfriends like you, Joshua. They think you're too darn arrogant. You have not earned an ounce of their respect. Drusilla likes you the least. The others have learned to ignore you. It's not like you've been around all that much. So that means it didn't take too much time in your company for them to come to those negative conclusions about you. You feeling me?"

"I feel you. I never thought I'd be seeking advice about women from my pint-sized kid sister. I must be desperate."

Taleah punched him playfully on the arm. "Don't leave out lonely. And you need to watch your mouth, which is one of your biggest problems. You say way too much of what you're thinking. Listen, this is our wedding day. I've got to go back to the beautiful man who's sitting over there looking pitiful and lonely. Loneliness is something that I never want my man to feel, not for a single second. One more thing before I go. If you intend to pursue Brenda, please take your time to build a friendship with her first, Josh. Don't rush into anything."

"You mean like you and Lorenz and Charlie and Sherra just did?"

Taleah rolled her eyes at Joshua, although she knew he had made a valid point.

Joshua threw up his hands in mock defeat. "Okay, Taleah, I promise to watch my mouth from here on in."

Taleah hugged Joshua and then kissed him on the cheek before he led her back to Lorenz.

Taleah and Lorenz were prepared to make quick work of tossing the historical Taylor blue garter and the bridal bouquet. The blue garter had originally belonged to Allison, who had passed it down to her eldest daughter, Marsha. Marsha in turn had passed it down to her younger sister, Lynette, who had now passed it down to her younger sister, Taleah. With no more sisters left in line, the garter would then pass to the future wives of Joshua and Jared.

All of the five siblings hoped to pass the garter down to their future daughters or their future sons' wives.

The honeymoon suite at the Hollywood Renaissance Hotel was magnificent. Lorenz had carried a giggling Taleah over the threshold, kissing her all the while. Champagne and flowers awaited the arrival of the newlyweds, compliments of the prestigious hotel located on Hollywood's Walk of Fame.

After drinking a toast to their happiness, Taleah went into the bathroom to change.

Taleah's hands trembled as she undressed and then redressed herself in the sexy eggshell-white silk gown and matching robe that her girlfriends had given her as a wedding shower present. She brushed her hair and then her teeth. A few spritzes of Jungle Gardenia came next.

For all the hints and frequent come-ons to Lorenz, Taleah found herself more nervous about making love to him than she ever would've expected. Her physical desire for Lorenz had always been strong, and there had already been a good bit of intimacy between them, but the fear of not being able to please him had suddenly come at her right out of the blue. No matter how close they'd come to making love, they hadn't.

Taleah swallowed her fear as she emerged from the bathroom. Seeing Lorenz already in bed caused her heart to pound unmercifully. His chest was bared, so she assumed the lower half of his wonderful body was in the same state of undress. The thought of him totally nude beneath the sheets excited and frightened her at the same time. While they had done a lot of intimate touching, no clothes had ever been removed. The butterflies began to stir in her stomach. The heat of her passion was also making itself known. Fear and passion joined in a maddening rival, assaulting Taleah on all fronts.

Lorenz sat up straight in the bed. "Baby, are you okay? You look a little dazed." Though she had talked about this night with eager anticipation, he had to wonder if she was frightened.

Immediately calmed by Lorenz's voice, Taleah allowed herself to move toward the bed, though slowly. As she grew nearer, Lorenz stretched out his hand to her. His gesture gave her even more courage to move forward. Her heart rate escalated at the thought of his tender hands caressing her body all over. The passion was starting to win out over the fear. The nearer she got to him, the more her passion flared. As her hand joined with his, feeling his warmth all through her, passion crossed the finish line way ahead of fear.

The moment she reached him, Lorenz lifted up Taleah and brought her into the bed, laying her next to him. He turned up on his side and looked down upon her face. He saw so many different expressions in her eyes. But it was the love that excited him the most. This beautiful creature was all his. He was truly blessed to have her in his life. This wasn't an act of passion to be rushed, no matter how eager he was to be inside her. A slowly building crescendo to sheer bliss was what he had in mind.

Slowly, Lorenz lowered his head, caressing her lips with his own, his stroking hands heating up her tender flesh. Taleah moaned inwardly as his hands and mouth continued to knead and caress her body. Taleah had the desire to open up every part of herself to receive him. Fear kept trying to enter into another race with passion, but the passion had grown too strong to even entertain such a ridiculous notion.

Taleah's slightly trembling hands began to massage Lorenz's chest, loving the feel of his firm flesh beneath her fingertips. Feeling less fear now, she found his tongue with hers and they became entwined. As his hand closed around one breast, then the other, she gasped from the fiery flames flicking out at her flesh. His tongue replaced his hand, causing her heat to raise another notch. Even her mind felt singed. His tongue laving her nipples was nearly her undoing. The stabbing sensations she felt were indescribable, indescribably delicious.

With her eyes completely glazed over with passion, Taleah stretched her arms out on the bed, in a show of total surrender. If she'd had a white flag, she would've raised it high. Lorenz was her captor. She was his willing captive. Her body belonged exclusively to him now. "I need you," she whispered brokenly. "Make love to me, Lorenz."

Lorenz didn't need to hear Taleah's request a second time. He was ready to fulfill her every need, her every desire; the crescendo he hoped to take her to had not yet been achieved. Causing her to burn for him even more, he slowly removed her gown, kissing her shoulders and breasts, as he bared them first. As he methodically slithered the gown down over her body, his tongue and lips kept the newly exposed parts of her naked flesh warm.

Taleah squirmed uncontrollably beneath Lorenz's heated caresses, quickly losing all touch with reality. As his hands and tongue arrived at the soft flesh inside her thighs, Taleah had to fight hard to keep from shouting out loud. This was one fiery sensation that she never wanted to have end. Lorenz had been right. He was a master of physical expression. How she loved the way he was expressing himself now. Taleah couldn't wait for him to settle himself inside her, but this expression of physical love felt way too good for her to ask for more.

Although his tongue and hands had her nearly insane, Taleah did not want this moment to end.

Totally caught up in the fever, Taleah began to touch Lorenz in zones she hadn't dared to go before, causing his dangerously elevated fever to soar even higher. Her soft hands roving over his body had increased his desire tenfold. The softness of her touch had him trembling. Their passionate kisses also grew in intensity, becoming hotter and wetter.

Taleah's breathing was so labored she began to think it was impossible for her draw in another single breath. Dying in her husband's loving arms wasn't an option she wanted to entertain, not when they had everything in the world to live for. Taleah didn't think the passion between them could get any hotter than it was. She hoped Lorenz would prove her wrong, as her hands clawed about his shoulders and back frenetically, intensifying the heat.

Aware that Taleah had reached the point where reckless abandonment had taken her over, Lorenz entered his wife, sweetly, slowly, causing her to scream out his name. As his tantalizing assault on her trembling body continued, so incoherent was she, Taleah could barely even recognize her own threadbare, softly moaning voice. Continuously, she cried out her husband's name. Lorenz slow-dancing inside, kissing her breathless, while tenderly familiarizing himself with her secret treasures, had swept her mind completely away. His thorough seduction of her body had rendered her incapable of any sort of logical thought process. Taleah was lost to a world of erotica, one she didn't ever want to return home from.

All Taleah could do now was lie there and feel

the tremendous fire. And what Taleah felt so deeply far surpassed anything she might've imagined. Everything in her world was delectably topsy-turvy and she didn't care if it ever again turned right side up. Lorenz, her loving husband, had made her his woman, forever his wife, in every sense of the word.

Taleah shuddered violently as her world suddenly begun to spin around. Just as her entire being splintered completely apart, Lorenz's impassioned release came simultaneously. The couple trembled with the force of conjoined passions, wishing for this moment to never end.

Curled up in each other's arms, husband and wife had been utterly fulfilled; the marriage had been breathlessly consummated.

Jack and Allison embraced Taleah, hating to see her move so far away from home. Their sadness didn't stop them from being deliriously happy for their youngest daughter and newly acquired son-in-law. Joshua and Jared took turns fiercely hugging Taleah and then Lorenz.

Jared was actually heartbroken over Taleah moving away to another continent, but he'd never let her know how deeply hurt he was. Since they were so sensitive to each other's emotions, he figured she already knew. Aware that she was in such loving hands allowed Jared to express his joy for her without crying.

Both Jared and Joshua had also promised to visit the couple in Japan.

Taleah's best friends had also shown up at the airport. Because only passengers were allowed inside the international gate area, the farewells all had to be said before the couple moved through security. Taleah had already had her private mo-

ment with Brenda, Drusilla, and Sherra. Drusilla
had also talked of visiting the couple, since she
had flying privileges as a member of the military.
Keeping the tears at bay had been impossible for
these four female comrades. Knowing they'd always stay in touch, no matter what, was a comfort
to each of them. Their friendship was much stronger
than any distance. Each promised to write often.

While the time for departure was at hand, Taleah's
emotions began to get the best of her. Leaving
everyone behind was hard, only made easier because of the beginning of her new life with Lorenz.
Her tears trickled down her face as she waved her
final farewells, blowing kisses all the while. The
loud shouts of "so long" caused her to tremble inside. Everyone would be missed.

This was farewell, and not good-bye, she told
herself. Knowing she'd see everyone again, God
willing, Taleah turned back around and cast her
loved ones a brilliant smile. This was her way of
wanting everyone to remember her farewell smile
and not her anguished tears.

Ten

Although she had slept during most of the flight, Taleah was exhausted by the time she and Lorenz reached the Yokota Air Base housing area. Taleah had never flown this long a distance, nor had she ever been on a flight that was more than five hours in length.

One of Lorenz's friends, Marvin Lawrence, had picked them up in a top-of-the-line Japanese car, a Nissan President. Marvin was a black Canadian married to a Japanese woman name Yuki, whom Lorenz had spoken fondly of. Marvin and Lorenz had been friends for a few years now. Marvin was responsible for the DJs in the club where Lorenz was a DJ, which was where they'd first met.

A quick glance at the three-bedroom, two-story structure she was to reside in for the next two years brought a smile of relief to Taleah's lips. It was actually a very nice place, referred to as a garden home, but she hadn't known what to expect despite Lorenz's descriptions. Marvin helped put the bags inside and then left. Taleah felt good about him and hoped to meet his wife one day soon.

Marvin had been very nice to her, also extremely respectful.

So far, so good, she thought.

Taleah was about to precede Lorenz into the house when he suddenly picked her up and carried her across the threshold. Her laughter rang out, which was quickly silenced, as Lorenz captured her lips in a riveting kiss. "Welcome home, Mrs. Hampton."

Taleah kissed him gently on the mouth, as he stood her back on her feet. "Glad to have a home here with you, Sergeant Hampton. Thank you."

Taleah followed behind Lorenz as he showed her around the house. He took her upstairs first so that he could take their bags up with him. All three bedrooms were nice and spacious, as were the two and a half baths. Though equipped with government-issue furnishings, the furniture was rather tasteful and modern. Once the tour of the upstairs was complete, Taleah followed Lorenz back downstairs, where he turned on the hall light.

The guest bathroom was the first place he showed her, turning on the inside light so she could see it better. The kitchen came next, and it was a good size, housing both the washer and dryer. Taleah liked the stainless steel sinks versus the porcelain ones that had been in her apartment. There was also plenty of cabinet and storage space. The living/dining room combination, furnished with an olive-green sofa and chair, was warm, receptive, and comfy. The dining area portion held a large mahogany table, six chairs, and a matching buffet.

What Taleah saw stationed on top of the buffet had her heart racing like crazy. Stapled to a large poster board were dozens and dozens of pictures of Lorenz with other women, beautiful, shapely women. Taleah felt like dying on the spot. Why did he have this vulgar picture board in the home they were to share together? It was so insensitive.

Lorenz noticed the horrified look on Taleah's face. "What's wrong, Taleah? You look so pale all of a sudden." It never dawned on him that the picture board was what had her looking so upset. "Taleah, what's going on?"

Taleah glared ferociously at him. "If this is your idea of a joke, it isn't the least bit funny. How could you flaunt these pictures of you and other women in my face like this? I guess I never thought you'd do something so insensitive, let alone something this downright cruel. This is totally unbelievable. What a sight to welcome me home to, Lorenz."

Taleah was too angry to cry. All of her insecurities about men came rushing back.

Lorenz heard the echo of his friend's voice. *"Get rid of those pictures. You don't want to leave them on display for your new wife to see. She won't take it very well. I can assure you of that."* Lorenz had really believed that the pictures wouldn't be upsetting to Taleah; otherwise he would have taken his friend's advice. He had collected these pictures from all over the world, and not one of them was of someone he had been involved with prior to meeting Taleah.

Lorenz looked chagrined as she tried to take Taleah into his arms. "I had no idea the pictures would upset you, though I was warned that they might. I'm sorry, Taleah. But these are just pictures that I collected during my travels. I don't even know some of the women I posed with. A lot of the pictures were the normal tourist types."

Taleah pushed him away, looking at him as if he were a perfect stranger. "Are you really that naïve or just plain stupid? How would you feel if I had a bunch of pictures of me with guys posted all over our place? I don't think you'd appreciate it one bit." Taleah immediately regretted her sharp tongue. This was not the way for them to start a new life together. She had to foster some sort of understanding to get through this situation.

Without uttering a word, Lorenz took the board down and headed toward the front door. Taleah followed behind him out of sheer curiosity. When he opened the door and went outside, she stood in the doorway watching his every move. Her heart thumped hard inside her chest as he walked across the street to the Dumpster and tossed the board inside.

Taleah suddenly had mixed emotions. Had she overreacted to the pictures? Had she been immature about it? According to him, they were only representative of his world travels. Besides, everyone had a past, though she didn't think it should ever meet up with her and Lorenz's present. She hadn't asked him to throw the photographs away, nor had she insisted on it. But she hadn't stopped him either.

At any rate, the photo board was right where it should be, in the trash. The pictures had bothered her to no end, but only because no newlywed, male or female, wanted to come home to something as visual as that. It was one thing to know your man or woman had a past, but it was an altogether different story to see the evidence of such staring you right in the face. No woman wanted to see a bunch of barely clothed women draped all over her man.

What a hell of a first night in her new residence, as a new bride. Ten thousand miles away from home with no one to call for advice, not without it costing a fortune, wasn't a good feeling. Taleah began to think that this wasn't something she and Lorenz couldn't work on without any outside interference. It now seemed to her that she might've made a mountain out of a molehill.

Without the slightest bit of reluctance, despite the possibility of rejection, Lorenz walked up to Taleah and took her in his arms. When she didn't pull away, his eyes searched hers, hating to see the pain of confusion staring back at him. "I'm sorry. I never intended to come off as insensitive. I just didn't think it was a big deal. It looks as if I still have a lot to learn about sensitivity. Those pictures were mostly of female friends despite the fact I was warned by my friend Rob to take them down. I'd never flaunt in front of you a picture of someone I'd been recently dating. Taleah, those pictures were not meant to hurt you or make you jealous. Can you please forgive me? I don't want our marriage to start out with issues of trust."

Wiping a tear from the corner of her eye, Taleah smiled warmly at her husband. "Of course I can forgive you. I think I may've overreacted. Still, it wasn't a pleasant situation for me to find myself in. I'm so far from home, Lorenz. This is all so new for me. I've never been married before, but I know what it feels like to be badly hurt. I was once involved with a cheater, and that was my first thought of you when I saw the photo board. What man flaunts his past conquests in front of his new wife? was one of many questions that came to mind."

"Don't worry about me going astray, Taleah. I'm not the cheating kind. The vows I made to you are sacred. But I can understand what you must've felt. Your question about how I'd feel if the situation were reversed made things crystal clear. Seeing a group of men all around you would've made me insane with jealousy. I'm sorry. This won't ever happen again. I promise."

Rubbing her body against his, Taleah stroked

his face with her forefinger, kissing him softly on the mouth. "Let's get unpacked. I'm extremely anxious to try out our new bed."

Lorenz's gushing relief was obvious, as it echoed off the walls. He kissed her lightly on the lips. "A shower before we unpack or afterward?"

Taleah grinned mischievously. "Let's leave the unpacking for the morning. I want to make love to my new husband in our new home."

Lorenz laughed. "You get no arguments here."

No longer feeling nervous about making love to Lorenz, Taleah took the initiative by helping him disrobe. After her own clothing was peeled away, Taleah climbed into bed to await her husband, who'd gone into the bathroom. Knowing she had satisfied him to the fullest on their wedding night and the morning after had helped her to lose the fear of not being able to please him. Being a wife was so new to her. She used to wonder if the love-making would be different during the course of their marriage. She'd heard enough stories about men losing interest in their wives soon after the vows were taken. Although she knew that wasn't the case with her sisters or even her mother, she still thought about it from time to time. Had the pictures prompted her musings? Lorenz closing the bathroom door caused Taleah to stray from her worrisome thoughts.

Lorenz slid into bed next to Taleah and instantly pulled her into his arms. His mouth instantly sought out hers, wasting no time in bringing her pleasure. While Lorenz massaged each of her nipples with the pads of his thumbs, she felt a fiery sensation rip right through her. Then she felt an incredible tingling as his mouth took over.

As his hands smoothly roved over her flat abdomen, Taleah felt an astonishing rush of warmth between her legs. Slowly, Lorenz moved his hands down to where her molten treasures eagerly awaited his tender touch. He was a man with a slow but sure hand. Taleah loved the way he took his time with her, how he made time for arousing foreplay. He showed no signs of being in a hurry. Lorenz's main goal was to bring his wife to utter fulfillment while savoring each heated caress and every sweet kiss.

Desiring to be a part of the act of seduction, Taleah used her hands to seek out her own pleasures, loving the feel of his rock-hard abs, touching and massaging his silky-smooth flesh. Caressing his manhood also made her body shudder with need.

Lorenz covered Taleah's hand and then guided it up and down the shaft of his hardened sex. They both moaned with undeniable pleasure. The sudden positioning of his hands between her legs caused her to moan even louder. The tips of his fingers had torched a fire inside her, threatening the control she held over a premature release. His wildly manipulating fingers had her squirming, making her wishing he'd hurry up and enter her. She wanted to explode with him inside her, craved to have him join her in the sizzling eruption. Taleah desperately desired to have the erotic agony live on and on.

Lorenz turned over and lay flat on his back. He then lifted Taleah and positioned her on top of him. As his hardness seared itself onto her flesh, her eyes closed. Biting down on her lower lip was all she could do to keep from screaming.

"Look at me, baby. I want you to see what you do to me, how you make me feel. Look into my eyes,

Taleah. See the love there, see the raw passion burning out of control just for you."

As Taleah slowly opened her eyes, a single tear escaped, her emotions oozing out from her heart. The love and the passion for her were unmistakably there in his dark, smoldering eyes. Lowering her head until their lips met, she kissed him passionately, continuing to keep eye contact with him. His every wish was her command. If he wanted her eyes open, then she'd accommodate him. If he wanted the world, she'd try to give it to him.

Too weak and too close to release, desperately wanting Lorenz to resume command, Taleah slowly dismounted and then stretched out on her back, begging him to fill her up with his hardened flesh. "Take me," she whispered, "all of me. Make me scream out your name."

Lorenz kissed her hard on the mouth, his tongue stroking her lower lip. "I want you, Taleah. All of you."

"I'm all yours. Every inch of me." Lifting his hand, Taleah sucked Lorenz's forefinger into her mouth. The incredible feeling of eroticism nearly drove him insane. With neither of them able to hold the flood back a moment longer, their torrential release burst forth, each screaming out the name of the other.

During the Yokota Air Base tour, Lorenz pointed out the commissary for Taleah, explaining to her its function, which she was somewhat familiar with from having heard her sisters talk about it. They had referred to the big grocery store as the "commisery."

"A lot of the items in the commissary are frozen.

So you'll have to get used to that, too. The navy brings in most of the goods. Meat is scarce here in Japan and it's very expensive when you can find it, so it has to be imported. The meat is shipped here from the States."

"That's interesting information." Taleah pointed at another big building. "I can see that that's the BX. I've heard my sisters talking about shopping at the exchange, but I've never been inside one. I hear you don't pay taxes on the purchases you make. Is that true?"

"Just another great fringe benefit. It's true. No taxes. But we do pay a nominal surcharge at the commissary. You have a temporary ID card, Taleah, so you won't be able to say you haven't been in these places much longer."

By the time Lorenz had completed the hour-long base tour, Taleah was familiar with all the important places. She saw that military bases were like a city within a city. They had their own banks, grocery and department stores, restaurants, parks, pools, golf courses, bowling alleys, clubs, and a host of other amenities found in stateside cities. Taleah was thrilled to see the tennis courts, where she hoped to continue honing her game.

The brief tour Lorenz had given Taleah of the military health and dental clinics had sparked an interest in her working there. Prior to the clinics, Lorenz had taken her by the building that housed the civilian Department of Human Resources. Lorenz had promised to take her there to fill out an application for employment as soon as she was better settled in. He was more than capable of taking care of them on his salary, but Taleah was an independent spirit, a characteristic that he had no desire to tamper with.

Lorenz reached across the seat and put his hand

on Taleah's thigh. "Do you want to eat out tonight? We can go to the club for dinner. They serve great food."

Taleah shook her head in the negative. "I'd like to eat at home if you don't mind. I saw some hamburger in the freezer so I took it out for spaghetti. Spicy spaghetti is something a friend of the family taught all of us to make. It's really good but hot. Can your stomach handle cayenne pepper? If so, we need to get some. I didn't see any in the pantry."

Laughing, Lorenz rubbed his stomach. "This baby is structured out of steel, woman. You already know how hard it is." He grinned with devilment. "I've noticed that you can't keep your sweet hands off it. By the way, my abs love your gentle, fire-filled paws."

"Are you trying to tell me you love it hot and spicy?"

Lorenz winked at her. "You know darn well I love it spicy. The hotter the better."

Taleah grinned mischievously. "We are talking about food, aren't we?"

He wiggled his eyebrows. "I guess you'll find out when we get home."

Taleah's flirtatious smile came lazily. "Positively intriguing. I can't wait."

Taleah pushed back from the table. Now that the delicious spaghetti dinner had been devoured, the dishes were calling. Knowing how Lorenz liked to take care of things immediately, she wanted to get in that mode and stay in it. In just a few days she had learned that he was more than just a neat freak. He was almost fanatical about keeping things in order. He hung up his clothes as soon as he took them off and he put everything back in its place the moment he was finished using it. While preparing meals, Lorenz kept hot, soapy water in the sink, washing and drying each cooking item once he was through with it.

Keeping things in order was going to be a challenge for Taleah, but she was willing to work hard on it. She wasn't the neatest person in the world, but neither was she a superslob. Taleah was messy at times, even a little junkie, as she often failed to put things back in place, but never had her place been dirty or nasty. As for her personal hygiene, they didn't come any more squeaky clean than Taleah. Bathing in hot scented water was her favorite pastime.

Lorenz refused to let her do the dishes alone, but she got the distinct impression that he'd rather do them by himself, though he only assisted. He mentioned using a system when getting things done. So it seemed to her that he wanted things done his way. Rather than requesting her to do it his way, she sensed that he preferred doing it himself. Taleah's feelings were a little hurt, but she opted not to make an issue of it for now.

Leaning over Lorenz as he read all the mail that had accumulated in his post office box while away, Taleah flicked at his ear with her tongue. When he didn't respond to her affectionate advances, she came from behind him and sat back down at the table.

As Taleah glanced over at her husband, she didn't like the horrified look on his face. In fact, the hard scowl he wore scared her. As it always did when she was frightened or upset, her heart began to race. "Is something wrong, Lorenz?"

Looking terribly upset, Lorenz held up a brown

envelope, shaking it back and forth in the air. "This important piece of information has been sitting in the post office box for more than a week now. I read the follow-up letter before I opened this one, which fully explains the legal documents that were in the brown envelope. Something awful has happened, Taleah."

"What, Lorenz? Please get on with it! I'm terrified over here."

Lorenz leaned forward and took Taleah's hand. "This contains information about my divorce. It's not final. My wife contested the divorce at the eleventh hour. Taleah, we're not legally married."

With her body trembling all over, Taleah looked stunned out of her mind. "But your lawyer . . ."

He nodded, feeling as anguished as his wife looked. The horrified expression on Taleah's face caused Lorenz to wince inwardly. "I know, Taleah. Mr. Saxon told me it was okay for us to marry, that everything was fine. He said that the paperwork would be finalized before September twelfth and that he'd send the final decree here the minute he received it. No one ever thought she'd wait so long to contest things. I'm sorry, baby. I know how tough this has to be for you. I'm also devastated by this horrific news. But it's you I'm worried about. I should be used to these games, but I guess I'm once again caught unaware."

"What does this all mean? Are you still married to her? Oh, my God, you are, aren't you?" Taleah began to cry softly, disappointed and discouraged beyond belief.

Lorenz took her in his arms, squeezing her tightly. "The divorce isn't final, Taleah." He couldn't bring himself to tell her that he was still married. "I have to go back to the States to appear in court. Both she and I have to be present. Saxon tried to reach me the day before we got married to stop the wedding, but to no avail. Neither my parents nor Saxon had a number to make contact with me. I always called them. I called Saxon before I left Japan and right after I arrived in California. According to the letter, my lawyer only received the document contesting the divorce the day before we got married. I don't know how this could've happened, but it has."

Moving out of his arms, she dropped back down in her chair. "So that means our marriage is null and void. Right?" Taleah knew the answer to her question, but she just couldn't bring herself to believe what was happening. She hoped by asking questions that Lorenz might give her a different answer, one that was more believable than the ugly truth. What was she to tell her family and friends? They would also be devastated.

He nodded, his expression painful. Lorenz sat down across from Taleah. "So it seems, but we'll still have to get an annulment."

"Why, if we're not legally married?"

"We're legal, as far as the state of California is concerned. I also have to talk to my new commander about this situation, since you were issued a temporary ID card at Los Angeles Air Force Base. It was based on the marriage certificate we received from the chapel. This is complicated, more complex than we both know. Her ID card would no longer be any good the instant the divorce had gone through. But since it hasn't, that means two dependent ID cards have been issued under my name and Social Security number. That also should've been caught. But the card was only temporary, so the mistake probably would've been noticed once we applied for the permanent one. A lot will have to be undone before we can get married again."

Taleah blew out a gust of uneven breath. She felt and looked frustrated. How could something like this happen? If only Lorenz's lawyer had been able to contact him, this entire mess could've been avoided. This was all too complicated for her to make any sense of—and she was too weary to try and figure it all out. As the chills of cold reality raced up and down her spine, Taleah's head began to throb like crazy. Tears filled her eyes.

That they weren't really married crushed her. She fought hard to breathe evenly. She wasn't his wife. Lorenz wasn't her husband. *I'm not Mrs. Lorenz Hampton. Oh, my God,* she cried inwardly, wishing she could wake up from his awful nightmare she felt trapped in.

Noticing that Taleah's anguished state had progressed, Lorenz got out of his seat and knelt down before her. She bent forward and moved to the edge of the chair, resting her chin on his shoulder. Hard sobs racked her body.

Lorenz stroked her back, doing his best to comfort her. "Are you going to marry me again, Taleah, once we get this all straightened out?"

Remarry him? Did Lorenz really think she'd leave him over something like this? It wasn't his fault. It bothered Taleah that he sounded so fearful, as if he really believed she'd bail out on him at a time like this.

Taleah lifted her head and looked him in the eye. "I'm already married to you, Lorenz. Our hearts are married. When we took those vows until death do us part, we believed that you were free to commit to them. Do you want to keep me, Lorenz?"

Lorenz breathed a huge sigh of relief, taking her

in his arms once again. "I love you, Taleah. You're a keeper. I knew that from the moment I saw you. We'll get through this. Together. I promise you that."

Taleah's cage had been rattled. She had to admit that. Could she and Lorenz get through this? Until things were resolved would she have to leave Japan? Although the government hadn't sponsored her, they were residing in base housing. So many unanswered questions now had her head spinning and throbbing. She didn't have to be a legal eagle to realize she'd lose her ID card, along with all the other benefits awarded her as a military spouse. The more she thought about things, the more complicated the situation seemed.

Seeing Taleah looking so anxious broke Lorenz's heart. Her vulnerability was shouting out to him loud and clear. Knowing he was solely responsible for her anxiety nearly brought him to tears. There was no comfort to be found in this situation. Pain and rain were often synonymous. Still, Lorenz knew that God was in total control of this situation. God knew their hearts, knew their every thought. A silver lining would eventually be found in all this. The reason for it all couldn't come too soon for Lorenz.

Lorenz couldn't help but bring Taleah close to him again, dropping kisses onto her face and in her hair. "This should be over rather quickly, baby. The court date has already been set for the end of next month, a little more than six weeks from now. I'll schedule my leave when I go in on Monday. It's a good thing I have so much leave on the books; otherwise I'd be in trouble timewise. Money for the trip might have to be borrowed from the credit union. Another expensive trip wasn't planned for. Space A won't work because of time restraints."

"What's space A?"

Lorenz kissed the tip of her nose. "Space available. Military members can fly on military or government-chartered aircraft for free when there's space available. But if you have to be somewhere and back within a certain time frame, flying that way can be pretty iffy. If your trip had been government sponsored, we would've flown here on orders."

Taleah massaged his cheek with the back of her hand. "We still have all that money you were sending me. Remember? I didn't spend a dime of it."

Lorenz smiled gently. "Thanks, Taleah. I had forgotten all about it, but I don't think there's enough for us both to fly at the high cost of tickets."

She looked perplexed. "You would want me to go?"

"Don't you want to go with me?"

"Not unless I have to. That would be so awkward for all of us. Besides, I'm supposed to fill out a job application next week." Her heart fell. "I won't be able to apply now, will I? Am I going to be forced to leave Japan? Oh, God, this is awful."

"Try to calm down, Taleah. I know this is upsetting for you. As a civilian, you can apply for a civilian job, regardless."

"Will they make you give up the house since we're not legally married?" She winced at her last question. The idea of having to go to the States without Lorenz was killing her.

What would her family and friends think about this situation? As she thought about it, she realized she really didn't care what anyone thought. This wasn't something Lorenz had planned out. A terrible mistake had been made, but not by him. On that note, she decided no one would know, not unless she was forced to leave Japan. There'd have to be an explanation for that.

"Honey, they might do anything, but I don't know, so I don't want to speak out of turn. I don't want to borrow trouble either. Moving out of base housing won't be a problem if that should occur. We can live off base with my allotted quarters allowance. But you won't have any benefits. If you got sick, you can't be treated at the military hospital. Something as simple as a toothache could cause major discomfort if it can't be treated."

Taleah slapped her palms on the sides of her face. "This is getting worse by the second. Maybe I should just go back home. That would solve everything." Her stomach turned at that.

"Taleah, let's not go there yet. If you have to leave, then we have to do what we must. But that hasn't been determined yet. I'm going to see my new unit commander on Monday. As I've already mentioned to you, Zurich Kingdom is an old friend of mine from my days at Buckley Academy. I can be honest with him. Besides, we have nothing to hide. He'll give me the best advice that he possibly can. If there's a way out of this, Zurich will know what path to take."

"I sure hope so. This court date, what is your lawyer saying might happen?"

"Let's get out of this kitchen." Lorenz led Taleah into the living room, where they both sat down on the sofa. Taleah immediately curled herself up against Lorenz.

"My attorney thinks the divorce will be granted the day I appear in court. According to his letter, he doesn't believe the judge will be too happy about this last-second filing. He told me to make sure I wear my uniform, but I don't like the implications of that. I don't like using my uniform to gain sympathy or to get the edge, which is what I plan to tell him. He may still insist that I wear it. He'll more than likely say that it won't hurt my case, but it might not help it either. I got a feeling that he believes it will have a tremendous impact on the outcome. No matter what I wear, it'll be okay, Taleah. I'm not too worried yet."

"But I am! Worried that I'll lose you. I don't want that to happen," she cried. "I just found you. Promise that you won't ever leave me."

Hating the pain he'd heard in Taleah's voice, Lorenz knew that he had to convince her that he wasn't going anywhere. He would marry her over and over again, as many times as it took to make it legal. He prayed hard that this horrendous situation could be resolved easily, quietly, and quickly. He and Taleah wanted desperately to get on with their lives as husband and wife. Although he couldn't understand what his estranged wife could possibly gain by contesting the divorce, he knew she was enjoying putting him through this hell.

It was obvious that she didn't want him, but it appeared as if she didn't want anyone else to have him either. He had hoped that she didn't find out from his mother that he'd remarried. But if his lawyer had contacted his mother, she would know the situation and would know not to say a word about it. He had planned to tell his estranged wife about remarrying but not until after he'd received the final dissolution decree.

Lorenz now wished he hadn't married Taleah until after he'd received all the paperwork, despite the fact he'd been assured by his lawyer that everything was in order. He hated putting her through this nightmare. She didn't deserve to have her first days of marriage suffer so many unsavory complications. Taleah had been so excited and happy to become his wife.

Taleah's anguished cries came suddenly and softly.

She had tried to hold up, had now failed at it. The realization that she was not legally married to Lorenz had overwhelmed her. Thinking about how everyone would react to this situation if they ever found out was daunting. Everyone concerned would be brokenhearted. None would ever be more brokenhearted than she and Lorenz. Their bitter disappointment ran soul deep.

All Taleah wanted to do right now was to make love to Lorenz, whom she could no longer refer to as her husband, hoping it would somehow ease the torturous pain. She desperately wanted to lose herself inside their passion.

Taleah's hand reached up and caressed his face. "Please make love to me, Lorenz. Please. I need to feel you inside me. I need you so much."

Wanting her every bit as much as she wanted him, Lorenz instantly, hungrily took possession of Taleah's mouth with his own. Convincing her that he'd never leave her was first and foremost.

No matter what any piece of paper said, legal or otherwise, Taleah was his wife in every way. Their spirits and souls were linked together in an unbreakable bond; their hearts were fused as one. This would be all over in due time. Lorenz had to believe that, had to hold on to that belief with all his might. God would make this situation right. He undoubtedly knew that because God hadn't failed him yet—and Lorenz didn't expect Him to start now.

Awakening in the middle of the night, tortured by the worst nightmare she'd ever had, Taleah stifled the screams welling up in her throat. Her trembling was nearly uncontrollable. Before she could awaken Lorenz she had to calm down. She didn't want him to see her so shook-up. Taleah's night-mare included a ghastly scene of Lorenz telling her that she had to leave Japan right away. The worst part of the dream was when he'd told her that he had decided against divorcing his wife, that he had make a big mistake by asking her to marry him in the first place.

Taleah slowly inched her way out of the bed, doing her best not to disturb Lorenz. Once she was upon her feet, she slowly headed for the bath-room. Unable to dam up the flowing tears, she just let them fall. Taleah felt sick inside. If Lorenz didn't already know how badly she was hurting, she didn't want him to find out. He already had enough to deal with. With sickness churning inside her stom-ach, Taleah wet a washcloth and then held it up to her face. She couldn't help wishing this ordeal was only a doubly bad dream, but she knew better. This was for real.

All she could do now was pray for her and Lorenz to have a happy ending.

Eleven

Lieutenant Colonel Zurich Kingdom, an officer and a gentleman, was extremely handsome. His sienna-brown eyes were a perfect complement to his sun-bronzed complexion. Thirty-six years old, with a hulking, athletic physique, Zurich stood a proud six-feet-plus.

His private office housed inside the weather squadron unit he commanded was as neat as a pin. Not so much as a paper clip was out of place. Numerous educational and award certificates hung on the walls in strong wooden frames. Several model air force planes were displayed on a large corner table. A stunning picture of him and his beautiful wife, clad in full military dress, sat atop his desk. The silver bars she wore on her shoulders represented the rank of first lieutenant.

Master Sergeant Lorenz Hampton and his newly appointed commander, Zurich, quickly got all the formal and not so formal greetings out of the way before they settled down to business. Lorenz had had the base tailor sew onto his uniform his new master sergeant stripes soon after returning from his TDY to California. Five months prior to coming to Japan, Zurich had been promoted from major to lieutenant colonel.

Lorenz found it much easier to talk with Zurich than with his last commander, though they'd also had a great rapport. But what Lorenz had to tell Zurich was so emotionally charged that someone who didn't know him on a personal and social basis might not understand his state of mind. It was a difficult situation to have to explain to anyone.

Lorenz was a military man first, always showing his strength and pride, but he was terribly passionate and emotion filled regarding matters of the heart. When it came to Taleah, Lorenz had a wide-open heart, and his sensitivity toward her was quite obvious. Seeing Taleah hurt was like having a dagger shoved into his stomach.

As Zurich was an old friend of his, Lorenz could relax with him and relate to him on a more personal level. At Buckley Academy Lorenz was never an integral part of the group often referred to as the fabulous four, Zurich Kingdom, Haughton Storm, Neal Allen, and Nelson Wainwright, but he had built a special friendship with each of the guys. The four best friends were all into playing multiple sports, but Lorenz only played basketball; he was one of the best guards to come out of the prestigious Dallas prep school.

Lorenz's anguish was apparent as he told Zurich every minute detail of what had happened with him and Taleah. He then spoke about the grim situation he was now faced with. Lorenz had to be brave for both himself and Taleah, since she had no idea of the enormity of the situation that had been visited upon them. She hadn't fared very well over the last twenty-four hours and he was gravely concerned about her. Taleah wasn't eating or sleeping properly.

Zurich shook his head. "This past year has been one hell of a humdinger for quite a few of us Buckley Academy jocks. Haughton, Neal, Nelson, and I have also had our share of megadrama. Welcome to the military drama club, my brother. Lorenz, I agree that you're in a tough situation, but I don't see it as insurmountable. Here's what I think you should do."

Zurich went on to explain in depth his point of view to Lorenz, giving his old friend the best advice possible. Zurich was mindful that he was wearing two hats. He saw the situation Lorenz was in as both personal and professional. As Lorenz's commander, he had to be careful not to show bias. As his friend, Zurich had to stand behind Lorenz, but he had to do it in a way that wouldn't jeopardize either of their careers.

Lorenz listened intently to every word Zurich spoke. Though he was making good sense, Lorenz was still somewhat worried. To simply do nothing didn't seem to him as if it were the greatest game plan to use, but it would keep Taleah in the country.

"What do you think, Sergeant Hampton?"

Lorenz leaned forward in his chair. "Despite my concerns, I think I have no choice but to go for it. Keeping Taleah here with me is very important. The embarrassment she'd have to face if she had to go home isn't something I want to see her go through. How do you go home and tell your family and friends that your marriage was just a sham, that the man you married was still married to his first wife? I don't know if she could handle that or the possibility of being forced to leave Japan alone."

Zurich stroked his chin. "Are you concerned about your reputation with her family or the embarrassment and pain she might have to suffer by leaving?"

Lorenz was taken aback by the question for a brief moment. He then gave the pointed query a few moments of thought. "I guess that's a fair question. I hadn't thought about it before now. What her family thinks of me is very important. But I would take all the family's wrath if it meant sparing Taleah. This wasn't a malicious act on my part. I went ahead and married her on the advice of my attorney. I never dreamed something like this would happen. But I feel totally responsible for this mess we're in."

"If Taleah can stay healthy, you two can manage everything else. Not being able to get medical care for her is the biggest immediate concern I have. You can do the grocery shopping and pick up whatever she may need from the BX. She can still work as a civilian, which might keep her from feeling like she's on lockdown. As your guest, Taleah can get into the majority of the other base facilities. You're not into the government for a single dime thus far, especially since she hasn't had to use her temporary ID card for medical or dental services. If the divorce is going to be final at the end of next month, we're not talking about a long time here. This matter should be resolved very soon."

"What about base housing?"

"What about it? They're taking your quarters allowance for it. You're paying to live there. I understand that all this is rather mind-boggling, but you have to sit down and weigh things out rationally, Lorenz. The fact that this is going to be over soon is the main reason why I'm encouraging you to hold on and wait on this matter to resolve itself.

Once you have the divorce decree in your hands, you two can get married by an official at the U.S. embassy. Taleah can then be issued a permanent ID card."

"All of what you've said makes perfect sense to me. I admit that I've been too emotionally involved to think everything through with a clear head. Although we have to get the annulment first, Zurich, I'm feeling more optimistic now."

"Glad to hear it. As for the other matter, I can get from the legal office a host country attorney referral for you. He or she can probably handle the annulment for you guys from here. That may be the only cost you'll have to incur." Zurich reared back in his chair. "Now let's get into something pleasant. We can start by you telling me all about Taleah. By the way, the other part of our conversation never happened."

Lorenz acknowledged Zurich's statement with a curt nod. Then a wide grin spread over his face. "Taleah is an incredible woman, both beautiful and intelligent. This girl has a gold medal for a heart." Lorenz then told Zurich how he and Taleah had come to meet and how they'd instantly fallen head over hills in love. Lorenz's love for Taleah was written boldly upon his face. His eyes carried the look of a man deeply in love.

Zurich smiled at how familiar Lorenz's story sounded to him. "Your experience sounds a lot like what happened with Hailey and me. She and I went through a lot of scary drama as well. An officer and an NCO involved in a love affair is against the rules, as you very well know."

"How'd you manage to handle that serious situation?"

"I married her before it could become an issue, though she had become an officer at the time.

There were a few questions thrown at me when the 'powers that be' found out about our marriage. I did just as you've done here today. I was honest with my commander. Hailey and I fell and love and got seriously involved before even knowing we were both in the military. It could've been disastrous for both our careers, but I had a great commander. He was as sympathetic to my situation as I am to yours."

"Thanks, Zurich. I'd love for you to meet Taleah and we'd love to meet Hailey. When do you think we can all get together for dinner at our place? I'd be happy to burn you some ribs."

"Oh, man, that would be a real treat. Meeting Taleah and eating your ribs are going to be two awesome experiences. When we get together, the guys always mention how delicious the ribs were that you used to cook for us. We missed you at the last reunion."

"I couldn't make it, though I tried. It's been a while since I've seen everyone at one time. I was surprised to see Mark in California. We had a great reunion."

"I'm sure you're grateful to him, since he introduced you to Taleah. How are Mark and his wife doing? I haven't seen Mark in umpteen years."

"Mark is fine; still the macho man. He's been assigned to Germany, Ramstein."

"I'd love to see old Mark again. He was a riot. About us getting together, we can do so as soon as Hailey gets back from her TDY. She's in Virginia, at Langley. Hailey is also a great woman. She makes me laugh like I've never laughed before. The girl has me sprung. Make no mistake about it. As the daughter of a meteorologist, the sister knows her weather, too. It drives my mother-in-law insane when all the weather nuts are under her roof at the same time. I guess you can imagine the conversations. I never thought I'd get married while still in the military."

"Yeah, I remember you swearing off marriage, period. But that was back in the day."

"This job has been my wife, my life for a very long time, Lorenz. But having someone that understands firsthand the commitment and sacrifices that have to be made in serving your country makes it so much easier to be married. Hailey is just as committed to the air force as I am. Our marriage is clicking on all cylinders."

"It sounds as if you two are happy, Zurich."

"Oh, yeah! We're an extremely happy couple. Love at first sight. Who would ever have thought that crazy emotion could happen to both of our military-hardened hearts? Our other boys have been bitten hard too. Neal and Haughton are both with women they'd known for a long time but had been separated from through time and circumstances. It seems like Cupid's arrow struck all of us around the same time frame."

"Man, my heart was gone before I knew it. Taleah and I had this spiritual connection thing going on from the very start. We think so much alike it's uncanny at times. We were happy until this latest drama came into play. I realize I'm going to have to give Taleah time to get used to us not being legally married. She says she still wants to marry me once everything is settled, but I'll just have to wait and see. She's beginning to take it hard now that reality has sunk in. I just hope that she doesn't change her mind, but it wouldn't surprise me under the circumstances. This has been so tough. For such a strong person, she seems to be cracking under the pressure."

"We can't have that. As soon as Hailey gets back,

I'll have her contact Taleah. With the relationship complications in common, those two will probably hit it off just fine. Hailey can certainly help her get over some of the rougher spots, since she's also been through a trying relationship ordeal. We'll also keep close tabs on Taleah when you go back to the States."

Lorenz got to his feet and extended his hand to Zurich. "I can't thank you enough, man. Good having you here in Japan. I'm already hearing great things about you from some of the other guys. You've always been commander material. Since I wasn't here when you first arrived, welcome aboard, Lieutenant Colonel Kingdom."

"Thank you, Master Sergeant Hampton. Thanks also for the kind and encouraging remarks. We'll see each other around the office. Looking forward to meeting Taleah. I can't leave out getting a taste of those mouthwatering ribs again."

Lorenz grinned. "You'll have them, sir. Have a great day."

In the quiet of the evening, all settled comfortably in bed, Taleah set her novel aside. Since she was home alone, Taleah thought this was as good a time as any for reflection. Lorenz was at the base gym playing in a basketball game. He had invited her to come along, as he always did, but she had opted out. Time alone would help her sort some things out. The past couple of weeks had been grueling. Being involved with a military man was harder than she'd imagined. Their home phone rang constantly from calls coming in after his normal duty hours and it seemed that he was always on some sort of base alert.

As the acting first sergeant of his unit, Lorenz

was called on all during the night and on weekends to handle the ever-present problems that had
a tendency to arise on a daily basis. The things
needing immediate attention ran the gamut, from
minor issues to quite serious ones. Twice in one
week he'd had to go out in the middle of the night
to counsel a couple of his troops who'd gotten
themselves involved in volatile domestic disputes.
His duties seemed never-ending.

Although Lorenz had explained all that to her
beforehand, Taleah hadn't understood the full
meaning of things. Not until she found herself
smack dab in the middle of so many crises that
were his duty to attend to. He had no choice but to
stand ready when duty called.

Being thousands of miles from home would be
scary if it weren't for Lorenz. Taleah felt safe with
him. But was she secure? Each word had a separate
meaning. He would protect her, fiercely. Never
would he wittingly allow anything to happen to her.
Yes, she felt secure with him as a man. But her security with him as her husband was no longer a
certainty. He hadn't yet been able to secure their
future, which delicately hung in the balance. Did
they love each other? Undoubtedly.

As of late Taleah had even become fearful of
making love to Lorenz. Without explanation, she
had thwarted his sexual advances over the past few
days. Conceiving a child amidst this turmoil was
not the smartest thing for her to let happen. He
could use condoms, but they were no more fool-
proof than any other method of birth control. She
was grateful that she had gotten a three-month sup-
ply of her contraceptives before leaving the States,
but they still weren't a guarantee against pregnancy.
No prescription meds of any kind were available to
her without the ID card. It was an unsettling feel-

ing to know that if you got sick you couldn't seek medical attention. Taleah thanked God for her excellent health.

Taleah was no prude, but it no longer felt right for her to share a bed with the man who wasn't legally her husband. Although she had wanted to make love to Lorenz before the wedding even occurred, she still wasn't feeling too good about her present living arrangements. She had never lived with any man before; she recalled with crystal clarity telling Lorenz that she'd never come to Japan just to live with him, that she didn't cohabit with the opposite sex.

All in all, Lorenz was a wonderful human being. Outside of his team sports activities, she was amazed that he'd never once mentioned wanting a night out with the boys. A lot of the airmen stopped off at the club before going home, but Lorenz hadn't done so thus far. That he didn't drink very much could be the reason for that, but some guys just liked to stop at the club to shoot the breeze with their friends and coworkers.

Every Friday she received a beautiful bouquet of flowers from Lorenz. He also called her several times a day during his workweek; as soon as the workday was over he hightailed it straight home to her arms. There were many days during the week that he came home for lunch just to eat with her. She was aware that things were often like that in the beginning of a relationship or a marriage, but she felt that Lorenz was the one man who'd be all things to her.

Taleah loved Lorenz with all her heart and soul, but she wasn't sure that she could continue living with him. There were only a few weeks left before he returned to the States for court, so she had to make up her mind about her future with Lorenz rather quickly. Staying in this relationship under the present circumstances wasn't something she favored. Before giving it a lot of thought, she had believed she could handle it. If she were to decide otherwise, the hardest part of all would be explaining her final decision to Lorenz. Causing him even an ounce of pain wasn't something she'd stomach with ease. Both she and Lorenz had been hurt enough.

Taleah had only been in Japan a few weeks, which wasn't enough time to make a full assessment of what life would really be like with Lorenz. But she had a feeling that he would be as perfect a husband as possible. She missed her parents badly. Unable to pick up and call them at any moment of the day was also hard for her. She couldn't remember a day ever going by that she hadn't spoken with Jack and Allison over the telephone.

International long-distance charges could be a bear if you talked longer than a few minutes. Every now and then Lorenz had one of his military base operator buddies put a call through to the States for them through a special routing number. Those calls were always short and sweet. Taleah had never even imagined not living in the same city as her parents. That alone had been a real challenge for her. Being with Lorenz helped to ease the pain of missing her parents and friends so much. The letters from home were a huge comfort to her, especially those from Jared. It had been hard for her not to confide in him in her letters, but she thought it best not to say anything to anyone unless she had to.

If only this messy situation hadn't occurred, she mused with regret. She and Lorenz would be happier than two bugs in a rug if this madness hadn't happened. Of that she was sure.

The night of their honeymoon came to mind and she smiled brilliantly. Lorenz was a patient lover. He had sensed her anxiety about making love to him for the first time. He'd had no problem guiding her through their first sexual encounter. The physical side of their relationship was unbelievably incredible. Each time was always better than the last. She had grown comfortable with him rather quickly.

Lorenz was also secure within himself. That was another thing she loved about him. A very confident man, he knew exactly who he was. How he'd handled the incident with the photo board had been admirable. Taleah had come to understand that he really hadn't believed the pictures would bother her. Although he'd said that he would've been jealous if the circumstances had been reversed, she now didn't think he would have come close to reacting the way she had. He wouldn't have been threatened by what was over or by what or who had been in her past. His knowledge of self was another incredible thing she admired about him.

In thinking all of this through, while reflecting on everything that had thus far occurred in their relationship, making up her mind about what to do was going to be even harder. Though she'd come to no final decision, she had come to realize that leaving Lorenz would be hard indeed. Her love for him was deeper than anything she'd ever experienced. Before picking up her novel, Taleah threw up a silent supplication. God would tell her exactly what she should do.

Lorenz rushed home only to find Taleah fast asleep. Much to his dismay, she had fallen asleep in one of the guest bedrooms. He didn't know exactly why she'd gone into one of those rooms in the first place, but he had a pretty good idea. Taleah hadn't been in the mood for lovemaking over the past several days, but Lorenz suspected that the problem went much deeper than any lack of desire. The fact that they weren't legally married was more than likely the root cause. Taleah hadn't pulled any punches regarding how she felt about cohabiting with a man she was romantically involved with. No matter how he summed it up, or what he thought of it as, they were living together out of wedlock. Her discomfort with their present situation was no secret. Taleah had married him believing she was getting one thing, only to end up with something totally different—and that which she hadn't bargained for.

Deciding to let Taleah sleep, Lorenz went off to take a shower. He'd worked off a lot of his aggression and frustration on the basketball court, but what was he to do with his pent-up passion and his dire need for her? Distance was starting to settle in between them, uncomfortably so. He feared that the gap might very well widen. That Taleah might be considering leaving him caused him considerable grief yet he understood. He quickly made up his mind not to try and change hers if she came to that end. He wouldn't try to pressure her into staying. No coercion whatsoever would come from him. To leave him or to stay would have to be her decision.

Surprised to find Taleah standing outside the bathroom door when he exited, Lorenz could only stand there and stare at her. Clad only in one of his long-sleeved shirts, she looked beautiful. It was his guess that she wore no other article of clothing beneath the shirt, since there was no evidence of such. As Taleah wended her arms about his neck, the towel he wore around his waist fell to the floor. She immediately reached down and picked up the towel.

Looking into his eyes, Taleah wrapped back around his waist the large white bath sheet and then tucked it in. "Can we talk over a cup of hot tea, Lorenz?"

Talking about their dilemma wasn't something he wanted to do tonight, but only because he feared what Taleah might have to say. Prolonging the agony wasn't going to make things any easier for him, but Lorenz didn't think he could stand to hear any more bad news. That she hadn't asked him who'd won the basketball game was another indication of her mood.

He stroked her cheek with the back of hand. "Is it something that can wait until the morning, Taleah?"

Disappointed by his response, Taleah bit down on her lower lip. "I guess it can wait. Too tired, huh?"

"Extremely tired but not sleepy yet. I had planned to eat something before I went to bed, but I don't have much of an appetite right now. I'm normally starving after a hard game. But that doesn't seem to be the case tonight."

Taleah clearly sensed that Lorenz wasn't in the right frame of mind to deal with anything that had to do with their dilemma. With that in mind, she stood on her tiptoes and kissed him on the cheek. "You'd better get dressed before you catch a cold. Flu season is in, you know." Feeling downright dejected and rejected, Taleah turned and walked back toward the guest room.

Lorenz cursed himself under his breath. How could he have even thought of making her wait until tomorrow to talk to him when her chaotic state was so evident? "Taleah, wait."

Taleah turned halfway around and looked back at him. "What's up, Lorenz?"

"I'll talk with you as soon as I slip on my robe. Do you still want that tea?"

Wondering what had made him change his mind, Taleah shook her head in the negative. That Lorenz really didn't want to get into any tough issues tonight was obvious to her. "We'll talk in the morning, when we're both more rested." Without uttering another word, Taleah went on down the hall and entered the guest room.

Lorenz mentally scolded himself for thinking of his feelings over hers. She had been home alone all evening, which had given her plenty of time to reflect on all the events of days past. Taleah had had something specific on her mind when she'd asked him to talk with her. The least he could've done was to hear her out. That she'd gone back into the guest room let him know he'd be sleeping alone tonight. Another sleepless night wouldn't come as a surprise to him.

Clad only in pajama bottoms and a white T-shirt, Lorenz slipped into the room where Taleah had chosen to sleep. His heart skipped a beat at the sight of her. She was all curled up in a fetal position, looking like a live baby doll, gazing up at the wall. The only lighting in the room came from a small lamp powered by a soft white low-wattage bulb.

It bothered Lorenz that Taleah hadn't yet looked

his way. He was positive she'd heard the door opening. "Hey, baby, are you okay?"

"I'm just fine," she responded, keeping her eyes trained on the wall.

"Okay, Taleah, I blew it, didn't I? I'm sorry I rejected your suggestion of talking. I'm really fearful of what you have to say."

Finally deciding to make eye contact with him, Taleah sat up in the bed. "Why's that?"

"Taleah, I came home and found you asleep in the guest bedroom. If you hadn't come to some final decision about our future, I can't think of any other reason why'd you be in this particular room and not in ours. I have no clue as to why you moved out of our bedroom."

"Who said I moved out? Isn't it possible that I came in here just to lie down?"

Lorenz let out a frustrated sigh. "Let's not play games, Taleah. You've never come in here before to rest." He came over to her and sat down on the side of the bed. "Let me try a different approach here. Why are you in this room instead of in ours?"

Taleah's fingers worried the lace on the pillow slip, nervous about Lorenz's right-to-the-point question. "I guess I need to go ahead and spell it out. I don't like our living arrangements. I think I should go back to the States. I'm not happy or content with our present situation."

Agitated now, Lorenz raised an eyebrow. "And you think I am?"

"Are we going to argue about this or talk it through like adults?"

"I only asked a simple question, Taleah. It wasn't meant to be argumentative."

"It wasn't the question, Lorenz. It was your tone of voice."

"Sorry about my tone. If you really think you should leave Japan, I'll support your decision, Taleah. I won't try to change your mind. Just tell me what you want to do."

"Just like that, huh? Is it that simple for you?"

Disliking the direction their conversation was heading, Lorenz wrung his hands together to ease the anguish. For someone who'd just asked a question about an argument, Taleah was sure trying to get one going, or so it seemed to him. "None of this is simple, baby. I know you're not happy and content here. I feel your discontent. I just don't know what I can do about it. I can't make you comfortable with what you're clearly not at ease with."

"You're right, Lorenz. It's up to me to come to terms with what's been happening. But it's not just the marriage situation. I think I'm in too deep with something I really don't understand. I don't think I can be a good military wife. I hate it when you're gone so much, especially when they call you out in the middle of the night. Maybe our illegal marriage is a blessing in disguise. Perhaps I needed to experience a taste of this life to be able to make a sound determination. I don't know if I'm cut out for this lifestyle. I'm beginning to believe my heart is not as fearless as it needs to be."

Where before had he heard similar words? *"Military life is not for me. I need to be around my family. I can't stand living overseas. I hate you being gone so much and never knowing when they're going to ship you off to some desolate, godforsaken place."*

Lorenz had heard those types of comments practically every single day, starting shortly after they'd gotten married. His estranged wife had worn into the ground her constant messages of unhappiness and discontent. Her bitter nagging about his military career had often been without cessation. He could now admit what he couldn't admit to himself back then. He had actually felt relieved when she'd finally made the decision to pack up and leave him. She had ended what he hadn't been able to bring to a close for fear of devastating both her and Amir. He was the one who'd ended up distressed. Now it looked as if history was about to repeat itself.

Would he be relieved to see Taleah go? *Not for a second, not in a million years.* How was a man to find peace devoid of his soul? A man without his spirit was simply a dead man. She had taken up permanent residence inside his heart. Their souls and spirits were eternally entwined. She was in his blood to stay. Taleah lived in every vital part of him. How was he to live without her? He didn't want to live a single minute without her, but the choice wasn't his to make.

"Do you want me to try and book you a ticket right away, Taleah? Or do you want to wait and fly back to the States with me? We'll only go as far as San Francisco together. That's where we'll catch our connecting flights to L.A. and Hartford."

"Right away works for me, Lorenz. The sooner the better."

Twelve

Within a few minutes of being introduced to one another, Taleah and Hailey Hamilton-Kingdom began carrying on a conversation as if they were lifelong friends. Taleah was still fascinated with the fact that Hailey was a first lieutenant in the air force, never dreaming that a female airman could be so pretty and delicate. Hailey also wore striking fashionable civilian clothing, giving her the ordinary girl-next-door appearance. Taleah had always imagined women in the armed forces as being big, strong, and rough and tough both inside and out. It was hard for Taleah to conjure up an image of Hailey going through the rigors of basic training or the dangers of engaging in hand-to-hand combat.

The two women continued their conversation while handling the final dinner preparations. Hailey had jumped right in to help Taleah set the table and fill the drinking glasses with ice. Taleah had wanted to make potato salad to go with the meal, but Lorenz had already made tuna-macaroni salad before she'd even gotten out of bed. It frustrated her that he didn't leave her much to do around the house. She wasn't sure what, if anything, it had to do with. She often wondered if Lorenz thought her incapable. On the other hand, she got the sense that he just loved to cook and clean up around the house. He *was* a product of southern parents.

Lorenz and Zurich were out on the back patio, where Lorenz was keeping a close eye on his prize beef and pork ribs and his much-praised barbe-cued chicken. This would be Taleah's first time to taste the ribs she'd heard so many raving reviews about from Mark and others.

"How's it going for you as a brand-new military wife, Taleah?"

Taleah was careful not to show any dismay regarding the subject matter. *Military wife* was the only job she'd ever applied for that she felt totally inadequate where executing the duties of her job description was concerned. As of late, Taleah often felt like she'd just jumped out of a plane, only to learn that her trusty parachute wouldn't open up.

Taleah's laughter sounded forced. "I'm afraid I'm still learning the job description, Hailey. It's not an easy assignment by any stretch of the imagi-nation. How do you manage to have a career in the service and be a military spouse, all at the same time?"

"The only plausible answer is that I love both my career choice and I revel in my wifely duties as Mrs. Zurich Kingdom. As with any newlyweds, there are bound to be a few challenges. Being married to a service man can make those same challenges seem doubly hard. Making sure we get assignments on the same base is one of our biggest challenges. Being together at all was our hardest challenge ever. I guess Lorenz has told you about all the difficulties we had in the beginning of our relationship."

"Yeah, he has mentioned it. I'd never even heard of 'fraternization' before that. I think I'd rather have that problem versus the current issues Lorenz and I are faced with. This problem of ours seems insurmountable at times. I find myself getting totally lost in it. Since Lorenz has talked to Zurich about it, I'm sure you have some idea of what I'm talking about."

"In this case, yes, I do. Zurich has never told me anything about his troop's private issues. He's duty-bound not to. That Lorenz is his friend and Zurich wanted us to give you guys our support is the only reason he shared your story with me. He also had Lorenz's permission to do so. You don't have to worry about us discussing your private affairs with anyone but you two. I want you to know I'm here for you whenever you need me. It's tough being far away from home without a support system. You and Lorenz will have that in us. Military families are pretty much there for each other. We have a tendency to pull together, especially when living overseas."

"Thanks, Hailey. Knowing I have your support means a lot to me." Taleah suddenly caught a glimpse of Lorenz though the sliding glass door. "Looks like the meat is ready. At least, that's what I think Lorenz's waving gesture means. Let's put the rest of the food out."

Ten minutes later the two couples sat down in the dining room to the informal meal the Hamptons had prepared in honor of their dinner guests, the Kingdoms. One look at Zurich's face, as he bit into one of the juicy ribs, was enough to let Lorenz know he'd once again attained cooking perfection. Taleah's and Hailey's delightful moans of appreciation put a smile on his face.

Once the dessert was devoured, peach cobbler baked by Lorenz, the two couples retired to the living room, where Taleah and Lorenz served coffee and hot tea.

Zurich put his arm around Hailey, kissing her softly on the mouth. "Hailey and I have some good news. We'd like to share it with you." His hand went to his wife's stomach, massaging it tenderly. "We're expecting a baby!"

Beyond excited for the future parents, who looked so elated, Taleah clapped her hands at the same time Lorenz shouted out his hearty congratulations. For the rest of the evening the two animated couples engaged in a zealous "baby talk" discussion.

Instead of using the dishwasher, Taleah and Hailey had opted to do the dinnerware by hand. Taleah handled the dishwashing while Hailey took care of drying off everything with a thick terry cloth towel. Once dried, the dishes were then stacked on the kitchen counter for Lorenz to put away later.

Taleah handled Hailey a dinner plate. "How do you and Zurich handle the chores around your house?"

Hailey shrugged with nonchalance. "We share the duties for the most part, but that can vary depending on the situation. Whoever gets home first starts dinner. If we're going to eat out, we normally make that decision before leaving for work. Zurich takes care of all the big jobs around the house, like scrubbing the floors and keeping the bathrooms clean. We each handle our own personal laundry, but Zurich usually changes the beds and washes the bedclothes. He also runs the vacuum. I get the feeling you have a specific reason for asking. Am I right?"

Taleah's laughter was a little shaky. "Yeah, Hailey, you are dead right. I honestly want to take care of Lorenz and our house, but he doesn't give me much of a chance to accomplish either. He does everything around here. A lot of it gets done before I even get out of bed. When I do take the initiative to tackle some of the lighter chores, I almost have to muscle him out of the way to do it. He either loves doing everything himself or he doesn't think I can do it good enough. What do you think? Could it be that I'm making too much of this?"

Laughing, Hailey shook her head. "Do you know how many sisters out there would love to have your problem? I've had some of my females friends tell me they can't even get their man to pick up his dirty clothes and put them in the hamper. It may be his military training or it could be the fact that he's been by himself for the past four years. If the latter is the case, he hasn't had anyone to handle the chores for him. It may also have everything to do with his upbringing. My mother-in-law taught all her boys to be self-sufficient. Zurich, Zaire, and Zane Kingdom can all cook and clean. They each know how to do more than just get by. Bernice Kingdom taught her sons everything she knew about cooking and cleaning."

"I hadn't thought of most of those things, except for the military training. It seems that you and Zurich have all your domestic issues worked out. I think I just need to come right out and ask Lorenz why he doesn't want me to do the chores. I'm sure he'll be honest with me."

"I think so, too. Getting it out in the open will at

least get your questions answered. As for Zurich and me having it all worked out, not everything. He's a neat freak and I'm not so neat. It drives me wild when he picks up after me, especially when I'm not through with the item. He hates to have anything out of place, so he jumps on it the minute he sees something amiss."

Taleah howled. "You and Zurich, too? Lorenz and I go through that also. At least I don't feel so alone anymore in this."

"Feel alone in what?" Lorenz asked, entering the kitchen with Zurich right behind him.

Taleah stifled a giggle. "It's nothing, Lorenz. Just girl talk."

Zurich chuckled. "That means they were talking about us, man. Now I know why my ears were burning like crazy." Zurich pulled Hailey into his arms, pressing his lips into her forehead. "You been out here dissing me to Taleah, girl?"

"Who, me? No, I've had nothing but wonderful things to say about you, Commander."

Everyone laughed at Hailey's comical expression. Once the laughter died down, Zurich regrettably announced his and Hailey's imminent departure. Early morning duty was cited.

Lorenz sat on the edge of the metal chair looking grim-faced as he consulted with the female ticket agent at the base's Tickets and Tours Office. This was the last place he wanted to be. The agent had just finished going over the various airfares with him, none of which were cheap. Buying Taleah a return ticket to the States was the last thing he wanted to be doing. Taleah hadn't said a word since they'd first sat down, other than to politely greet the agent. Lorenz had never seen her as quiet as she'd been over the past few days; it worried him.

"Sergeant Hampton, I'm sorry I can't offer you a better discount on the one-way ticket," the agent mentioned. "I could've done a slightly better fare with a round-trip purchase. Last-minute tickets are always grossly overpriced. Have you made a final decision on the time and date you'd like to travel?"

"The tickets are actually for my wife . . . Taleah here," he quickly corrected himself.

The agent looked a bit confused as her eyes darted from Lorenz to Taleah.

Taleah suddenly came out of her trancelike state and covered Lorenz's hand with her own. "Can I please speak to you in private, Lorenz?"

"Without question." Lorenz got up out of his seat and guided Taleah out of earshot of the agent. "What's your mind, Miss Taleah?"

Taleah shuffled her feet, looking as if she might be a tad embarrassed. "Is it okay for me to change my mind about leaving, Lorenz? If so, I want to stay here in Japan."

Lorenz was stunned but thrilled. His sudden euphoria died just as quickly as it had come upon him. "What has changed your mind?" He had an idea that her change of heart might have come from the enormous cost of the ticket. He wished the change had only to do with her love for him.

Taleah nervously cleared her throat. "I don't think I've given us a fair chance, Lorenz. I may've been using the divorce issue as an excuse to bail out on you, when my restlessness is based solely on your busy work schedule. I admit to feeling a bit neglected by you. I thought we'd have more time to spend together. I've never been this alone before. I'm scared of my feelings of isolation becoming worse. I know your duty to your country has to come first, but I rather thought I'd be number one the majority of the time." The support from and the newly acquired friendship of one Hailey Hamilton had also had a tremendous impact on her decision.

Lorenz wanted desperately to take Taleah into his arms and kiss her until they were both panting for air. Knowing that the agent was waiting on them to make a decision kept him from acting on his impulse. "Hold your next thought, Taleah. Stay put. I'll be right back." Lorenz walked back to the desk and told the agent there had been a last-minute change in plans.

Lorenz couldn't whisk Taleah out of the Tickets and Tours Office fast enough. He was still astonished that she'd had a sudden change of heart. A quiet, romantic dinner at the Yokota Air Base Club would give them a chance to talk things through, without the worry or hassle of preparing the meal.

The moment they reached the outdoors Taleah turned to face Lorenz. "I want to stay here because I sincerely love you, Lorenz. Our relationship is worthy of us putting our every effort into it. However, I'd prefer to move into the guest room until we're free to resume our lives as husband and wife. Will you be okay with that?"

Lorenz rubbed Taleah's shoulders in a soothing manner. "Baby, I always want you to sleep right next to me, but I'm willing to concede to the temporary arrangements. They *are* only temporary. It's going to be tough as nails not to sleep in the same bed with you, but if it means keeping you here in Japan you can sleep anywhere you want."

Taleah laid her head against Lorenz's broad chest, inhaling the lemony scent of his captivating aftershave. "You are the best man, Lorenz. What if we eat at the club tonight? We can talk over dinner, without the bother of cooking it."

Lorenz busted up laughing. They were still in tune with each other, still on the very same wavelength. Their thoughts often ran on the same parallel.

Taleah eyed him curiously. "What's so funny?"

"I'm only laughing at how much we think alike. I also thought of going to the club for dinner. You see what I mean?"

Taleah laughed at the revelation. "Perfectly. We've always been tuned in like that. We're so inside each other's heads it's almost laughable." Taleah's expression grew soft and her eyes suddenly became moist. "Thanks for letting me stay, Lorenz. Had you turned me down I don't think I could've handled it."

Lorenz brought Taleah to him. "I should be thanking you. Since we're both so happy with your decision to stay on and in our decision to give our love every possible effort, let's get our celebration on over a nice romantic candlelit dinner."

The club's formal dining room was elegantly appointed, dimly lit by chandelier lighting and softly glowing candlelight. Only sparsely populated with diners, with light jazz playing, the romantic aura made a lovely backdrop for couples in love, both single and married.

Taleah had changed into a cute, hot little black number and Lorenz had exchanged his denim jeans and polo shirt for dark dress slacks, dark jacket, and an open-collared cream-colored dress shirt. Taleah wore a hand-knitted sweater around her shoulders.

Yakatori, a Japanese dish consisting of stick-skewered meats cooked over an open grill, and served with a dipping sauce, had been served as an appetizer. The couple enjoyed an order of fried *gyoza*, a Japanese dumpling that could also be steamed. Chateaubriand for two, along with fresh-steamed vegetables, baked potatoes, and garden salad, were Taleah's and Lorenz's choices for their early evening meal. Cognac was poured over the beef before it was set afire. As this was her first time trying the delicious beef entree, the sight of the flaming meat excited Taleah.

The firelight in Taleah's eyes mesmerized Lorenz, making him feel all warm and fuzzy inside. Conversation was kept at a minimum as the couple enjoyed the superbly prepared meals, though they were barely able to take their eyes off each other. Taleah found it hard to believe that just a short time ago she had been all set to abandon their relationship because of her numerous fears.

In hopes of them working out all their issues, Taleah now felt secure in her decision to stay in the country. It was the only right thing for her to do. Going back home and facing the music with her family and friends would have been daunting, to say the least, but that wasn't the reason why she'd chosen to stay. Her deep abiding love for Lorenz had caused her change of heart. Taleah's shoulders felt much lighter since the weight of defeat had been lifted from them.

"Dessert, Taleah?"

"I'd like to save it for later, at home, since I've chosen you for my after-dinner treat."

Lorenz chuckled. "I can easily give in to becoming that."

Slightly embarrassed, Taleah lowered her lashes for a brief moment. "I probably shouldn't have gone there. It's so natural for me to flirt with you and desire you at the same time. Because I've opted to sleep in the guest room, I should play by my own rules."

"Are there rules, Taleah? If so, you'd better lay them out on the table for me. I don't want to go breaking them."

"Lorenz, I'm not a Goody Two-shoes, but there are some rules of conduct that are drilled into you while growing up, some that you can't ever seem to escape, things that you'd be loath to forget. There's always that little voice inside your head to steer you back on the right path, before and after you've gone astray."

"That doesn't mean we have to take all the fun out of our relationship, Taleah. There's not a thing wrong with flirting and tempting the hand of fate. It should come naturally for us. It's all a part of what happens between a man and woman who are lucky enough to find themselves deeply in love and physically attracted."

"You're right, as usual. Can you bear with me on the sleeping arrangements, Lorenz? Maybe it's some sort of endurance test for us. Are we capable of passing it?"

"Not only can we can pass, we can ace it, baby. Ready to go home?"

Taleah yawned involuntarily. "I'd say so. I'm a little tired, but will you dance with me before we go to bed?"

"Slow?"

Taleah gave Lorenz her brightest flirtatious smile. "Especially slow."

Dancing in Lorenz's arms allowed Taleah to relax even more. Listening to the old-school album *Rufasized* featuring Chaka Khan, now available on CD, gave Taleah goose bumps. She couldn't remember how many times her parents had played the album that they used to love so much. Taleah grew up on seventies music, loving it as much as her parents did, if not more. She and her siblings had the best times of their lives while watching Jack and Allison dancing all over the place. Every other year the Taylors threw a seventies party and invited all their friends from back in the day. It was always a blast from the past. The Taylors were still forever young.

Since both Taleah and Lorenz loved the music and the movies from the seventies, the couple had chosen several CDs to play from Lorenz's Chaka Khan, The Spinners, and The Iseley Brothers collection. When the cut "Sweet Thing" came on, Taleah whirled away from Lorenz and began lip-synching to the still very popular tune.

Taleah's tantalizing dance routine had Lorenz paying close attention to the swaying and subtle grinding of her hips. He was relieved to see her looking happier and content. He believed that her positive interaction with Hailey Hamilton-Kingdom was in part responsible for Taleah's peaceful state of mind. Joining in the fun, Lorenz began lip-synching to The Isley Brothers' "For the Love of You," another of the couple's favorite oldies.

It took only a few verses of the song for Taleah to realize that there was no place she'd rather be than with Lorenz. They already had a lot of memories to drift on and a lot more precious memories to create. Seeing Lorenz's divorce situation through to the end was the vow she'd recently made to their relationship. Lorenz deserved all the loyalty she could give him. Although she'd chosen to sleep in one of the guest rooms, her heart would rest wherever Lorenz's was; their hearts were entwined.

Taleah was tickled to death by Lorenz's singing

performance. This was so much fun for her. She'd nearly lost sight of what they had by letting her fears rule. She silently thanked God for showing her the light of day. Being more spiritual than religious, Taleah had no desire to fall out of favor with her Savior. Living with Lorenz under the present circumstances was against the laws of God. Her discomfort with their sleeping arrangements had everything to do with her spiritual beliefs despite the fact that she'd lost sight of them for a short time. That Lorenz understood where she was coming from made her decision much easier to execute without taking the drastic measures of leaving the country.

As Taleah dressed for bed, Lorenz came up behind her and then wrapped his arms around her waist. He buried his nose in her hair, inhaling deeply of the flower fresh scent. Taleah tilted her head back, resting it against his broad chest.

Lorenz kissed the tip of her ear. "Would it be too much for me to lie down beside you in here until you fall asleep? I promise to be a perfect gentleman."

Laughing softly, Taleah turned around and touched her forehead to his. "I'd love that. You've always been a gentleman with me. I'm not worried about that. Having you to hold me until I fall asleep sounds so sweet. Are you going to dress for bed first?"

"I had planned on it. Would you rather I keep my clothes on?"

Taleah laughed. "Of course not. You should make yourself comfortable." She then snapped her fingers. "I've got an idea that might work. Since there are twin beds in the other guest room, we can sleep in there together but in different beds."

"Does that mean I won't get to hold you?"

"Nothing about that has to change. Instead of you going into the other room after I go to sleep, you can just cross the room and get into the other bed." She suddenly looked downhearted. "Am I asking too much of you? I know sleeping in separate beds may seem juvenile to you, but I just want to do this by the book until we're legally married."

He brushed her hair back from her face. "I like your idea of us sharing the same room. That'll at least keep us close together. Separate beds can work for us for now."

"They certainly can. Why don't you go change while I shower and then brush my hair?"

Lorenz kissed Taleah lightly on the mouth. "Be back in a jiffy."

Once Taleah finished her nightly ritual of showering, cleansing and moisturizing her face, and brushing her hair out, only to tie it back in a ponytail, she went across the hall and loaded the CD changer with oldie tunes only, the one in the other spare bedroom. She then walked back into the bedroom where she'd been sleeping. Taleah hadn't yet broken the habit of falling asleep with music playing, doubted that she ever would. Music soothed her and allowed her to relax.

Lorenz reappeared in the doorway, smiling warmly at Taleah. "Want a cup of tea?"

"Only if you'll join me."

"I had exactly that in mind. Finish making yourself comfortable. I'll bring the tea into the room we're going to sleep in, along with a few white chocolate, macadamia nut cookies. Are you up for watching a movie?"

"Hmm, I'm glad I didn't have dessert at the club. Can't wait to bite into your freshly baked cookies. You are a man of many talents, Sergeant Hampton. A movie sounds good to me."

Taleah now wished she hadn't eaten the cookies. Her stomach had been hurting for the past hour or so. The pain wasn't tremendous, just enough dull aching to make her uncomfortable. She also felt slightly nauseated. The stomachache wasn't her only dilemma; Lorenz had fallen asleep. He was positioned on his side with his arm draped over her abdomen, making it impossible for her to move without waking him.

Wondering if she was being too silly about their sleeping arrangements, Taleah mentally checked herself. Why she had been making such a big deal over them sleeping apart was the first question she asked herself. Taleah gave the question a lot of thought. She already knew that it was a morals issue with her, but she soon discovered that her motivation also went much deeper than that.

Taleah was quite fearful of the impact it might have on her if they ended up not getting married. Not only would she have the serious worry of missing him emotionally, she'd have to deal with craving the physical side of their relationship as well. Although she'd decided to deal with their situation as it was, that didn't mean there weren't deep concerns. Getting pregnant had crossed her mind a few times.

Panic suddenly welled in Taleah as she thought about her nauseated stomach. Had she already conceived? That was too awful a subject to entertain, yet she delved right into it. She hadn't missed taking any of her birth control pills, but that wouldn't prove anything either way. Women on the pill got pregnant all the time.

Taleah then tried to recall the dates of her last cycle. Upon realizing her period wasn't late, she breathed a deep sigh of relief. Thinking about the possibility of getting pregnant before they were legally married caused Taleah to risk awakening Lorenz. Moving over to the other bed was the lesser of the two evils. He could go back to sleep, but if she ended up with child she couldn't ever go back. Not tempting the hand of fate was the best way to resolve that issue.

An hour after moving over to the other bed Taleah was still wide-awake. On the other hand, Lorenz was knocked out cold. Reading always helped her to relax. Instead of picking up a novel, she retrieved a couple of letters from off the nightstand.

Delighted to know that Sherra and Charlie were still happy and madly in love with each other made Taleah smile. She cherished the letters she received from her family and friends at home. It kept them close and helped to ease the pain of distance. Her parents and Jared wrote every week. Although the letters from her friends arrived with less frequency than those from her family, there was consistency. It was a pleasant surprise for her to receive three letters from home at the same time.

Jared wrote to her more than anyone. His letters spoke of missing her and barely being able to wait until he saw her again. He also wrote about his recent exciting encounter with a San Francisco socialite, which had him wondering if she might be Miss Perfect. Jared had also asked Taleah about coming to Japan to visit them within the next month or so. But with her and Lorenz's issues unresolved Taleah knew she'd have to put Jared off a bit longer. Otherwise, she'd have to explain their private matters, which she had no stomach for at the moment.

Brenda's version of her experiences with Joshua differed greatly from his. Brenda wrote about Joshua being really hard to get to know, while Joshua had told Taleah that he and Brenda were getting along famously. Joshua's letter said that he was flying down to L.A. to see Brenda on a regular basis, mostly on the weekends; Brenda had spoken of infrequent visits.

Since Joshua wasn't one to share too much of his private business with anyone, Taleah believed Brenda's account over her brother's. Joshua was never known to paint an exact picture of his encounters with others. There was one area where the couple's accounts were exactly the same; they were taking things very slow.

All of her girlfriends wrote mostly about the very same events, since they did a lot of things together. Each of them added pinches of their own spicy flavor to the spirited typewritten communications, along with interesting bits and pieces of comical drama. Just as Matthew, Mark, Luke, and John had recorded their individual accounts of their experiences with Jesus, Brenda, Sherra, and Drusilla were doing the same exact thing with Taleah.

A short time after reading the three letters at least twice each, Taleah felt that she might be able to fall off to sleep. She then turned off the bedside lamp and made herself comfortable. Upon closing her eyes, the heartfelt prayer for a brighter tomorrow was the low whisper that came from her lips.

Thirteen

After making it through the first series of interviews, Taleah thought her chance of landing the administrative assistant position in the medical clinic were looking real good. She had to have one more interview and would also have to wait for her security clearance to come through. There wasn't anything in her background that would keep her from passing the clearance, so she wasn't the least bit worried about that. Taleah had been praying fervently over the job, since she believed that working would take her mind off all the nerve-racking things going on in her life.

Lorenz's busy lifestyle hadn't calmed down one bit. In fact, Taleah thought it had gotten much worse than before. They'd spent very little time together over the past week. Anything akin to socializing hadn't happened since Hailey and Zurich had come to dinner. While both Taleah and Lorenz had hoped he wouldn't have to go away before the scheduled trip back to Connecticut for the divorce hearing, things hadn't turned out that way.

To fulfill his duties as a member of the unit's

flight crew, Lorenz and his crew were taking off for Alaska the next morning. Within a couple of days of his return from the TDY, Lorenz would then leave for the States. Since Zurich also had a scheduled TDY at another base in Japan, within the same time frame as Lorenz's, Taleah and Hailey had promised to keep each other company. Any sort of get-together between the two women would be contingent upon Hailey's work schedule, which was a demanding one. To Taleah it seemed as if everyone but her had something worthwhile to do. Taleah had never felt so worthless. Landing a job was an absolute must.

Taleah was having a cup of hot tea, as she looked over the job listings she'd had Lorenz pick up for her from the civilian personnel office. There were several new jobs posted on the weekly sheet; nothing akin to her qualifications had come open in the dental clinic. The dental field was where she had garnered the most experience, but she had also worked as administrative assistant to the administrator of a large Los Angeles hospital. Although she still hadn't heard anything from the medical clinic, she expected to. Taleah thought the interviewing process had gone very well. It had seemed to her at the time that the director had all but offered her the job.

Lorenz entered the kitchen, kissed Taleah softly on the mouth, and then sat down at the table. "Good morning. Surprised to see you up so early." He picked up her mug and took a swallow of the hot liquid.

Taleah got up from her seat and rushed over to the oven and pulled out a plate covered with aluminum foil. She removed the silver wrapping and then placed the dish in front of Lorenz. "Breakfast is served! I finally beat you to the punch." Taleah then retrieved from the refrigerator a pitcher of freshly squeezed orange juice. "Do you want hot tea, too?"

Lorenz was genuinely surprised by Taleah's unexpected breakfast of scrambled eggs and turkey sausage. "No tea, thank you. I can't believe you got up this early just to fix me breakfast. Thank you so much. That was really sweet of you. I'm also flattered. I'm not much of a breakfast eater, Taleah, but I'm going to eat this because of all the trouble you've gone through."

Taleah scowled hard. "Trouble? It wasn't any trouble at all. As for you not being fond of breakfast, I obviously didn't know that. Since you're always up way before me and the sun, long before the rooster's first crow, how would I know that you don't normally eat breakfast, Sergeant Hampton?" Taleah was clearly agitated. Her body language spoke to that.

Lorenz was slightly taken aback by Taleah's attitude. "It's obvious that I've offended you, but I don't understand how. What did I do or say that upset you?"

Taleah threw up her hands, wishing she hadn't had the moment's loss of temper. Her issues seemed silly to her now, yet they were still extremely bothersome. "It's nothing. I'm just a little on edge this morning. Maybe I got up way too early." Her last statement was meant as a joke, but the unmistakable biting sarcasm in her tone gave Lorenz nothing to laugh about.

Lorenz pulled Taleah down onto his lap. "Something's wrong. What is it?"

Taleah shook her head from side to side. "I'm just frustrated with a few things that go on around here. My biggest issue is that you never let me do anything for you, or for myself, for that matter. By

the time I wake up every household chore is done—
and most of the time you've already cooked or have
at least taken out of the freezer what we're having
for dinner. This hasn't been exactly paradise for
me. It would be nice if I got a chance to take care
of your needs once in a while. The problem is I
don't know what your needs are. What's this all
about? Don't you think I can cook and clean? Or is
it that I'm just not good enough at it for you,
Lorenz?"

Lorenz knew that he had to be careful not to
take lightly her issues with him. A blind person
could see that all the things she'd mentioned to
him hotly bothered her. "Taleah, it's never been
my intention to offend you, but that's clearly what
I've done. I don't think you're incapable of cooking and cleaning, not at all. Those are things that
I've always done. They come natural to me. In case
you haven't noticed, though I believe you have,
I'm rather hyper. I have to stay busy. Besides that, I
love to cook and clean. Unusual for a man, huh?
It's really not. My dad is the same way. I was taught
by my parents to take care of myself at an early age.
I'm sorry you've been hurt by this. I never realized
I was depriving you of taking care of me."

"Trust me, Lorenz, I have noticed your Energizer
bunny activities."

Taleah really felt silly now. Stuffing her foot in
her mouth was becoming a habit, a very bad one.
Lorenz seemed too good to be true, but he was just
that. He was also the same kind of wonderful man
her mom had married. There were probably women
who'd darn near kill to have a man who loved to
cook, clean, wash clothes, and take good care of
them. The things she'd taken such issue with seemed
so trivial now. Why was it so hard for her to accept

that Lorenz was an extraordinary person? What he did for her was simply a part of who he was.

As Taleah's mind suddenly settled on Bradley Fields, one thing had already become crystal clear for her. Lorenz was not Bradley, was nothing like him. Perhaps she was waiting for Lorenz to do a Bradley on her. Her fear of exactly that happening could be at the crux of her imagined problems with Lorenz, which really weren't problems at all. Where Lorenz's treatment of her was concerned, the first shoe hadn't fallen, so why was she constantly waiting for the other one to drop?

Lorenz was a good guy, plain and simple. Since there were no comparisons, she had to stop comparing bitterness with sweetness. Lorenz was definitely the latter. They didn't come any sweeter than Lorenz Hampton.

"Will you fix lunch for me today, Taleah?"

His attempt to please her and make her feel needed caused Taleah's heart to flutter. He came home for lunch a lot, but he normally brought with him meals already cooked. "That's one request I'd have a hard time denying you. Do you have anything in particular in mind?"

He wiggled his eyebrows flirtatiously. "Besides you?"

Taleah laughed at his suggestive comment. "That would be called *dessert.*" She placed two of her fingers onto his lips. "Don't respond to my earlier question. I'll just surprise you."

"I like intrigue. That's why I love you so much. You're full of it."

Taleah raised a questioning brow. "Full of what?"

"That, too, on occasion."

As he lifted her off his lap, they both laughed.

"I'm not even going to try and interpret that

one." Taleah looked at the plate in front of Lorenz. "Now that your food has gotten cold, I guess I should warm it up."

"While you do that, I'll go grab my briefcase. Once I've eaten, I've got to make a mad dash for it. Extra duty calls this morning. According to the phone call I received earlier, one of my troops didn't show up for work last night. He didn't show at the clinic for sick call either. That means I have to stop by the barracks and see what's up with him. I hope this one doesn't turn out to be something serious or even an AWOL."

"Away without leave, right?"

"Hey, girl, you must be hanging around with some military guy. That's exactly what the initials stand for."

While watching Lorenz rush out of the room to retrieve his briefcase, Taleah chuckled, beaming with pride at her right answer. Taleah picked up his plate and covered it with a paper towel. She then placed the dish in the microwave oven and set the timer for less than a minute.

Lorenz had been long gone when Taleah noticed the folded letter lying on the nightstand in the master bedroom. The envelope it had come in was right beside it. Taleah picked the envelope up and read the return label. The correspondence was from his mother. That made her curious as to why Lorenz hadn't mentioned the letter to her; the postmark was a recent one.

The moment Taleah picked the letter up, she noticed a second letter beneath the first one, which had her name written upon it. Since it had her name on it, Taleah couldn't find a single reason why she shouldn't read it. But she could think of several reasons why Lorenz should've told her about it. With one of the letters being addressed to her, his reason for keeping the correspondence a secret puzzled her.

A few minutes into the reading revealed to Taleah the main reason Lorenz hadn't shared the letter with her. His mother was opposed to their marriage, had been opposed to it from the very beginning, according to what was written. Since his mother knew that the marriage hadn't taken place, and why it hadn't occurred, she was now trying to convince Taleah that she should leave Japan immediately before Lorenz got into serious trouble. Taleah noticed that the words *living in sin* were written in darker ink than the rest of the letter.

Highly curious about what was said in the letter addressed to Lorenz, Taleah picked it up and began to peruse it. The phrase *know your enemies* gave her just cause to read it, though she would probably later regret invading his privacy.

That he wasn't yet divorced was another reason cited by his mother for him to alter his present living arrangements. The letter went on to say that Lorenz should see his current situation as a blessing in disguise; that he should consider himself lucky to get out of this second marriage without it costing him an arm and a leg. The letter was basically telling him to run for his life and to get out of his present situation before it ended up costing him his prestigious career. Cynthia Hampton also warned him of what might happen if his estranged wife ever found out that he was living with another woman, not that she would be the one to tell her.

It was an unpleasant experience for Taleah to learn that she had enemies that she'd never before met. That Lorenz's mother was vehemently opposed to their wedding came as quite a shock to her.

Lorenz not mentioning it was the biggest shocker of all, though Taleah was in no doubt that he more than likely thought that he was protecting her.

Taleah believed that she now understood why Lorenz's parents hadn't come to Los Angeles for their wedding. With Lorenz as their only child, Taleah had thought his family would've jumped at the chance to see him get married, despite the fact it was his second marriage. This letter made better sense of things for her.

Adding yet another strike to their situation made Taleah feel even worse than she already felt. His mother, or perhaps both parents, being opposed to the marriage was another hard blow for her to endure. How could she start out in a marriage where her future in-laws were at odds with her, without them having met? As if they didn't have enough to contend with already.

Lorenz not mentioning his mother's position regarding their marriage was just another insult to the numerous injuries that had already been inflicted upon her. That it was a no-win situation for her was becoming painfully obvious to Taleah.

Taleah didn't feel an ounce of guilt about reading the letter with her name on it, but she felt deep remorse over reading Lorenz's. Did she confront Lorenz with what she now knew or just act as if she'd never pried into his private affairs, which weren't all that exclusive to him since one letter was specifically addressed to her?

It suddenly dawned on Taleah that she'd never even spoken with either of his parents over the telephone. Neither one had called to congratulate them on their engagement, nor had they phoned to tell them that they shouldn't get married. Taleah hadn't given much thought to it, but it was now clear that she should've at least questioned the lack of communication.

Cynthia Hampton's attempt to get her to leave Japan, when she couldn't get her own son to listen to reason, was a strange approach for a mother, in Taleah's opinion. Taleah didn't see herself as an enemy to anyone. If Cynthia felt so strongly about her convictions, why hadn't she tried to convince Taleah of such before the wedding had actually taken place? Lack of an address or telephone number for Taleah could possibly be Cynthia Hampton's defense.

It was feasible that Lorenz wouldn't give his mother Taleah's private information if he thought his mother would possibly use it to confront the woman he loved. He had to already know what his mother was or wasn't capable of. She was certainly outspoken and opinionated.

Taleah felt like crying. Instead of giving in to her emotions, she simply willed herself to go numb. Feeling wasn't in her best interest at the moment. This disturbing chain of events had already caused enough pain for everyone involved. Her friends and family had no clue what was happening to her, while it looked as if Lorenz's family had already gotten themselves emotionally involved. Mrs. Hampton had every right to offer advice to her son, but did she have the right to make assumptions of any kind about Taleah, especially without the benefit of knowing her?

To be accused of "living in sin" with Lorenz was a boiling point for Taleah.

For the umpteenth time in one day Taleah looked at her suitcases, which were stored in the master bedroom closet. It would be so easy for her to pull them out and start packing; so hard to come to that conclusion. Taleah couldn't even build any anger toward Lorenz. How could she be angry with him for him merely wanting to protect her? She had convinced herself that Lorenz keeping this secret from her was nothing more than his desire to shield her from more heartache.

Taleah inhaled deeply of the roses Lorenz had presented to her upon his return home from work. The red buds had yet to blossom. The heavenly scented beauties would be something spectacular once fully bloomed. After thanking Lorenz with a passionate kiss, Taleah arranged the dozen dark red roses in the clear glass vase Lorenz had provided her with.

Roses are red—and Taleah is blue, because she might never truly be a wife to you. Taleah's mental rhyming nearly brought tears to her eyes. Becoming Lorenz's wife seemed like a dream never to come true for her.

Lorenz took a seat at the kitchen table. "How was your day, sweetheart?"

Full of surprises. She fought hard to keep from saying her thoughts aloud. "Interesting."

"What made it so interesting?"

"I don't really know. It just was." Taleah looked over at Lorenz, doing her best to keep the rest of her answer to herself. If she were to remain quiet, wouldn't she be guilty of keeping secrets, too? Before she could continue in her response to his question, Lorenz announced his intention to go upstairs and change clothes.

"Will you be ready to eat when you come back down?"

"I'm ready to eat now. What did you cook?"

"Stewed chicken wings and wide egg noodles, one of my childhood favorites."

"Sounds good. I'll be ready for a big bowl of chicken and noodles once I make myself more comfortable. I'll be right back."

"Hurry up, love. I'm hungry, too."

Taleah had done a remarkable job in setting an elegant table, though the meal was a simple one. There was nothing gourmet about chicken and noodles. But she saw no use in their having recently purchased the new beautiful china, crystal, and flatware only to keep their beauty hidden away in a buffet. With Lorenz giving her more of an opportunity to shine in the kitchen, she wanted to make a wonderful showing with her brand-new dinnerware.

Although both of them had a lot on their minds, neither made a query into such. Taleah and Lorenz seemed content to eat in silence. If it weren't for the complimentary moans and groans over the delicious food, the room would've been soundless.

The moment Lorenz finished eating he pushed back from the table. He then stood up and took something out of his back pocket. Lorenz handed to Taleah the letter with her name on it. "I meant to give this to you earlier, but I forgot." His expression turned pensive. "Taleah, the letter is from my mother. I don't know what's in it 'cause I haven't read it. However, if the content is anything like what mine says, you're more than likely going to be hurt. My mother thinks it's her God-given right to say whatever's on her mind, no matter who gets hurt in the process."

"Why didn't you tell me she was opposed to us getting married?"

"So you've already read it."

Taleah nodded in response, although he'd made a statement, as opposed to asking her a question. "I'm not sorry about it either. I won't apologize."

Lorenz raised an eyebrow. "Okay, Taleah. There's no need to apologize. Glad we got that out of the way. Was the letter as hurtful as I suspect it of being?"

"Very. But not so hard to understand. Her concerns are quite real."

"Being concerned and highly opinionated are two very different things. I bet more opinion was given than concern was shown. I'm sorry if the letter caused you pain."

"I'll get over it. Pain has been a frequent visitor lately. Since you're going TDY in the morning, the letter is rather untimely. I won't have you here to help allay my fears." Taleah chuckled, her laughter belying the awful agony she felt deep down in her gut. "You know this girl needs you to reassure her on occasion."

Lorenz reached for Taleah's hand and squeezed it gently. "Any time you need reassuring, I'll be here for you. Although I'll only be gone a few days, I'm sure it'll feel like a month." He looked deeply into her eyes. "Taleah, I need you to believe that we're coming up on the end of this thing. It's almost over. Can you please hang in there awhile longer?"

Taleah smiled broadly. Bending her head, she kissed the back of his hand. Lorenz needed reassuring, too. They both did. "As I've said before, I'm in this for the long haul. I must admit that there are times when I want to run away and never look back, but my love for you always manages to override those terribly anxious moments. Are you going to hang with me?"

"By both my feet and hands," Lorenz joked. "We're going to hang together."

"Yeah, that'll make it a lot easier. I have questions as to why you didn't tell me about your mom's feelings on our marriage, though I have somewhat of an idea. I just don't want to spend time dwelling on it the night before you go away. Will you agree to discuss it with me at a later time, after you come home?"

"Of course, Taleah. I know that it needs to be addressed. But also know this. My mother doesn't rule me. I listen to what she has to say, and I respect her at all times. But I always do what I feel is best for me and what's best for whatever the situation may be. In case you're wondering, my dad rarely shares in her sentiments. He's all for whatever makes me happy. Your leaving Japan right now is not in our best interest. We can't work through this being apart. I know I've said this a hundred times, but I don't want you to leave."

"And I don't want to go."

Lorenz got out of his seat and came over to stand before Taleah. He reached down and took both of her hands. "Let's go into the living room and curl up on the couch. The dishes can wait until later."

"Maybe we should do them now. We'll only have to come back in here and tackle them before we go to bed."

Lorenz grinned. "What happened to your old habit of rinsing them and stacking them until the next day?"

Taleah laughed. "You happened. I know you like everything to be put back in its place right away. I'm trying to get in the habit of keeping things in order around here."

"Then we shouldn't tamper with that. We'll also use the dishwasher this time."

Taleah moved right along with Lorenz until they reached the sofa, where they both sat down. Lorenz got right back up so that he could put some mood music on. He had to leave Taleah early in the morning and he wanted their evening to be a romantic one. While he was up, he also went into the kitchen and poured chilled sparkling cider into the new crystal glasses he and Taleah had recently purchased from one of the specialty vendors located out in the mall area outside the exchange. Choosing their dinnerware together had been an awesome time for them. Their decision to purchase the chinaware was an attempt on their part to move forward with their plans despite the holdups.

Remembering how animated Taleah had been on that day caused Lorenz to smile brightly. After several minutes of browsing separately through the shop, they had each settled on a china pattern to present to the other. Taleah and Lorenza had chosen the very same pattern.

Lorenz brought the glasses into the living room and set them down on the coffee table. Once he'd reseated himself next to Taleah, he picked up a glass and handed one to her. He then retrieved his own, raising it in a toast. "To us, Taleah. May we get through this brief separation without incident. May the Lord keep us both safe and secure. I love you."

Taleah carefully clinked her glass against his. "Hear, hear, my love."

Taleah took a sip of cider and then set her glass back down on the table. She watched Lorenz down his drink in one huge gulp, smiling warmly. The thought to light a few candles suddenly came to her mind. It seemed as if Lorenz had been trying to set a romantic mood by serving the sparkling cider in crystal glasses. The soft music was also an indication of his intent. Lighting candles would hopefully show him that she loved the mood he'd set for them.

Mindful of how fast time was ticking off the clock, Taleah hurried through her mission. Once all the candles were lit, she turned off the lights. "How's this for a romantic atmosphere?"

"As usual, we're on the same page."

Lorenz couldn't help wondering if Taleah was thinking of breaking her rule of waiting to make love until after everything was finally resolved. He wouldn't press the issue, though he wanted her in the worst way. Now that he knew what it was like to make passionate love to Taleah, waiting had been pure torture for him. His delightful memories of them entwined together as one served him well, but he wanted to once again experience the real thing with her. Thinking of them together in a passionate coupling only heightened his physical desire for her.

Instead of seating herself on the sofa, Taleah positioned herself on Lorenz's lap. Making love to him was also heavy on her mind; getting his mother's untimely letter out of her thoughts was harder than anything Taleah could've imagine.

Living in sin were the words now ruling her head. It seemed that her heart had been left with no say in the matter. If only she could drown out the little voices inside her head . . .

Deeply satisfied, both physically and emotionally, Taleah lay in Lorenz's arms, attempting to shut out the loud ticking sounds of the clock. In knowing that Lorenz might be going on a dangerous mission the next day, since it was classified, Taleah had allowed the needs and desires of her weakened flesh to completely overtake her nagging mind. The only sounds she'd heard while Lorenz made love to her was her own voice screaming out his name. At the time she'd come to that conclusion, she was in no doubt that regrets might come later. But later wasn't now, so she'd told herself she'd deal with it then.

Taleah looked up at Lorenz while stroking his cheek. "Should I be fearful of your TDY since it's classified?"

"All we can do is pray on it, Taleah. Prayer, not fear, is what will get us through the separation. Fear won't comfort you in the middle of the night. God will. Just stepping out the door can be a dreadful experience if we let fear rule our hearts. It doesn't matter where we are when it's our time. If I thought I was going to die every time a mission came about, I'd hope by now that I would've come to the conclusion that I was in the wrong line of work. A mission being classified doesn't necessarily mean it's a dangerous one. Living life is dangerous, Taleah. Living in fear of danger increases tenfold the likelihood of such an occurrence. You get my drift, sweetheart?" He kissed the tip of her nose.

"You've made a few good points. I'll concede that to you."

Lorenz rifled his fingers through her disheveled tresses. "How gracious of you!" He pulled Taleah into his arms. "Would you consider me as a greedy man if I asked for an encore of our physical farewells?"

"As long as you don't consider me a needy woman if I give my consent too readily."

"Let the encore begin."

* * *

While looking into the mirror, Taleah noticed the dark circles under her eyes. Lack of sleep was the culprit. It was one thing to live in a two-bedroom apartment alone, but staying by herself in a two-story house, especially at night, had Taleah completely unnerved. Every little sound she heard coming from the downstairs areas caused her heart to leap into her mouth. The creaking of the steps in the middle of the night kept Taleah in constant prayer. She would never have bought into the theory that wood steps had a tendency to settle after a day of heavy traffic. No one could've convinced her that someone wasn't climbing the steps just to get to her.

There had been times when Taleah had reached for the phone to call Hailey and Zurich. That they would think she was downright crazy had thus far kept her from dialing their number. How was a twenty-seven-year-old woman supposed to tell her friends that she was scared to death of being alone in her own house? Lorenz definitely didn't know that much about her. There was no way she could've brought herself to tell Lorenz that she was afraid of being home alone at night. Though he would've taken things seriously at the time, the unmerciful teasing that might come much later because of her fears was the strongest deterrent for not telling.

That which had defined her heart as *fearless* had rapidly changed.

Fourteen

Lorenz figured he should be nervous about this dissolution of marriage hearing, but oddly enough he wasn't. He was positive that he had given his very best during the marriage and had continued to do so even after Loretta had insisted on the legal separation. He had to believe that the judge would grant him his divorce so that he could get on with his life.

That four years had passed by without so much as a note from Loretta stating her desire to stay in the marriage should be taken into account by the judge. In his opinion the divorce had been put on hold without good reason. Loretta would never be able to convince him that spite wasn't her sole reason for contesting their divorce.

The crisply pressed black robe that Judge George Fullerton wore made the tall, powerfully built African-American man appear somewhat formidable; Lorenz was not intimidated, dressed in his full air force blues, a uniform that he took great pride in wearing.

Because Lorenz was in the military and had had

to take off precious duty time to fly back to the States for this hearing, John Saxon, Lorenz's lawyer, believed that this special set of circumstances should gain his client more than a little empathy from the judge.

Both Lorenz and Saxon were both highly aware that anything could happen during what Lorenz saw as a useless hearing. All Lorenz could do was hope and pray that his situation would find favor with God. He had to think positively, had to believe that his stressful ordeal would be over on this day, not resolved on a day six months from now.

Lorenz wasn't sure how much more of a delay Taleah could take either. Her patience had already been stretched to the absolute limit. Their earlier phone conversation had further convinced him of that much. Taleah had not only sounded harried to him, he had also heard disillusionment in her voice. The phone call had been ever so short, though he would've spent his last dime talking with her in hopes of assuaging her anguish.

Lorenz quickly turned his thoughts back to the hearing. Thinking of what Taleah must be going through with him away from her again wouldn't help him to stay focused on the daunting task before him. He had to remain strong and confident in order to fight this uphill battle. Adopting a defeatist attitude at this final stage of the game was not going to help matters.

The fact that his estranged wife hadn't bothered to show up for court wasn't a smart move on her part. That the defense had allowed Loretta to be a no-show was a stunning revelation to Lorenz. It appeared to him that she wasn't interested in making an appearance, which made him wonder what had possessed her to file papers to contest the divorce at the last possible hour. Her negligence in showing up might garner him a win by default. Lorenz was sure love had nothing to do with any of this.

However, Lorenz did not rule out monetary gain as a motive. Loretta could be seeking spousal support. Since she'd always received steady child support from Amir's natural father, Lorenz didn't think that receiving an award of that nature from him was a motivating factor.

As the law clerk read the opening remarks, Lorenz gave fifty-three-year-old Judge George Fullerton his undivided attention. Court was now in session.

Lorenz listened intently as John Saxon presented his case before the judge.

"As an active duty member of the United States Air Force, my client, Master Sergeant Lorenz Hampton, has had to take precious time away from his important military duties to fly here all the way from Tokyo, Japan. We are looking to bring this case to a close today. It has been delayed long enough. Their differences in this marriage have been proved as irreconcilable; therefore, my client is not seeking ways to try and work things out. This couple has already been estranged for four years. The emotional bond has been long since broken."

Saxon went on to explain how the estrangement had come about in the first place. Lorenz's lawyer then made it clear that his client had not been the one to initiate the legal separation and that he had only filed for the divorce after the separation had become a lengthy one. Mrs. Hampton's desire to be around her stateside family, as opposed to living overseas with her husband, was the main reason she'd given for wanting the separation. Her lack of commitment in being a military spouse was yet another reason cited by her for leaving him.

"My client is always on call to serve his country.

He often does it at a moment's notice. That's enough of an uncertainty for one man to have to deal with constantly. Although Loretta Hampton initiated the legal separation, she has contested the divorce, but only at the last possible second. To add insult to injury, Mrs. Hampton doesn't even bother to show up today for these important proceedings. On the other hand, my client has flown halfway around the world in hopes of resolving this matter expeditiously. It is our hope that Your Honor will grant Sergeant Lorenz Hampton his dissolution of marriage without any further delays."

The judge then gave the opposing attorney his chance to represent his absentee client.

With no client there to help prove his case, Wilkes Stafford attempted to convince the judge as to why there was a need to delay the final dissolution of marriage. Stafford's case was weak at best. Loretta's attorney mentioning that his client wasn't emotionally prepared to have this sudden end to her marriage had Lorenz cursing softly under his breath. He'd never heard anything so ridiculous. There was nothing sudden about a chain of events that had occurred over a period of four years.

"My client, Mrs. Loretta Hampton, also seeks spousal support in the amount of one thousand dollars a month, not an unreasonable amount. The child involved, Amir Spencer, is the natural child of Mrs. Hampton and a stepson to Sergeant Hampton."

Lorenz had paled at the requested amount for spousal support. While the United States granted a lot of wonderful benefits to its military members, the salaries were in no way competitive with the money allotted for employment in the private sec-

tors. To pay out that amount of money to his ex
would prove to be a tremendous burden on Lorenz's
finances. Loretta had once again managed to floor
him with her selfishness and disregard for others.

Judge Fullerton first thanked Sergeant Hampton
for his dedicated service to his country. The judge
also took a moment to speak on his own illustrious
military career with JAG, office of the judge advocate general. He then asked Lorenz a few personal
questions, which Lorenz answered honestly and
succinctly.

Lorenz made it known in a very respectful manner that he had no desire to save what hadn't existed between him and his estranged wife for a
very long time. Time for reconciliation had long
since come and gone. Lorenz spoke about his stepson, Amir, in a loving way, which clearly showed
how he truly felt about the young child. He talked
of how it had devastated him once he no longer
had the little boy in his life. Though he hated to
address it in such a public forum, Lorenz mentioned the financial burden that would come as a
result of paying spousal support. Without sounding as if he were complaining about his military
salary, he thought it was in his best interest to address it in front of the court. He told the judge
that he didn't mind paying a fair amount, but he
hadn't expected to pay such an exorbitant amount
to his estranged wife.

The judge encompassed Lorenz in his thoughtful gaze. "I understand your concerns, Sergeant
Hampton, and I appreciate your honesty. I also
have firsthand knowledge of the limited finances
when serving in the military. With that in mind, I
will grant the sum of one dollar to Mrs. Hampton
for spousal support. However, the amount is subject to change at the court's discretion. After hear-

ing both sides, I see no good reason why this court should delay this divorce another minute. I don't see any reason why you shouldn't be granted a final dissolution of marriage."

Judge Fullerton turned to look at the opposing attorney. "Mr. Stafford, you haven't presented me with a solid enough case for me to grant your client any further delay in this matter. Also, your client couldn't care too much about saving this marriage; otherwise, she would've been present today to at least try and fight for it."

"With all due respect, Your Honor, my client lives in another state."

"I beg your pardon, Mr. Stafford. Sergeant Hampton lives on another continent—and he's certainly present and accounted for. If he could make it here from the other side of the world, surely your client could've made it in from another state. Without further delay, I hereby grant on this day the dissolution of said marriage between Lorenz Hampton and Loretta Hampton. This court is now adjourned. Good luck, Sergeant Hampton."

Lorenz was so full that it was hard for him to keep his emotions inside. He and Taleah could marry right away. The moment they'd both been longing for was now upon them.

Thinking of Taleah anxiously awaiting his next call had him blinking back the tears. She would be so happy. The night before he'd left Japan they'd completely broken the rules regarding remaining celibate until they were married. Now, with his divorce finally being granted, he was sure it would be so much easier for Taleah to bear the decision she'd made.

The surprise Lorenz had in store for Taleah was about to be revealed. Jared had played a huge role in helping him plan the upcoming surprise. He and Taleah were finally going to have a proper honeymoon, though they'd have to wait a few months longer. All of her friends and family would be invited to join them, although they'd have to fund their own trips.

Without telling Jared about Taleah's and his marriage dilemma, Lorenz had asked Jared to check with all the family and close friends to see if they'd be interested in celebrating with them in Jamaica in the not so distant future. Jared had also agreed to research group rates through the travel agency he frequented. Lorenz had given Jared an early spring date to work with just to ensure that everything would be resolved by then.

Little did Taleah know that she would one day soon be Jamaica-bound; Lorenz couldn't be more thrilled about the upcoming surprise honeymoon. Taleah deserved to have the best honeymoon money could buy, the best of everything that life had to offer, period.

Hailey had helped Taleah put up all the grocery items before the two women sat down at Taleah's kitchen table to have a cup of hot tea. Before shopping at the base, Hailey had taken Taleah to her favorite off-base haunts, where bargain shopping was at a premium. Taleah enjoyed the outdoor markets more than shopping at the department stores Lorenz had taken her to. The marketplaces were colorful and the shoppers were quite animated.

Taleah had purchased one of the finest bolts of raw sea-green and gold lamé silk she'd ever laid her eyes on. She picked up the bolt of fabric and held it up to the light. "Have you ever seen anything more beautiful, Hailey?"

"I'm afraid that I have, Taleah. Fine raw silk can

be found all over the Far East. The color you've chosen is exquisite. What are you going to have made from it?"

"An after-five dress for starters. There's more than enough material to do an evening gown and a shoulder wrap. Since Lorenz's favorite color is blue, I want to go back one day and get a bolt of royal-blue silk with tiny flecks of gold in it. If I can't get a perfectly matched pair of shoes, I can always wear gold ones. I love the bright colors the vendors had on display."

"The marketplaces are an unforgettable experience. I've been TDY to Japan a couple of times, so that's why I know all the fabulous places to shop. Yokota is my first permanent-duty station in this country."

"Where did you meet Zurich?"

"We met on South Padre Island near Brownsville, Texas, the southernmost part of the state. I later found out that we were both in the military—and that he was an officer. A relationship for us was off-limits since I was an NCO."

"How'd you all handle that?"

"Shortly after landing in Germany, I learned that Zurich was also stationed there. I eventually went back to the States for officers' training school, but not before Zurich and I went through a whole lot of drama. After graduation from OTS, I was sent back to Germany, but only for a short while. Zurich and I got married in Texas right after I graduated. He wasn't taking any chances. He was prepared to resign his commission if our marriage became an issue. It didn't."

Taleah shook her head from side to side. "You two seem like you belong together. I'm glad that everything turned out okay. Zurich's mother, how do you two get along?"

Hailey's eyes grew misty. "Mama Bernice is an absolute angel. You'd think I was her daughter if you ever saw us together. We get along very well; hit it off from the very beginning, though I was concerned that she might not like me. You know how some mothers are about their sons; no woman is good enough for their can-do-no-wrong boys. Bernice Kingdom has three grown boys, gorgeous Texans. And she's actively looking for wives for Zane and Zaire. Mama Bernice is dying to become a grandmother. We haven't told her I'm pregnant yet. We plan to do that when we go there for Christmas."

"You won't have to tell her. She'll be able to see for herself, since I'm sure you'll be showing by then." Taleah suddenly got a worried expression on her face. "I don't think Lorenz's mother likes me, and I haven't even met her yet. She doesn't approve of our present living arrangements. She wrote a letter telling me exactly how she feels about us living together."

Hailey looked shocked. "You're kidding! I can't believe people do things like that. What's Lorenz saying about it?"

"He assured me as a matter of fact that his mother doesn't rule him. We were supposed to talk about it when he got home from his TDY. But once he got back he barely had time to breathe. Then it was time for him to leave for the States to attend the divorce hearing. Oh, Hailey, I have been a basket case since he walked out that front door. If he knew what I've been putting myself through, he'd be so unhappy about it. Waiting for his call has me on pins and needles."

"I'm glad shopping took your mind off the hearing, if only for a little while. I have a good feeling about this, Taleah. I think it's going to be okay.

Lorenz will get his divorce. How can they deny him? They can't force him to stay married."

"I hope you're right, Hailey. I want this divorce to be over with in the worst way. I want to marry Lorenz. He wants to marry me. I wouldn't ever have gotten involved with a married man, period. If Lorenz hadn't been separated for such a long time, I wouldn't have considered him as a date. I had already fallen for him when I learned he wasn't yet divorced. So you see, this is one of the reasons why I want it over so badly."

"It's going to happen. Don't worry."

"I'm trying not to, Hailey, but it's hard. When does Zurich get back?"

"Three days from now. I can't wait. We hate being apart, but we've learned to handle it. I don't know what's going to happen once the baby comes. Right now I'm planning on staying in the military. But only God knows what's going to happen after I hold that sweet bundle of joy in my arms for the first time. My mom was a stay-at-home mom; she loved every minute of it."

"How does Zurich feel about it?"

Zurich thinks it should be my decision to stay in the military or get out. He's not opposed to retiring and becoming a stay-at-home dad. We'll settle it all before my last trimester."

"Oh, I have something to show you, Hailey. I need to know what you think." Taleah retrieved a fancy envelope from off the kitchen counter and handed it to Hailey. "I'm terribly intimidated by this invitation for more than one reason."

Hailey perused the gold-embossed invitation for a welcome reception in Taleah's honor. The military wives married to members from Lorenz's weather unit had sent the invitation.

"You shouldn't let this intimidate you, Taleah.

The invitation is par for the course. This is the way the unit wives have chosen to welcome you as one of them. Welcome receptions are held all the time for base newcomers. It's almost a tradition in some squadrons."

Taleah pushed her hands through her hair, feeling extremely anxious. "Hailey, I'm not a unit wife yet." Taleah scowled hard. "You couldn't have possibly forgotten, have you?"

Hailey's hands flew up to her face in a show of embarrassment. "I hadn't forgotten, but I certainly wasn't thinking of it at the moment. I now understand why you feel the way you do, Taleah. Turning the invitation down is unheard of, so you can't possibly do that. You'd be labeled a nasty snob for sure. We've got to figure a way to get you out of this, at least until after you guys get married."

"I agree. But what can I do to get out of it?"

Laughing, Hailey reached over and felt Taleah's forehead. "You're going to have to develop a sudden fever the night before this shindig. No, several days before might be better."

"I don't know about that, Hailey. They're not going to wait until the last minute to order everything for the reception. Maybe I should tell them I already have something scheduled for that date. That way, I might be able to put it off a couple of weeks. If the divorce goes through right away, perhaps we can be married by then. Ugh, this is so unreal, so tasteless."

"Decisions, decisions," Hailey remarked. "We'll come up with something, but we have to do it rather quickly. The reception is scheduled for next Friday. We don't have much time."

"Don't I know it, Hailey! Maybe Lorenz will come up with something, since he already knows all the wives. I don't want to offend anyone in or out of his unit. A welcome reception is a very nice gesture. I like the idea."

"It really is a nice thing for them to do. The officers' wives did one for me. Mine was done as a surprise get-together. We should thank our lucky stars that yours isn't a surprise party. That would mean no way out, but more than likely dates would've been checked out with Lorenz. Things will work out." Looking at her watch, Hailey got to her feet. "I've got to run."

Lorenz sat in his mother's kitchen eating a slice of her freshly baked lemon meringue pie. His parents had already gone to bed, and he wasn't far behind. He was too tired to do anything else but shower and leap into bed. He had called Taleah twice, but she hadn't answered. He planned to keep trying until her got her. The time difference made it difficult for him to reach her at a decent hour.

Cynthia Hampton walked into the kitchen and took a seat at the table. She was a very attractive woman whose hair had turned completely white at an early age. The whiteness was striking against her beautiful cocoa complexion. "How's the pie, son?"

"Oh, come on now, Mom. You already know the answer to that. Fishing for compliments, huh? If so, the pie is delicious, as usual." Lorenz gave his mother a thoughtful glance. "I thought you were in bed already. Couldn't you sleep?"

"As a matter of fact, I couldn't get comfortable. I had a hard time getting my mind off the court hearing. Are you pleased with the outcome?"

"I think everything went the way it should've

gone. I'm glad I didn't have to pay a thousand dollars a month in spousal support. That would've killed me financially."

"Had the court ordered you to pay it, would you have given more serious thought to this idea of marrying again so soon?"

Lorenz saw where this was conversation was going; he didn't like it. But he knew that Cynthia Hampton would continue to give the matter her best shot. She never knew when to let go of something, especially if she was on the losing end. Being the victor was important to her.

Lorenz stroked his chin. "Had the court ordered me to pay the money I would've had no choice but to comply. To pay it or not to pay it has nothing to do with me getting married again. I'm going to marry Taleah, Mom, as soon as I get back to Japan. I wish you could accept my decision. I'm the only one who knows what's best for me. Taleah is the best thing that has ever happened to me. I know that for a fact. If you'd give her a chance, you'd see that for yourself."

"I've seen quite enough for myself. I don't think she had your best interest at heart when she picked up with you before you were divorced. That alone tells me a lot about her."

Lorenz would never disrespect his mother, but he wasn't about to let her unkind remarks about Taleah go unchallenged. "Taleah didn't know my marital status right away. She's nothing like you're making her out to be. Your assumptions are unfair ones."

"I just call it like I see it, Lorenz. There's nothing unfair about that. The fact remains that you were married when you met her."

"If you can call living by myself for four years being married, then so be it. Let me reiterate my

position to you. As soon as all the legal documents
are filed, and everything is finalized on paper, I'm
going to make Taleah Taylor my wife. Nothing anyone can say will make me change my mind. Can
you please respect my right to make my own decisions? I have been an adult for a very long time."

Cynthia pushed her chair back from the table
and got to her feet. "As you wish, but don't say I
didn't warn you when this marriage blows up like
the first one did. Good night, Lorenz."

"Sweetheart, it's finally over," Lorenz shouted
into the telephone. "I'm free! Free to marry you as
soon as I get back to Japan. The judge granted me
the divorce. We're going to run right down to the
U.S. embassy and tie the knot. Are you happy,
Taleah?"

Taleah was so choked up she found it hard to
speak. "I'm free." The very words she'd longed to
hear. They were finally free to marry. *Thank you,
Jesus,* she cried inwardly. "I can't define what I'm
feeling right now, Lorenz. It's a weird one, but so
darn close to euphoria. When does your flight land
at Narita?"

"Late tomorrow night." He hesitated for a mo-
ment. "Taleah, would you mind if I popped over to
Loretta's to see Amir? I miss the little guy. Seeing
Amir means I'd also be seeing Loretta. It would
also delay my return to Japan for at least a day.
How do you feel about that?"

"It won't bother me, Lorenz. At least I don't
think so. Since you haven't seen him in a while,
are you sure it won't be disturbing for you?"

"Why would it be?"

"I don't know. It upset me when Bradley came
by to see me after such a long—"

"When did that happen, Taleah?" Lorenz interrupted. "When did you see Bradley?"

His question made Taleah realize that she'd never mentioned Bradley's impromptu visit to Lorenz. When was she going to stop shoving her feet into her mouth? Her mouth was big, but not large enough to hold both feet. "I'm sorry. I just realized I hadn't mentioned it. He just dropped by to see if I would forgive him and take him back."

"Is that all, Taleah? If so, he wasn't asking for much, was he?"

"Don't be facetious, Lorenz. This call costs too much for that."

"I see your point. Was seeing Bradley a deciding factor in your decision to marry me? Did you agree to see him to make sure you were marrying the right man?"

Taleah wished she could throw her arms around Lorenz's neck. He sounded hurt. "Oh, God no, honey! I'd already decided to marry you when I saw him. He just showed up at my door. I had no advance warning. Trust me, Bradley doesn't have that kind of power over me. However, there were some questions about him and me in the back of my mind. Seeing Bradley helped me see that all I ever could've felt for him was infatuation. It was good for me to have the air cleared. I love you, Lorenz. I was only infatuated with Bradley. Big difference, baby."

"Thanks for reassuring me, Taleah. As for Amir, what I'll do is call Loretta and ask her if it's even possible for me to see him. She may not want me to have any further involvement in his life. I hope that's not the case, but I'd have to accept it."

"Do what you think is best. Just know that I can't wait to be in your arms again."

"Same here. I'll let you know if my plans change. Good night, love."

"Wait, Lorenz. Don't hang up. I have a question for you."

"What do you want to ask me, Taleah?"

"Your mother. Was she at the hearing? And did you have a chance to talk to her about the letters she sent us?"

"My mother was simply there in support of me. She wasn't asked any questions by either of the lawyers. As for the letters, we didn't come right out and discuss them, but we did talk. I told her my feelings on certain issues and she reiterated hers. It wasn't a pleasant conversation, nor was it that unpleasant. We just both took a stand."

"Were you able to get her to see things differently?"

"She still feels that I'm getting married too soon after the divorce. She's not going to change on that issue. She hasn't stopped trying to get me to wait at least a year before marrying again. I'm not going to change my mind where marrying you is concerned. We have a wedding to attend at the first possible date. Getting the final decree in my hands may take a week or two. We'll wait on it to come, though I don't think anything can happen to stop the divorce again. We probably should've waited the first time, since we didn't have the document in hand. We might have been spared some grief. The divorce is final now and we will be married."

"Do you think I'm going to have a problem with your mother from here on in?"

"More than likely."

"Lorenz, I'm serious."

"I'm serious, too, Taleah. My mother is a very

difficult woman at times. As wonderful as you are, she's probably going to continue to find fault with you. That's her problem, not yours. But please remember this. You are marrying me, not my mother. She can't do what we don't allow her to. Taleah and Lorenz will be the only Hamptons running the younger Hampton household. Have I made things clear for you?"

"You couldn't have made them any clearer. See you soon. I love you."

"Love you, too. It won't be as long as it's been. Good night, Taleah."

Taleah couldn't stop smiling as she slid out of bed. That her family and friends would never have to find out about their awkward situation pleased her greatly. She'd now have to plan a small second wedding. None of her family and friends would be present for the second ceremony, but they'd witnessed the first one. Taleah wondered if she should ask Hailey to stand up for her. Perhaps Zurich would agree to be Lorenz's best man. Hailey and Zurich would be the only two people on their guest list.

Seconds later Taleah scrapped the entire idea of a second wedding. She and Lorenz would just go down to the U.S. embassy and get married. Besides, they didn't need to go through an additional expense to pull off a wedding. They just needed to be together.

The bolt of beautiful green silk came to mind. Taleah thought it would make a perfect dress for her second wedding day. Now all she had to do was find someone to fashion the material into a stunning dress for her. Hailey had mentioned knowing several shops where they offered the very best in tailoring services. Taleah also remembered Hailey saying that Japanese seamstresses could fashion an entire outfit from merely looking at a picture in a magazine.

Taleah thought it was perfect timing for her to have landed the job at the base clinic. Everything had been moving so slowly; now things were suddenly moving very quickly. She and Lorenz could now have a double celebration when he got home. He was flying in as was originally planned, since he hadn't been able to get a hold of Loretta.

Learning that Loretta's phone number had been disconnected had come as quite a shock to Lorenz. She had moved and had also quit her job. He didn't know when either event had taken place. With no means for Lorenz to contact her, other than to call Amir's father, something he wouldn't think of doing, his plans to see Amir and spend time with him had gone up in smoke.

Although Lorenz had sounded upset over the latest discovery, he had assured Taleah that he was going to be okay. He was certain that Loretta would let him know where Amir was once they got settled in to wherever they'd moved. However, he thought it was a strange occurrence for Loretta to up and move away without so much as a word to him.

Seated at the kitchen table, Taleah was busy making a list of the things she needed to get at the commissary for their dinner celebration. Lorenz wouldn't get home until after midnight, but the dinner she was planning for them was for the next evening. It was times like these when Taleah was happy that Lorenz had insisted on her getting her driver's license, though she only drove around on the base. Taleah would never venture out the gate in a motor vehicle. Driving in Japan was much worse than operating a motor vehicle in Los Angeles. It was also just as scary.

Taleah stepped back and looked at her handi-work, hoping Lorenz would be pleased with the fresh flower arrangement she'd purchased for him at the base florist. Taleah planned to position the vase of flowers and welcome-home greeting card out in the hallway, where he'd see them as soon as he entered the house. She'd never given a man flowers before, but she had the feeling that Lorenz would appreciate the loving gesture, especially since he brought home fresh flowers for her every Friday.

What to wear to bed was her next thought, since she planned on bending the celibacy rules yet again. Wearing nothing at all came to mind first. Then she thought that the black lace teddy that Sherra had given to her as a gift would certainly make Lorenz stand up and take notice. But, then again, so would the red lace gown, she considered. Both pieces of filmy lingerie were hot and seductive, perfect for the prelude to a night of sensuous love-making.

Taleah had even purchased a new fragrance trio to wear for their special night. The heavenly scented bath gel, body lotion, and perfume had all been packaged together in a gift set. Taleah desired to smell as good as she planned on looking.

Taleah was still wide-awake when she heard the front door open and close in the wee hours of the morning. She thought of how the day and evening had dragged on and on as she had waited for this very moment. It had been hard for her to find something to occupy her mind. Reading hadn't helped one bit, because she hadn't been able to concentrate on the story.

However, Taleah had succeeded in writing lengthy letters to each of her friends and also to Jared and Joshua. Once the letters were written, all Taleah had been able to think of was Lorenz's homecoming.

As Lorenz slipped into bed with Taleah, she felt an overwhelming sense of joy and relief. He was now home with her, holding her in his arms, taking possession of her lips. The brief separation, which had seemed like an eternity to her, was now over. Lorenz was right beside her, right where he belonged.

Their forever could now get under way.

Fifteen

Taleah couldn't stop the happy tears from flowing. Marrying Lorenz for the second time in a period of a couple of months had her completely overwhelmed. Her emotions had been on a roller coaster for what seemed like forever. The shaking of her knees had nothing to do with her fears, since she believed she'd conquered them on all fronts. Taleah had come to terms with so many of the unsavory things that had affected them while waiting for things to be resolved.

Eight pounds that she couldn't afford to lose had dropped off Taleah without any effort on her part. The amount of weight loss didn't fully come to her attention until after the seamstress had taken her measurements. Her clothes had been fitting a lot looser, but she hadn't thought too much about it. Nervousness had tampered with her appetite something terrible, which was the reason for the weight loss. Although Taleah was eating normally now, she hadn't gained any of the weight back.

A short note of Godspeed from Lorenz's parents had given rise to hope in Taleah. It was her constant prayer that her awkward situation could be resolved. Taleah didn't expect her and Cynthia Hampton to become great friends overnight, but she was happy that their love for Lorenz at least gave them something in common.

Lorenz was adamant about not letting anyone or anything come between them. Loretta had finally sent Lorenz a note informing him of her new address and phone number. The promise of Amir being able to visit with Lorenz in the near future was also made. Although no specific date had been set, Lorenz was already looking forward to the visit. Lorenz was excited about being able to be a part of Amir's life. He'd also made the vow to call Amir at least twice a month. Now that he had the new address, Lorenz would also resume writing to Amir.

The dress fashioned for Taleah out of the raw green silk was exquisite. She looked as beautiful as she had on the day of their first wedding. Her friends and family not being there was deeply felt by Taleah, but the importance of this day hadn't been diminished by their absence.

Zurich and Hailey were proud to stand up for Taleah and Lorenz. As Taleah and Lorenz's only guests, Zurich and Hailey felt honored to be a part of their wedding ceremony. Hailey wore a loose cream-colored silk sheath, simple but elegant in style. The slight bulge in Hailey's stomach was barely detectable. Zurich wore a dark blue suit with a cream-colored shirt.

The U.S. embassy wasn't the ideal setting for Taleah and Lorenz's wedding, but the fact that this marriage was legal made it an acceptable backdrop. The couple would always regard the first wedding as their very favorite one. Taleah and Lorenz also

planned to celebrate both anniversary dates for
the rest of their lives. Both ceremonies held signif-
icant meaning for each of them.

An appointed government official presided over
the nuptials and two civilian government employees also stood by as witnesses.

While holding on to Taleah's hand, handsomely
dressed in his full military uniform, Lorenz promised to be there for Taleah through sickness and
health, for richer or poorer, until death parted them.
Taleah vowed to do the very same for Lorenz in
voicing her segment of "repeat after me." The passionate kiss after the pronouncement of them as
husband and wife was the most moving part of the
simple vow exchange.

The master bedroom was beautifully decorated
with fresh flowers and colorful balloons. Candles
burned softly in every corner of the room. A dozen
red roses in a crystal vase had been placed on the
dresser. When Lorenz had mentioned getting a
hotel room in downtown Tokyo for their wedding
night, Taleah had told him she'd be happy for
them to stay right at home.

Taleah was genuinely flattered that Lorenz had
taken the time to try and make things special for
her. She loved the outcome of his efforts. When
she couldn't figure out how he'd found the time
to decorate the room, she had asked him about
that. It was then that Lorenz told her that Hailey
and Zurich had done the honors.

No one other than the Kingdoms had been priv-
ileged to their private information. Inviting others
to the wedding wasn't possible since everyone
thought they were already married. Taleah and
Lorenz had shared a superb Japanese meal with

Zurich and Hailey after the ceremony, which had been the extent of their reception. The Kingdoms had given them their only wedding gift, a pair of crystal flutes.

Taleah sighed with total satisfaction as Lorenz slid into the bed next to her and rested his hand on her bare abdomen. As his mouth captured her right breast in a warm embrace, her fingers wended their way through his hair. Lorenz then brought his lips up to Taleah's, kissing her deeply, passionately. Taleah couldn't get enough of her husband's sweet kisses. Lorenz's kisses were physically arousing, the kind of kisses a woman lived for.

The flame of Taleah's desires burned white-hot for Lorenz. This wasn't a fantasy. His naked flesh felt so wonderful beneath her hands as she kneaded and massaged his firm muscles. "Baby, I need you," Taleah whispered. "Make sweet love to me."

"I'll make love to you as often as you need me to, Taleah, over and over again."

Lorenz stroked Taleah's body with slow, tender hands. Her heat was reaching out to him, drawing him into the warmth of her inner sanctum. Lorenz didn't want Taleah to forget one moment of their time together, but he especially didn't want her to forget this night. They'd waited too long to make love as husband and wife.

Lorenz's teeth nipped at her skin, causing Taleah to shiver and shake. Her flesh craved him, hungered for his tender touch. His mouth and hands all over her body made her feel so good. His tongue circling her nipples felt even better. Taleah was more than ready to experience the ultimate feeling, but she was content to let the slow hands work their seductive magic.

His tongue probed her intimate treasures, making her squirm beneath him. Taleah felt herself los-

ing control as her fingers tightly gripped his hair.
The wild sensations coursing through her made
her even crazier with desire. As he entered her,
Taleah rose up to welcome his hardened flesh inside her. Slowly, with sweet determination, his manhood inched its way down to the core of her essence.

Taleah had lived for the moment when she and
Lorenz would make love as husband and wife; now
she wanted to live in it. She bit down on her lower
lip to keep from screaming out his name. She
could hear the raggedness of their uneven breathing. Taleah kept her legs wrapped tightly around
his waist as she rode out the storm of passion. His
gentle rocking inside her had her craving for more,
dying for him to go deeper and deeper, until he
completely filled her up.

As if Lorenz had read her mind, his maniacal
strokes and deep thrusts increased in intensity.
Taleah's gyrations moved beneath him in perfect
harmony with the frantic grinding of his hips. The
gentle in-and-out plunging of his thickened organ
had Taleah so near the edge she feared falling off.

Before she could gasp for her next breath, a
powerful explosion erupted inside her.

As Lorenz joined Taleah on the fiery path to fulfillment, her name came across his lips as softly as
a whispering breeze. His body shook uncontrollably with the force of his staggering release. Unable
to move another muscle, his breathing labored beyond his control, Lorenz lay perfectly still atop his
wife, praying for sweet mercy to deliver him.

Once Lorenz finally found the strength to move,
he rolled over and turned up on his side. A few
seconds later he reached up under the bed and
pulled out a large brown packet, which he handed
to Taleah. "This is my wedding present to you, Mrs.
Hampton. I hope you like it."

Taleah wasted no time in ripping the package open. Her eyes immediately became as bright as the crown jewels. "Jamaica! Pamphlets for Jamaica," she screeched, laughing and crying at the same time. "Does this mean we're going to Jamaica, Lorenz?"

"Although we're in paradise right this moment, Taleah, we're going to have that proper honeymoon in an idyllic setting very soon." He kissed her gently on the mouth. "You've had some very trying times over the past few months; you've also been very brave. Bravery should always be rewarded." Lorenz removed a jewelry box from the packet and handed it to Taleah.

Tears welled in Taleah's eyes as she gently fingered one half of a delicate gold heart pendant. "It's so beautiful. Thank you, Lorenz. I love you." She kissed him softly on the mouth.

With tears in his eyes, Lorenz held up the other half of the gold heart for Taleah to see.

"May we always own each other's heart, Taleah. Just as these two hearts joined together make one, our fearless hearts will always and forever be united."

Dear Readers:

I sincerely hope that you enjoyed reading from cover to cover FEARLESS HEARTS. I'm very interested in hearing your comments and thoughts on the romantic story of Taleah Taylor and Air Force Master Sergeant Lorenz Hampton, who fall in love at first sight. I love hearing from my readers and I do appreciate the time you take out of your busy schedule to write to me.

If you'd like a reply please enclose a self-addressed, stamped envelope (SASE) with all your correspondence and mail to: Linda Hudson-Smith, 16516 El Camino Real, Box #174, Houston, TX 77062. Or you can e-mail your comments to *LHS4romance@yahoo.com*. Please feel free to visit my Web site and sign my guest book at *www.lindahudsonsmith.com*.

ABOUT THE AUTHOR

Born in Canonsburg, Pennsylvania, and raised in the town of Washington, Linda Hudson-Smith has traveled the world as an enthusiastic witness to other cultures and lifestyles. Her husband's military career gave her the opportunity to live in Japan, Germany, and many cities across the United States. Linda's extensive travel experience helps her craft stories set in a variety of beautiful and romantic locations. It was after illness forced her to leave a marketing and public relations career that she turned to writing.

Voted the Best New Author by the Black Writer's Alliance, Linda received the prestigious 2000 Gold Pen Award. She also won two *Shades of Romance* magazine awards in the categories of Multicultural New Romance Author of the Year and Multicultural New Fiction Author of the Year 2001. Linda was also nominated the Best New Romance Author at the 2001 Romance Slam Jam, and was recently named Best New Christian Fiction author by *Shades of Romance* magazine for 2003. Linda is a member of Romance Writers of America and the Black Writers Alliance. She enjoys poetry, entertaining, traveling, and attending sports events. The mother of two sons, Linda shares a residence with her husband, Rudy, in Texas.